Also by Sidney St. James

Beneath the Waves Series
Throwback - Terror Beneath the Waves

Bridget Flynn Detective Series
Bridget Flynn - A Female Detective
Bridget Flynn - A Female Detective
A Prince of Their Own

Demon Gorge Trilogy
Room of Death - Here Today and Gone Tomorrow
Fate - Eventually Everything Connects
Standing in the Shadow of Death - The Sword of Damascus
Demon Gorge Trilogy Box Set

Gideon Detective Series
Rosenthall - Bete Malefique des Bois
Gideon Returns - A Damsel in Distress
The Dusty Adler Murder Mystery

Phantom of Black Rock Cove
The Transformist
El Transformista
Ace of Spades
Gideon - The Final Chapter (Volume 2)
The Final Curtain Call - The Illusion of Innocence
Lady in Red
Ace of Spades (Vol. 1) & Gideon - The Final Chapter (Vol. 2)
Gideon Detective Murder Mysteries Box Set: Books 7-9

James' Recipe Series
Wild Game Recipes - Squirrels, Bullfrogs, Alligators, Rabbits, Armadillos and More
Recipes that Won Chili Cookoffs in Texas
Duck and Goose Recipes from the Wilds of Eagle Lake, Texas and the Rock Island Prairies
Grandma's Homestyle Cooking Recipes

Lincoln Assassination Series
The Lost Cause - Lincoln Assassination
Lincoln Assassination Series Box Set: Books 1 - 5
Lincoln - Pursuit and Capture of John Wilkes Booth
Lewis Thornton Powell - The Conspiracy to Kill Abraham Lincoln
The Knights of the Golden Circle
Mary Elizabeth Surratt - "Please Don't Let Me Fall!"

Love Lost Series
It Takes Two to Tango (Volume 1)

It Takes Two to Tango (Volume 2)
Tears Are Words from the Heart
Let Me Drive
Belem Towers - Only Two Will Ever Know
The Curse of Knight's Island
Norderney Island
The Winds of Destiny

Omega Chronicles
Omega - The Lost City of Altinova
Nevaeh - The Lost City of Nemea
Bonaventure - Three Years on the Island
Crux Ansata - The Lost City of Ankara
Nevaeh & Crux Ansata Part I & 2 Anthology in the Omega Chronicles
Omega Chronicles Books 1 - 3 - An Anthology

Planetary Romance Trilogy
The Secrets of the Mist
Secrets of the Golden Cliffs
Wrath of Nevaeh

Self-Guided Creative Writing Series
Taglines Unveiled - Crafting Memorable Dialogue Hooks

Texas Outlaw Series

Sam Bass - A Dead Man's Hand, Aces and Eights

The Faith Chronicles
The Rose of Brays Bayou - The Runaway Scrape
Adversity - Keeping the Faith
Faith - Seventy Times Seven
Genesis - Stepping Onto the Shore and Finding It is Heaven
Hallelujah - He is not Here; He Has Risen (Luke 24: 6)
Seeing the Power of God
Living in God's Word
The Faith Chronicles: Books 1 - 3: An Anthology
The Faith Chronicles Box Set: Books 4-6

The Storm Lord Trilogy Series
The Flaming Blue Sword
Nine Months Will Tell
The Three Keys to Armageddon
The Storm Lord Trilogy Box Set: Books 1 - 3 An Anthology

The Whodunnit Series
Murder in Horseshoe Bay - Death Comes Quietly
Jaded Lover - Things Are Getting Heavy
Under Cover Queen - Sequel to Jaded Lover
The Amaryllis Murder Mystery
Murder at Morgan Park
Checker Cab Murder Mystery
Destiny Waits - Murder at the Lakeside Museum
Lollapalooza - The Case of the Woman in Black

Time Travel Series
Quantum Echoes - RX-7: An AI Detective

Victorian Mystery Series
This Old House - A Lily Blooms in the Jaws of Hell
I Am Woman - I Am Invincible

Victorian Romance Series
I Am Woman - Hear Me Roar

World War 2 Series
USS Houston - Galloping Ghost of the Java Coast

Standalone
True Love Ways
I Go to Pieces - Part 2: Sequel to True Love Ways
Guitar - Truth is Strange - Stranger Than Fiction
Refuge of Death - A Kiss for a Kiss
The Runaway Scrape
Das Ausser Kontrolle Geratene Kratzen
La Raspado Fuera de Control

Watch for more at https://www.facebook.com/sidneystjamesshow.

Table of Contents

Published by BeeBop Publishing Group
Georgetown, Texas

This story is based on actual memoirs and told with a flare of suspense as Historical Fiction reflects actual events taken from memoirs of real sailors and Marines on the USS Houston.

FIRST EDITION

World War II Series

BOOK 1

This novel's jacket format and design are protected trade dresses and trademarks of Sidney St. James and the BeeBop Publishing Group.

Published Simultaneously in Canada

Library of Congress Cataloging-in-Publication Data

1 3 5 7 9 10 8 6 4 2

Available in eBook, Paperback, and Audio

Dedication

I dedicate this novel to the loving memory of the 1,064 brave souls who sailed aboard the USS Houston and lost their lives at sea in 1942. It was amid the treacherous waters and the impenetrable jungles of Java where fate took a turn. Three-hundred and Sixty-eight men found themselves captured by the relentless grip of the Japanese forces. Some of these courageous soldiers, their strength waning, found themselves adrift in the vast expanse of the ocean. And from the depths of that harrowing ordeal, 266 survivors emerged, each with their own tales of resilience and survival.

Years later, as the late 1960s embraced the small town of Eagle Lake, Texas, my uncle sat on the back porch, his weathered face etched with the marks of a life lived through an indomitable spirit. It was there, in the company of his brother-in-law, a crew member of the aircraft that dropped the bomb on Hiroshima, and my father, Elmer Struss of Operation Magic Carpet, along with other wartime heroes, that they shared their stories. These were tales of bravery, sacrifice, and the unbreakable bonds forged on the battlefields of World War II.

We will always cherish and hold dear the memories of those who have departed. Their voices, echoing the weight of history, actively bore witness to the unwavering spirit of those who fought and honored the memory of those lost, with each word standing as a powerful testament.

In this novel, I honor the memory of these brave souls, capturing their experiences in the indelible pages of time. May their stories serve as a poignant reminder of the enduring human spirit and the sacrifices made to pursue freedom.

With my most profound respect and admiration,

--—Sidney St. James.

waves

Prologue

USS Houston Commissioned During Great Depression

The **USS Houston, a shining example** of valor in over 240 years of naval history, met her heroic end 81 years ago in a fierce battle against overwhelming odds. Commissioned during the challenging times of the Great Depression, the Houston was a testament to resilience and ingenuity.

The USS Houston, crafted under the shadow of post-World War I naval treaties aimed at regulating naval armaments, emerged as a distinguished Northampton-class heavy cruiser. These international agreements, notably the Washington Naval Treaty of 1922, significantly influenced her design, mandating limitations on tonnage and armaments.

Despite these restrictions, American naval engineering ingenuity and resilience led to the construction of the Houston, a formidable vessel and a testament to their capabilities.

Captain Jesse Bishop Gay, the inaugural captain of the USS Houston, was a naval officer of remarkable distinction. An alumnus of the United States Naval Academy at Annapolis, his extensive career spanned across the globe, encompassing diverse assignments. His tenure in the U.S. Navy polished his skills in navigation and leadership, adeptly preparing him for the intricate challenges of diplomacy and warfare. Captain Gay's experience and acumen were pivotal in guiding the USS Houston through its early voyages and missions.

With his deep understanding of naval strategy and tactics, Gay was an ideal choice to helm the Houston. He brought with him a wealth of experience and a leadership style that inspired loyalty and bravery among his crew. Under his command, the Houston was more than just a ship of war; it was a vessel that carried the hopes and the fighting spirit of a nation still finding its footing in a world grappling with the aftermath of a global conflict.

The Houston, under Captain Gay's command, quickly gained a reputation for excellence. Her crew, a blend of seasoned sailors and young recruits, mirrored the captain's dedication and commitment to duty. Together, they navigated the challenging waters of the interwar period, a time marked by political shifts and emerging global tensions.

While constrained by treaty limitations, the ship was a marvel of naval architecture. The ship boasted formidable firepower, advanced navigational equipment, and a design that balanced speed and armor. Houston's sleek lines and imposing presence made her a symbol of American naval power and ingenuity.

As the world inched closer to another global conflict, the USS Houston and her crew, led by Captain Gay, stood ready to defend their country's interests. Their story, woven into the fabric of naval history, remains a testament to the skill and bravery of those who sail to defend their nation.

A series of notable events and the presence of distinguished guests marked the illustrious history of the ship, each adding a chapter to its storied legacy.

One of the most memorable moments was in 1938-1939 when President Franklin D. Roosevelt dined with the ship's officers in the wardroom. Among the distinguished guests were Admiral William

D. Leahy and Captain George N. Barker, the ship's Commanding Officer at the time.

Houston's prestige and the high regard others held her made this occasion a testament.

In the years preceding World War II, the USS Houston occupied a unique and cherished position in the life of President Franklin D. Roosevelt. As a passionate naval enthusiast and the former Assistant Secretary of the Navy, Roosevelt had a deep and abiding interest in maritime affairs, and the USS Houston, with her impressive capabilities and distinguished crew, became his warship of choice.

Roosevelt's affinity for the Houston was more than just a matter of preference; it reflected his profound appreciation for the sea and the naval tradition. He often admired the ship's sleek design, formidable firepower, and advanced technology, making her a jewel of the American fleet. The Houston, in turn, seemed to embody the strength and resilience that Roosevelt admired in the United States Navy.

His visits to the Houston were significant for the President and the ship's crew. Roosevelt would spend considerable time aboard the vessel, not merely as a figurehead but as an active and engaged participant in her voyages. These trips allowed the President to escape the pressures of his office and indulge his passion for the sea, but they also served a more practical purpose. They allowed him to witness firsthand the Navy's operational capabilities and understand the challenges and needs of a modern warship.

The crew of the Houston took great pride in these presidential visits. They saw in Roosevelt not just their Commander-in-Chief but a fellow sailor with a genuine love for naval life. His presence on board was a morale booster, validating their hard work and dedication. The President, in turn, enjoyed the camaraderie and straightforwardness of the sailors and officers, often engaging in conversations about their experiences and insights.

Roosevelt's trips aboard the Houston actively embodied a sense of adventure and discovery. He reveled in the ship's maneuverability and speed, often participating in exercises and drills. The President, keenly interested in naval strategy and technology, would spend hours discussing tactics and innovations with the ship's officers. These discussions were not just academic for Roosevelt; they influenced his thinking about naval policy and strategy.

During these years, the Houston became more than just a ship in the U.S. Navy; she became a symbol of the close relationship between the nation's military and its leadership. Roosevelt's repeated choice of the Houston for his voyages was a testament to his confidence in her crew and capabilities. On the decks of the Houston, Roosevelt found a temporary respite from the burdens of leadership, surrounded by the vastness of the ocean and the steadfastness of a ship and crew he deeply admired.

In 1937, the USS Houston assumed a role of immense pride and significance during the grand opening of the Golden Gate Bridge in San Francisco, California. This event was not just a ceremonial occasion but a celebration of engineering triumph and national achievement, marking the completion of what was then the world's longest and tallest suspension bridge. Houston's participation in this landmark event symbolized the might and reach of the U.S. Navy and underscored its role in the nation's progress and innovation.

As the Houston navigated the waters near the bridge, her presence was a commanding sight. With her sleek lines and powerful silhouette, the ship glided gracefully under the towering span of the newly completed bridge. The grandeur of the Golden Gate, with its majestic towers and sweeping cables, created a dramatic backdrop against the crisp blue of the Pacific Ocean. The bright red-orange hue of the bridge, known as International Orange, contrasted strikingly with the deep grays and blues of the USS Houston and the surrounding seas.

Dressed in their finest uniforms, the crew stood at attention along the decks, adorning the ship in her most splendid attire for the occasion. Flags and pennants fluttered in the breeze, adding color and movement to the solemn beauty of the warship. As the Houston passed under the bridge, a thunderous roar of applause and cheers erupted from the crowds gathered along the shores and on the bridge itself. The air was electric with excitement, pride, and shared national accomplishment.

Onboard the Houston, the crew felt profound pride in being part of such a historic moment. The bridge's grand opening was a celebration of an engineering marvel and a reflection of the era's optimism and forward-looking spirit. The Houston's presence at the event was a reminder of the Navy's integral role in the nation's journey toward growth and modernization.

Airplanes flew overhead in formation, ships sounded their horns in salute, and bands played patriotic music, creating an atmosphere of jubilation and festivity. The Houston, with her guns saluting in honor of the occasion, added to the spectacle, her powerful presence a symbol of the nation's strength and capabilities.

As the sun set on this momentous day, the Golden Gate Bridge shone like a beacon over the bay, illuminated by thousands of lights. The USS Houston, a proud participant in the day's events, continued to grace the waters nearby, her crew taking in the sights and sounds of the celebration.

The bridge's opening, with the Houston's participation, was not just a local or national event but a moment that captured the world's imagination, symbolizing hope, progress, and the indomitable human spirit.

In 1938, a year after her prominent role in the grand opening of the Golden Gate Bridge, the USS Houston embarked on another significant chapter in her storied history.

She received the prestigious appointment as the flagship of the U.S. Fleet, placing her at the forefront of American naval power. This appointment, under the command of Rear Admiral Claude C. Bloch, was a testament to the Houston's impressive capabilities and a clear indication of her esteemed status within the United States Navy.

Rear Admiral Bloch, a respected and seasoned officer, brought a wealth of experience and leadership to the Houston. His career, marked by a series of commendable assignments, made him an ideal commander for the fleet's flagship.

Under his guidance, the Houston became the symbolic and operational heart of the fleet, a role she fulfilled with distinction. The heavy cruiser's new role as the flagship required her to be more than just a powerful warship. She became a floating command center equipped with state-of-the-art communication and navigation systems. These upgrades ensured that she could effectively coordinate fleet movements and strategy, making her the nerve center of U.S. naval operations in the Pacific.

The ship's already seasoned and skilled crew adapted to their new responsibilities with professionalism and pride. They understood the importance of their ship's role and the trust placed in them by the Navy's leadership. The Houston's decks buzzed with heightened activity as sailors and officers worked tirelessly to maintain her operational readiness and fulfill her flagship duties.

As the flagship, the Houston hosted numerous high-level meetings and diplomatic functions. Her decks saw admirals, politicians, and foreign dignitaries coming to discuss strategies, forge alliances, or witness firsthand the U.S. Navy's might.

The Houston's officers' wardrooms and staterooms often served as the venues for critical meetings. Here, the ship's leaders actively made decisions that shaped the fleet's future and, by extension, influenced the nation's course. These areas on the vessel became central to strategic discussions and critical decision-making in naval operations.

The Houston's presence in fleet exercises and maneuvers was a sight to behold. She led from the front, cutting through the Pacific waters with an air of authority and grace. Her participation in these exercises demonstrated the Navy's tactical prowess and readiness to defend American interests. The Houston, with her imposing guns and sleek profile, was not just a warship but a symbol of American naval strength and innovation.

As the flagship, the Houston also played a crucial public relations role. She was often the centerpiece of naval parades and public demonstrations, where her impressive size and capabilities were on full display. Crowds would gather at ports and harbors to catch a glimpse of this magnificent ship, the pride of the U.S. Fleet.

Under Rear Admiral Bloch, the Houston's time as the flagship involved rigorous activity and heightened visibility. It was a time when the ship and her crew exemplified the very best of the United States Navy, showcasing their readiness, versatility, and commitment to duty.

In November 1940, as geopolitical tensions escalated in the Pacific, the USS Houston stepped into a role of critical importance, reflecting her rising prominence in the United States Navy.

Admiral Thomas C. Hart, the esteemed Commander of the Asiatic Fleet, designated the Houston as his flagship.

This appointment was not just an honor but a strategic decision, placing the Houston at the heart of the United States' naval presence in a region brimming with uncertainty and impending conflict.

Admiral Hart, a highly respected figure with a profound understanding of the complexities of the Pacific theater, brought a wealth of experience to his command.

Admiral Hart led with deep strategic foresight and a nuanced understanding of international relations. Under his command, the heavy cruiser transformed from merely a symbol of naval prowess to a pivotal player in the intensifying global political arena and the impending war. The selection of the Houston for this esteemed role was a testament to her capabilities and the confidence the Navy had in her crew.

As the flagship, the Houston received upgrades, including additional communications and intelligence-gathering equipment. This maintained its status as a formidable warship and elevated it to a floating command center.

From her decks, Admiral Hart would oversee the operations of the Asiatic Fleet, which required rapid decision-making and constant vigilance.

The Houston crew adapted to their new role with characteristic efficiency and professionalism. The ship buzzed with heightened activity as sailors and officers worked around the clock to ensure she met the demands of her new status. The responsibilities were immense, and every crew member felt the weight of the task at hand – they were now the vanguard of American naval power in a region on the brink of war.

In her capacity as the flagship, the Houston became a hub of strategic operations.

On the USS Houston, critical meetings involving senior naval officers and diplomats frequently occurred, focusing on strategizing and decision-making. These discussions significantly shaped the United States strategy in response to the growing tensions in the Pacific.

The USS Houston's officers' wardroom, usually a dining and leisure space, frequently became a strategic hub for critical discussions that charted the Asiatic Fleet's future direction. The Houston's presence in the Pacific was a clear signal of American intent and commitment. She participated in numerous fleet exercises and maneuvers, demonstrating the Navy's readiness to protect

American interests in the region. These operations, often carried out under the watchful eyes of potential adversaries, were as much a show of force as they were routine training.

As the political situation deteriorated and the threat of war grew more imminent, the USS Houston and her crew found themselves at the center of a rapidly changing geopolitical landscape. Their mission was to project American naval power, gather intelligence, and maintain a vigilant watch over American interests in the face of an increasingly aggressive Japanese expansion.

Under Admiral Hart's command, the Houston actively embraced its role as the flagship of the Asiatic Fleet, characterized by a sense of urgency and purpose. Her crew understood they were on the front lines of a brewing conflict that would soon engulf the world.

As the 1940s dawned, the world was on the precipice of a conflict engulfing nations and continents. The USS Houston, with her storied past and formidable presence, stood ready at the heart of this brewing storm. Her transformation from a proud emblem of peacetime naval strength to a warrior on the cusp of war mirrored the United States' own shift from a stance of isolationism to that of an emerging global power bracing for inevitable conflict.

The air aboard the Houston was thick with tension and anticipation. The crew, a mix of seasoned sailors and younger recruits, felt the undercurrents of change. There was a palpable sense of urgency as they went about their duties, each man acutely aware of the ship's critical role in the coming days. The usual routines of maintenance, drills, and exercises took on a new gravity, performed with a meticulousness borne of the knowledge that each task could be vital for survival in battle.

The ship itself seemed to sense the changing tide. The once gleaming decks and polished brass of peacetime now served as the backdrop to rigorous preparations for war. Crew members meticulously checked and rechecked the Houston's guns symbols of her might, and diligently replenished and secured her ammunition stores.

The crew expertly tuned the Houston's engines, the heart of the warship, ensuring they were ready to propel her through the upcoming treacherous waters.

Admiral Hart and his senior officers spent hours poring over maps and intelligence reports, strategizing and planning for the uncertain future. The atmosphere in the war room was tense, with the weight of responsibility hanging heavily in the air. Decisions made here could alter the course of the ship's fate and that of the men who served on her.

Conversations among the crew, previously brimming with stories of past shore leaves and future plans, now actively centered around speculation and rumors about the conflict's onset and location. The mess halls and sleeping quarters buzzed with whispered discussions about strategies, potential enemies, and the role the Houston would play in the impending war.

The crew maintained heightened alert as the ship sailed through the Pacific waters. Lookouts scanned the horizon with a vigilance born of the knowledge that the enemy could appear at any moment. The rumble of war, once distant, now loomed ominously close for every sailor on board the Houston. They understood they might soon face the battle they had been preparing for months or years.

The transition from a symbol of peacetime to a war-ready vessel was complete. The USS Houston, with its proud legacy and battle-ready crew, was a microcosm of the United States itself – poised on the brink of a conflict that would redefine the nation and its place in the world.

As the clouds of war gathered ever closer, the Houston sailed on, her journey from peace to war encapsulating a nation's evolution and readiness to face the challenges of a world at war. The Houston and her crew, poised for a significant chapter in their history, were ready for valor and sacrifice. This period would testify to their bravery and resilience amid the 20th century's most significant conflict... World War 2!

Chapter ONE

Pearl Harbor Attacked

In the early hours of December 7, 1941, violent actions abruptly shattered the serene tranquility of Pearl Harbor, a lagoon harbor on the island of Oahu, Hawaii.

The day broke not with the gentle hues of dawn but with the thunderous roar of warfare, a stark harbinger of the chaos to come. The sky, which moments before had been a canvas of peaceful azure, rapidly transformed into a churning mass of dark smoke, pierced by the relentless, ear-splitting loudness of explosions.

Japanese aircraft, having approached the harbor with stealth and tactical precision, commenced a surprise military strike of devastating efficacy. As the sun timidly rose above the horizon, its rays struggled to penetrate the thick, ominous smoke billowing from the stricken ships below. The normally placid waters of the harbor turned tumultuous, violently disturbed by the desperate activities of sailors and soldiers. They scrambled frantically to man their battle stations, their faces etched with shock, fear, and determination.

The harbor reverberated with explosions, each blasting a terrifying echo of destruction. Bombs and torpedoes, unleashed with ruthless accuracy by the Japanese attackers, found their marks on the mighty battleships. Once the proud titans of the U.S. Pacific Fleet, these vessels now lay heavily damaged or sinking, their steel frames grotesquely twisted and set ablaze. The USS Arizona bore the brunt of the onslaught, suffering multiple bomb hits that triggered a catastrophic explosion.

An instant transformed the ship into a fiery tomb, entombing hundreds of her crew in a searing inferno. Above, enemy planes dominated the sky, swarming like predatory birds. They swooped down in precise formation, their machine guns unleashing torrents of bullets in a deadly strafe across the naval base and airfields. On the ground, sailors and soldiers, stunned by the audacity and suddenness of the attack, mounted a desperate defense. Armed with whatever was at hand, they returned fire with small arms and anti-aircraft guns, their actions a defiant but outmatched response to the overwhelming assault.

Amid the chaos and horror, amid the smoke and the shrieking of metal, acts of extraordinary heroism and self-sacrifice emerged. Men risked, and many lost, their lives in valiant efforts to repel the attack and save their fellow servicemen from the fiery Hell that engulfed the harbor.

President Franklin Delano Roosevelt later encapsulated the enormity of this day in his historic address, branding it as a *"date which will live in infamy."*

The attack on Pearl Harbor, with its profound and far-reaching consequences, marked a pivotal turning point not just in American history but in the annals of the world. It propelled the United States, with resolute determination and a stirred spirit of vengeance, into the global conflict of World War II. A war that would rage across continents and oceans, forever altering the course of human history.

In response to this unprecedented attack, President Roosevelt addressed the nation with a speech that would echo through the annals of history:

"Yesterday, December 7, 1941 - a date which will live in infamy - the United States of America was suddenly and deliberately attacked by naval and air forces of the Empire of Japan... I ask that the Congress declare that since the unprovoked and dastardly attack by Japan on Sunday, December 7, 1941, a state of war has existed between the United States and the Japanese Empire."

With these solemn words, Roosevelt galvanized the American public, awakening a united resolve to face the trials of war and defend the principles of freedom and democracy.

During the turbulent times of World War II, the USS Houston carved its name in history with an almost mythical reputation, earning the moniker "Galloping Ghost of the Java Coast." This illustrious title was a testament to the ship's prowess and a symbol of hope and resilience for the Allied forces.

In the vast expanse of the Pacific, particularly around the Java Sea, the Houston was renowned for its elusive and resilient actions. Time and again, the ship demonstrated an uncanny ability to avoid destruction, deftly evading the formidable Japanese naval and air forces that sought to end its voyages. The Houston's skillful maneuvers, often in dire situations, painted it as a spectral entity, elusive and indomitable.

Adding to its ghostly reputation was the ship's persistent defiance in combat. Despite facing overwhelming odds, including damage and the absence of reinforcements, the Houston engaged the enemy relentlessly. Its refusal to succumb to the assaults it faced made it appear almost otherworldly to friend and foe alike.

The nickname "Galloping Ghost of the Java Coast" transcended beyond the mere physical presence of the USS Houston.

This moniker became a powerful talisman for the Allied forces in the heart of a desperate and harrowing conflict. During these dark times, when morale was as crucial as bullets, the legend of the USS Houston illuminated the war's grim landscape like a lighthouse of resilience and fortitude.

The Houston was more than steel and firepower for the sailors aboard other ships and the soldiers in the trenches; she was a mythic symbol of defiance and strength. Her story rippled through the ranks, spoken in hushed tones of reverence and awe. To them, the Houston wasn't just a ship – she was an indomitable spirit, gliding ghost-like through the treacherous waters, elusive and untamed, a constant thorn in the side of the advancing Japanese forces.

Back home, families huddled around their radios, clinging to every piece of news from the front. Or, they would attend the movie theaters, and there would be an entire update on the progress of the War. The "Galloping Ghost" tales, evading capture and fighting against overwhelming odds, became a source of national pride and hope. People spoke of this phantom cruiser in living rooms and local diners, factories, and farms, her exploits becoming part of the war's lore.

The image of a ghost ship, a ship Tokyo Rose and the Japanese reported as having sunk to the bottom of the ocean three times, was ceaselessly roaming the Java Coast, uncatchable and relentless, stirred the imagination, and bolstered the spirits of those fighting. It was a narrative that transcended the brutal realities of war, offering a glimpse of something unearthly... something unconquerable.

For those waiting anxiously for loved ones to return, Houston's legend was a comforting emblem of persistence and courage. It was as though there lay a promise of hope and a future victory in the very whisper of her name.

The "Galloping Ghost of the Java Coast" was not just a nickname; it was an enduring symbol of an unyielding fight against formidable adversaries, embodying the unbreakable spirit of all those who stood against tyranny.

As with many wartime stories, myth and legend intertwined with reality to enhance the ship's tale. The USS Houston's legend grew with each encounter, weaving a narrative of bravery, skill, and endurance larger than life.

A series of notable events and distinguished guests marked the illustrious history of the ship, each adding a vibrant chapter to its storied legacy. Among these events, the saga of the Houston reached a heroic but tragic climax during the Battle of the Sunda Strait in 1942. In this fierce confrontation, the ship valiantly engaged in its final battle before sinking. Despite this, the legend of the 'Galloping Ghost of the Java Coast' continued to thrive, symbolizing the ship's indomitable spirit and the unwavering bravery of her crew.

During World War II, movie theaters became more than just places of entertainment; they transformed into communal experiences and information hubs. As people flocked to these venues, drawn by the allure of the big screen and the need for news from the front lines, they further cemented the legacy of these theaters in the nation's collective memory. Stepping into a theater of that era was like entering another world.

In 1940, movie theater lobbies featured posters of several notable films. Some of these included Disney's "Pinocchio" and "Fantasia," Charlie Chaplin's "The Great Dictator," Alfred Hitchcock's "Rebecca," and "The Grapes of Wrath."

The scent of freshly popped popcorn mingled with a faint mustiness characteristic of the plush red seats and heavy velvet curtains. A sense of hushed anticipation filled the air as young and old audiences settled into their seats, the dim, warm glow of the aisle lights illuminating their faces. As the newsreels started, the room plunged into darkness, save for the flickering beam of the projector, cutting through the smoky air to hit the silver screen. The grainy black-and-white footage crackled to life, the monotonous yet compelling voice of the newsreel announcer filling the space. Images of the war – soldiers in trenches, airplanes in formation, and naval ships at sea – flashed across the screen, captivating the audience with their stark realism.

Through these newsreels, many learned of the USS Houston's fate. The footage, often accompanied by dramatic musical scores, showed the ship in its prime and in the heat of battle. The tale of the 'Galloping Ghost of the Java Coast' unfolded on the screen, a name given for its elusive maneuvers and unexpected attacks. The audience watched the ship's story with awe and respect as the narration detailed its exploits and ultimate sacrifice, leaving a profound impact.

These cinematic moments served a dual purpose. They provided the viewers with updates on the war's progress and brought the stories of ships like the Houston to life. The dramatic presentation, coupled with the communal viewing experience, etched the memory of the Houston and its brave crew in the hearts of countless individuals.

As the world teetered on the brink of global conflict in the early days of World War II, the enchanting allure of cinema offered a cherished escape. On a vibrant Saturday evening in 1941, the Majestic Theater, with its Art Deco splendor and dazzling marquee lights, welcomed eager moviegoers into its embrace for a night of captivating entertainment.

The downtown streets buzzed with the lively sounds of big band music and the excited chatter of people against the backdrop of trolley cars clattering in the distance. Couples, dressed in their finest attire, walked arm-in-arm towards the theater, their faces alight with anticipation for the night's featured films.

As the clock struck 7 PM, the majestic doors of the Cole Theater in Eagle Lake, Texas, and the Oaks Theater in Columbus, Texas, opened, revealing a grand lobby adorned with opulent mirrors and luxurious velvet curtains. The air was rich with the aroma of freshly popped popcorn, blending seamlessly with the subtle scents of elegant perfumes and distinguished colognes, setting the stage for an unforgettable evening.

Inside the opulent halls, ushers in pristine uniforms escorted the patrons to their seats, the soft velvet embracing them in comfort. The theater buzzed with anticipation, the audience abuzz with discussions of Hollywood's latest offerings. Tonight, they were in for a treat, with not one but two of the year's biggest hits gracing the screen.

The lights dimmed, casting the room into expectant darkness. The grand curtain slowly parted with its intricate golden embroidery to reveal the gleaming silver screen. The newsreel began the evening, briefly grounding the audience in the world's current events, but an animated short quickly followed, drawing laughter and applause from the audience. Then came the highlight of the night - the number 1 film of the year, "Citizen Kane," Orson Welles' masterpiece, which captivated audiences with its innovative storytelling and cinematic brilliance. The tale of Charles Foster Kane's rise and fall told through a series of flashbacks, had moviegoers hanging on every word, every scene a display of cinematic genius.

Following a brief intermission, the excitement built again for the second feature, "Sergeant York," the number 2 film of 1941. This gripping biographical film, starring Gary Cooper, told the story of a World War I hero, Alvin York. Its themes of courage and patriotism resonated deeply with the audience, particularly given the current global situation.

During these films, the audience escaped their own world's concerns, becoming deeply engaged in the drama and spectacle unfolding on the silver screen. They laughed, cried, and gasped together, united in their shared experience.

As the final credits of "Sergeant York" rolled and the lights gently brightened, the audience slowly emerged from their cinematic journey, reluctant to leave the magic behind. They stepped back into the night, now illuminated by the soft glow of street lamps, their conversations abuzz with reflections on the powerful stories they just witnessed.

In the face of the world's brewing storm, the Cole and the Oak Theaters offered a haven of joy, wonder, and shared human experience.

The magic of "Citizen Kane" and "Sergeant York" reminded them that the captivating world of cinema could bring light even in dark times.

When the newsreels ended, and the lights slowly brightened, the audience left their seats, carrying with them not just the entertainment of the films they had watched but also a deeper connection to the events and heroes of the war. In this way, movie theaters during World War II played a pivotal role in shaping public perception and keeping the home front connected to the distant battlefields.

Embark on the riveting journey of the USS Houston, a tale of valor and resilience on the high seas of World War II. Get ready to delve into a story that encapsulates more than just naval warfare — it's a saga of the human spirit, of bravery against insurmountable odds. Stay tuned for the unfolding chapters of this gripping narrative, where history and heroism intertwine. The story of the USS Houston awaits to captivate and inspire you.

Chapter TWO

The Crew of the USS Houston A Week Before

Almost a week before the infamous attack on Pearl Harbor, the crew of the USS Houston, particularly its Marine detachment, lived in a state of semi-normalcy, albeit with an undercurrent of anticipation for something significant and ominous on the horizon.

Lieutenant John Miller, part of the Houston's Marine complement, found a semblance of routine in their softball games. These games were more than just recreational activities; they were a brief escape from the growing tension that had been building up in the Far East.

The Houston's team, comprising about sixty-three Marines, was known for its skill in softball, a necessary adaptation due to the lack of space for baseball.

Standing on the deck, Miller often reminisced about their games against various teams in the Philippines. The Filipinos, particularly in places like Palawan and Cebu, had heard of their prowess and constantly challenged them to friendly matches. *"These games keep our spirits up,"* Miller thought, watching the calm sea, unaware of the impending storm.

Following a game against Canacao Hospital sailors one afternoon, the atmosphere around the USS Houston shifted dramatically. At 1300 hours, the ship buzzed with activity at the

Cavite Navy Yard, undergoing routine repairs. Filipino workers and American sailors collaborated on modifications and maintenance.

Amid the clatter of tools and shouted instructions, one sailor remarked to another, "She'll be in top shape after this overhaul, huh?" His colleague, passing by with a toolbox, replied, "Absolutely. These repairs are making her stronger than ever. She's going to sail smoothly after this." This industrious scene captured the essence of teamwork and dedication aboard the USS Houston.

"We're just sprucing up the old girl," Miller joked, hands busily installing new searchlights and anti-aircraft weapons on the USS Houston.

Private Johnson, wiping sweat from his brow in the sweltering heat, grinned in response. "Yeah, giving her a bit of a makeover, aren't we? She'll be the belle of the ball with these new lights."

Miller laughed heartily, his hands skillfully tightening a bolt. "Not just pretty, but tough too. These guns are going to pack a serious punch."

Johnson paused, taking in the formidable new armaments. "Feels like we're gearing up for something big," he mused thoughtfully.

"You bet," Miller replied with a sense of pride, stepping back to admire their handiwork. "The Houston's always been a force to reckon with. Now she's going to be even more formidable."

A moment of gravity passed over Johnson's face. "I just hope we're ready for whatever comes our way."

Miller clapped him reassuringly on the shoulder, his confidence unshaken. "We will be, as long as we've got the Houston and each other. We'll be ready for anything."

But upon their return at 1600 hours, the atmosphere had shifted dramatically. The Shore Patrol was rounding up all personnel, hurrying them back to the ship.

"Alright, everyone, let's focus on the degaussing system," the foreman instructed the Filipino workers. "These modifications are crucial for counteracting magnetic mines."

One of the workers, wiping his brow, nodded. "We understand the importance, sir. We'll work tirelessly to get it done."

Another added, "This system could save lives. We're committed to making sure it's fully operational."

As they delved into the intricate wiring and mechanics, there was a sense of urgency and determination among them. The task was complex, but they understood its critical role in safeguarding the USS Houston.

Miller felt a surge of unease. "Something big is coming," he said to Sergeant Davis, observing their frenzied activity. The urgency was unmistakable, the usual rhythm of the shipyard disrupted by a sense of impending crisis.

Over the next couple of days, the workers hastily completed the modifications. "No liberty now," Miller mused, sensing the tightening grip of war.

The Houston then set sail for Iloilo on the island of Panay, where they remained for about four days.

During this period, Washington intercepted communications indicating significant Japanese movements in the East Indies. *"They're up to something,"* Miller thought, his instincts as a Marine alert to the signs of impending conflict.

On the morning of December 8th in the Far East, the crew of the Houston, with the ship on high alert and standing gun watches, braced themselves. The games, the laughter, and the semblance of normalcy they had enjoyed seemed like distant memories now.

They were entering an unknown and dangerous phase, and Miller knew they had to be prepared for anything. The uncertainty was heavy in the air, starkly contrasting the calm seas surrounding them.

As tensions escalated in the Pacific, the Marines on the USS Houston, including Sergeant John Miller, were acutely aware of the changing winds of war. Miller, the gun captain of the five-inch dual-purpose gun, found himself standing gun watches with a reduced crew, reflecting the growing apprehension aboard.

On the morning of December 8, 1941, everything changed. Miller and his partial crew had just taken over the gun watch when the startling news came in: *"The Japanese have hit Pearl Harbor. We are virtually at war with Japan,"* echoed from the intercoms.

Miller felt his heart pounding as he absorbed the shocking news. With disbelief and resolve washing over him, he turned to his men, urgency clear in his voice. "Listen up, everyone, war has come to us," he announced, his tone firm yet controlled.

Private Johnson, wide-eyed, approached him. "War, sir? Are you sure?"

"Yes, Johnson," Miller replied, quickly taking charge of the situation. "We need to get this gun ready... now! Load the ammunition and check the mechanisms. We don't have a minute to lose."

As the crew sprang into action, Johnson's hands shook slightly as he handled the ammunition. "I can't believe this is happening," he muttered.

Miller, noticing his unease, clapped him on the shoulder. "Stay focused, Johnson. We've trained for this. We need to be prepared for anything."

Sergeant Davies, overhearing the exchange, joined in, his voice steady. "Miller's right. We've got a job to do, and we're going to do it to the best of our abilities. This is what we're here for."

The crew worked with increased fervor, checking and rechecking their equipment. Standing tall among his men, Miller knew the weight of responsibility on his shoulders. He bolstered the spirits of his crew, saying, "Every round counts, gentlemen. Let's show them what the Houston is made of." As they prepared the gun, the reality of their situation set in. They were no longer just a crew on a ship; they were warriors on the brink of a conflict that would test their mettle.

The Houston remained at anchorage that day, vigilant for any signs of enemy aircraft. Miller couldn't shake the feeling of being a sitting duck, knowing Japanese warships were likely nearby. *"We're on our own out here,"* he thought grimly, scanning the skies.

Later that afternoon, Admiral Glassford came aboard, bringing a semblance of reassurance. "At least we're not completely in the dark," Miller muttered to Private Johnson, watching the Admiral's staff bustling about the ship.

That evening, the Houston set sail from Iloilo under the cover of darkness, with rumors circulating about a return to the United States.

The crew's hopes briefly lifted, but the next morning's rendezvous with the USS Boise dashed them. "Seems like there's no way out of this," Miller sighed, his exhaustion apparent.

As they picked up their supply train, Miller learned of Admiral Hart's foresighted actions to move ordnance out of the Philippines. "Hart did what needed to be done," he remarked to Sergeant Davis, a sense of respect in his voice. "Pearl Harbor was a sitting duck, but at least we're moving."

The convoy's journey to the East Indies was tense, with the crew on high alert.

On the second evening, the crew spotted two Japanese ships as the sun dipped low. "Action stations," Miller barked, his adrenaline surging. The Houston and Boise moved to intercept, readying their eight-inch guns and star shells.

Miller explained to a younger Marine, "Star shells light up the night sky, giving us eyes in the darkness. Without radar, they're our best chance to see and hit the enemy."

As the sun set, painting the sky with hues of orange and purple, Miller and his crew prepared for what could be a defining moment in their battle against the Japanese. The uncertainty of night combat weighed heavily on them, but they were ready to face whatever came their way, armed with their training, courage, and a fierce determination to defend their ship and each other.

As the USS Houston braced for a potential encounter with Japanese scout vessels, Sergeant John Miller prepared his gun crew to illuminate the target area with star shells. These shells, essential for night combat in an era without high-tech radar, would light up the enemy ships, allowing the Houston and its companion, the USS Boise, to aim accurately.

Miller, responsible for the precise computations needed to deploy the star shells effectively, felt the weight of his duty. "We need to get this right," he thought, his mind racing through the calculations. The sun was setting, casting a golden hue over the sea, and the Houston was in a favored position with the sun behind them.

"I can see the Boise ready to fire," Miller said to Private Johnson, pointing to their companion ship. The Boise's guns, silhouetted against the fading light, were a sight of preparedness and power.

Admiral Glassford's decision not to engage unless necessary added tension. "They might not see us," Miller relayed to his crew, his voice steady but filled with anticipation. The Japanese ships, possibly unaware of their presence, continued their course.

As night fell, the Houston and its convoy remained cautious, heaving to avoid a potential ambush in the strait. The darkness enveloped the ship, the only sounds being the gentle lapping of waves against the hull and the distant hum of the ship's engines. Miller felt relief and frustration, aware of the delicate balance between attack and defense.

The following day brought clarity and a sense of cautious progress as a scout plane and destroyer confirmed that the path through the strait was clear. "We're moving again," Miller informed his crew, a sense of purpose in his voice.

In the following days, the Houston and a destroyer broke away from the convoy, speeding back in the direction they came. The night was a blur of rushing water and the roar of engines as the ship cut through the sea at high speed.

The ship called its boarding party to action early the following day, a rare occurrence in modern warfare. Miller watched as the team assembled, equipped with a mix of skills and weapons. "They're ready for anything," he thought, impressed by the efficiency and preparedness of the crew.

As a Marine, Miller armed himself and stood ready as part of the security forces to provide protection in case they met resistance. The tension was palpable, the unknown nature of their mission adding to the uncertainty. The sea stretched beyond them, vast and enigmatic, a mirror to the unpredictable nature of war.

In these moments, Miller and select marines demonstrated their adaptability, skill, and courage, ready to face whatever challenges lay ahead in the unpredictable waters of the Pacific Theater.

As the USS Houston cut through the waters of the Pacific, tension and anticipation were intense among the crew, particularly for Lieutenant John Miller and his Marine detachment. The ship was on high alert, with Miller leading the boarding party in case they encountered enemy vessels.

One morning, as a ship appeared on the horizon, Miller and his team prepared for a possible confrontation. "This might be it," Miller thought, feeling a mix of adrenaline and apprehension. The sight of the red ball on the ship's side seemed to confirm their worst fears - a Japanese vessel. Miller remembered their previous boarding experience with Norwegian vessels, but he knew this time would be different potentially hostile.

As they neared the ship, the tension among the Marines onboard the Houston was palpable. "Prepare for resistance," Miller ordered his gun crew, his voice calm yet firm. The Marines checked their weapons, ready for whatever awaited them. But as the destroyer moved ahead to investigate, the situation took an unexpected turn.

"It's an American vessel," came the radio call, much to the relief of Miller and his men.

The American flag's scraping off left a red mark of rust. The boarding party stood down, the immediate threat dissipating.

Back in Soerabaja, Miller missed the opportunity to serve as a bodyguard for Admiral Purnell, a role he had hoped for. Instead, he continued his duties aboard the Houston, feeling both disappointment and acceptance.

The Houston's role in the war effort primarily focused on convoy duty, a monotonous and exhausting task that tested the crew's endurance. "This convoy work is just endless," Miller mused, feeling the weight of the long hours on the guns and the reduced opportunity for rest.

Despite the tedium, there was an undercurrent of eagerness for action among the crew. When word came down from Captain Albert Rooks to prepare for combat, Miller felt a familiar surge of excitement. *"This is what we're trained for,"* he thought, his crew checking and rechecking their equipment, readying themselves for battle.

The anticipation of combat brought all sorts of emotions - not fear, but an eagerness akin to the nerves felt before an athletic contest. "We're ready for this," Miller reassured his men, his unwavering confidence in their training and abilities.

But the expected battle never came. The ship continued its convoy duties, navigating the treacherous waters filled with active enemy submarines. For Miller and his gun crew, each day brought the same routine, vigilance, and lingering question of when their actual test would come. In the meantime, they remained steadfast... a handful of Marines and Navy sailors united in their duty and prepared for whatever the war would bring their way!

Chapter THREE

A Northampton Class Heavy Cruiser

Let's back up and reminisce for just a moment. The USS Houston, a Northampton-class heavy cruiser, loomed majestically in the stillness of a brisk morning at the Philadelphia Naval Shipyard. Her sleek, formidable frame, stretching 600 feet from bow to stern, was a testament to American naval prowess. Equipped with nine 8-inch guns, her main battery commanded respect, capable of hurling shells up to 30,000 yards. Secondary armaments included four 5-inch guns, six 21-inch torpedo tubes, and a host of anti-aircraft artillery, making her a versatile threat in any naval theater.

The ship, powered by steam turbines, could cut through the ocean at 32.5 knots, a remarkable feat for a vessel of her size. Below deck, advanced communication systems, radar capabilities, and a well-appointed command center stood ready to execute complex naval operations.

Captain Albert H. Rooks was a beacon of calm authority and seasoned wisdom aboard the USS Houston. His journey to becoming the captain of this prestigious vessel unfolded through a remarkable career in the United States Navy, marked by significant achievements and unwavering dedication. Captain Rooks began his naval education at the United States Naval Academy, where his astute strategic thinking and natural leadership qualities earned him notable recognition. During his time at the Academy, he developed a keen interest in naval history and tactics, often spending hours in the library, poring over texts on maritime warfare and the evolution of naval technology.

In his rise to becoming the captain of the USS Houston, Rooks experienced a diverse naval career that began with his graduation from the Academy. He served in various capacities on different classes of ships, ranging from swift destroyers, known for their speed and agility, to majestic battleships, the heavyweights of naval warfare with formidable firepower.

This broad spectrum of assignments gave Rooks a wealth of experience and knowledge, shaping him into a well-rounded naval officer and preparing him for his eventual command of the USS Houston.

His early years in the Navy coincided with significant technological advancements in naval warfare, transitioning from the era of dreadnought battleships to more modern warships. This period of transformation profoundly influenced his approach to naval command, making him adept at adapting to changing tactical and technological environments.

His postings took him to various corners of the globe, allowing him to gain invaluable experience in international naval operations. He served in the Atlantic Fleet, honing his skills in large-scale naval maneuvers and joint operations with Allied forces. His tenure in the Pacific Fleet exposed him to the complexities of maritime operations in vast oceanic expanses, further solidifying his tactical expertise.

Before the Japanese bombed Pearl Harbor, Captain Rooks played a pivotal role in several vital naval exercises and was instrumental in testing and implementing new naval strategies and technologies. His insights and feedback often contributed to naval tactics and ship design improvements.

Throughout his career, Captain Rooks was known for his exceptional leadership qualities. He commanded with a blend of stern discipline and a fatherly concern for his crew, earning him respect and deep loyalty from his subordinates. His leadership style was not just about issuing orders; it was about mentoring and nurturing the growth of his officers and sailors, preparing them for the challenges of naval life.

As the world edged closer to the brink of World War II, Captain Rooks' vast experience and leadership abilities made him an ideal candidate to command the USS Houston. His wisdom, gained from years at sea and witnessing the transformation of naval warfare, equipped him with the foresight and strategic acumen necessary to navigate the imminent challenges of the conflict. His calm demeanor and fatherly approach to leadership would be crucial in maintaining his crew's morale and combat readiness in the face of adversity. Under his command, the USS Houston was not just a warship but a vessel steered by a leader whose life at sea had prepared him to face the greatest challenge of his career.

Executive Officer Commander Paul H. Rice was a pillar of naval efficiency and professionalism on the USS Houston. His journey to becoming the Executive Officer of this formidable ship unfolded through a series of distinguished achievements and a deep commitment to naval service.

Commander Rice's education began at the United States Naval Academy in Annapolis, Maryland, where he distinguished himself as a top student. His time at the Academy was not just an academic endeavor; it was a period of profound personal growth and the forging of a lifelong dedication to naval excellence. He excelled in subjects like naval tactics, engineering, and leadership, graduating near the top of his class. His sharp intellect matched his keen physical prowess, as evidenced by his active participation in varsity rowing, a sport that honed his teamwork and endurance skills. After graduating from the Naval Academy, Rice rapidly ascended through the naval ranks, a testament to his exceptional skills and leadership qualities. He served on various ships, from destroyers to aircraft carriers, each assignment adding layers to his understanding of naval operations and strategy. His postings were not just in the United States; he spent time in naval bases worldwide, gaining valuable insights into global naval dynamics.

Before his assignment to the Houston, Commander Rice, serving as a navigation officer on a cruiser, gained recognition for his innovative approaches to maritime navigation, particularly in challenging weather conditions. This experience was crucial in preparing him for the complex navigational challenges of the Pacific theater.

Throughout his career, Rice was known for his tactical acumen and ability to inspire and motivate those under his command. His leadership style was a blend of quiet confidence and unwavering discipline, earning him the respect and loyalty of his crew. Despite his often serious demeanor, those who knew him well were familiar with his dry wit, which surfaced during off-duty hours, revealing a more relaxed and approachable side.

His deep sense of loyalty to his men was not merely a professional obligation; it was a personal creed. Commander Rice believed that the strength of a ship lay in the unity and well-being of its crew, and he dedicated himself to their professional development and personal welfare.

As he stepped aboard the USS Houston as its Executive Officer, Commander Paul H. Rice brought with him a sterling resume of naval achievements and a history of leadership that inspired confidence and camaraderie among his crew. In the challenging times ahead, his strategic mind, meticulous attention to detail, and deep commitment to his men would prove invaluable in steering the USS Houston through the turbulent waters of World War II.

Captain John H. Lauterbach of the Marines was a man whose military bearing was unmistakable even at first glance. Standing well over six feet tall, his posture was always impeccably upright, a physical embodiment of the discipline and strength he brought to his role. His sharp, penetrating eyes, shaded by a prominent brow, seemed to miss nothing, conveying a sense of intensity and focus.

Years of service and exposure to the harsh elements at sea weathered Lauterbach's face, marking it with lines that spoke of his challenges and responsibilities. His jaw was square and set, often clenched in moments of deep thought or determination. His hair, cropped in a neat military style, had started to gray at the temples, hinting at his experience and the years he had dedicated to his country.

In his interactions with his men, Lauterbach was both stern and fair. He demanded the best from his Marines, never accepting anything less than their utmost effort. His men deeply respected and admired him for his unwavering commitment to their welfare and readiness to lead from the front. His voice, deep and commanding, could be both motivating during a rousing speech and reassuring in times of uncertainty.

Lauterbach was a skilled Marine and a tactician who understood the importance of strategic thinking in warfare. He possessed a keen mind, often found poring over maps and plans, always contemplating the next move in the chess game of naval warfare. Despite his tough exterior, he was known among his men for moments of unexpected compassion, revealing a leader who valued the lives and well-being of those under his command.

The deck of the USS Houston teemed with the vibrant enthusiasm of young sailors, each brimming with a blend of nervous excitement and earnest dedication.

Central to this youthful dynamism was Seaman John 'Johnny' Thompson. Johnny, a fresh-faced recruit hailing from a quaint

Midwestern town, stepped onto the Houston with awe and determined ambition. His broad, bright eyes, the color of the summer sky, mirrored the vast ocean that stretched before him, a symbol of the new world he was about to navigate.

Johnny's backstory was a tapestry of small-town life - Friday night football games, fishing in the local creek, and dreams that reached far beyond the cornfields of his hometown. He enlisted with a heart full of patriotism, fueled by stories of valor and adventure. His eagerness to learn every rope, bolt, and deck of the Houston was not just about proving himself; it was a pursuit of a dream, a longing to be part of something greater than himself.

Alongside Johnny were his newfound best friends, forming a close-knit group that embodied the spirit of camaraderie typical of young sailors in the Navy:

Seaman Peter 'Pete' Anderson, a lanky, freckle-faced youth from a coastal town in Oregon, shared Johnny's bunk. His love for the sea was as natural as his easygoing smile. Pete's knowledge about the ocean, a legacy from his fisherman father, made him an unofficial guide to Johnny in understanding the moods of the sea.

Seaman Mark 'Sully' Sullivan, from a bustling New York City borough, was the life of the group. He could lighten the mood in the tensest situations with a quick wit and a never-ending supply of jokes. His urban upbringing contrasted sharply with Johnny's, yet their friendship blossomed over shared dreams and aspirations.

Seaman David 'Dave' Johnson, a quiet and thoughtful soul from a dairy farm in Wisconsin, had a knack for mechanics. His fascination with the workings of the Houston's engines and machinery often led to lengthy discussions with Johnny, who was keen to absorb every bit of knowledge.

Seaman Luis Rodriguez, a vibrant and energetic Miami sailor, brought the group a touch of rhythm and warmth. His stories of sunny beaches and lively streets added a colorful dimension to their gatherings. His fluent Spanish often came in handy during their on-shore adventures in foreign ports.

This band of brothers from different walks of life found common ground aboard the Houston. Their shared experiences, from rigorous training drills to late-night conversations under the stars, forged a strong bond. They looked out for one another, growing together as sailors and men who were about to face the trials of a world at war. With his Midwestern charm, Johnny stood at the center of this group, his journey on the Houston interwoven with the lives of his newfound brothers.

Amid the diverse crew of the USS Houston, the presence of a detachment of Marines instilled a sense of gritty determination and unwavering resolve. These Marines, under the seasoned command of Sergeant William 'Bill' Davis, brought a unique element of combat readiness and stoicism to the ship.

Sergeant Davis, known simply as "Bill" to his peers and "Sarge" to his subordinates, was a man whose very posture spoke of battles fought and hardships endured. His rugged features, etched with lines of experience, were a canvas of his military career. The scars that adorned his weathered face and sturdy arms were not just marks of physical battles but also emblems of the emotional resilience forged in the fires of conflict. Bill's eyes, sharp and perceptive, missed nothing - a trait that made him an exceptional leader. His voice, when he spoke, was like gravel, rough yet reassuring, commanding respect and attention.

Under his command were several essential Marines, each with unique backgrounds and skills.

Corporal James 'Jim' Martinez, the second-in-command, is a quick-witted and agile Marine known for his sharpshooting skills. Jim's Hispanic heritage was a source of pride, and he often shared stories of his family in Texas. His loyalty to his squad was unparalleled, and he served as Sergeant Davis's right-hand man.

Lance Corporal Michael 'Mike' O'Reilly, a towering figure with a booming laugh, was the squad's heavy weapons expert. Hailing from a small town in Massachusetts, his easygoing nature belied a fierce combatant when the situation demanded. His expertise with machine guns and mortars made him an invaluable asset during skirmishes.

Private First Class Thomas 'Tommy' Lee was the youngest of the group. Tommy was of Chinese descent, having grown up in San Francisco's Chinatown. His sharp intellect and knack for languages (speaking both Mandarin and Cantonese fluently) made him the unofficial interpreter of the group. His youthful enthusiasm and curiosity about the world contrasted with the more jaded perspectives of his older comrades.

Private Samuel 'Sam' Johnson was a stoic and reserved individual from the Deep South. He was the squad's scout and reconnaissance expert.

His skill at moving silently and observing without detection made him the group's eyes and ears. Behind his quiet demeanor lay a deep sense of duty and a commitment to his fellow Marines.

These men formed a cohesive unit, each bringing their strengths to bear under Sergeant Davis's experienced leadership. Their camaraderie and mutual respect were the glue that held them together, creating a brotherhood forged through shared experiences and the unspoken understanding of those who stand on the front lines. As the Houston sailed towards uncertain waters, this group of Marines stood ready, a steadfast bulwark against the gathering storm of war.

Chapter FOUR

A Global Chessboard of Rising Tensions

The world of the early 1940s was a global chessboard of rising tensions and shifting alliances. In Europe, the shadow of war loomed large as Nazi Germany, under Adolf Hitler, aggressively expanded its territory, threatening the delicate balance of peace. Meanwhile, in the Pacific, the Empire of Japan, driven by imperial ambition and a voracious appetite for resources, cast an ominous gaze over its neighbors, unsettling the United States and its regional interests.

The USS Houston, therefore, was not just a ship; she was a symbol of American might and a sentinel in a world inching closer to the abyss of war. She was the flagship of the Asiatic Fleet. Her crew, a microcosm of the nation, came from all walks of life, united by their common purpose to serve and protect their country in the face of an uncertain future. As the Houston prepared to set sail, the weight of this responsibility rested on the shoulders of every sailor and marine aboard, their destinies intertwined with the fate of nations.

So, with that said, let's now back up ten days and prepare for the beginning of World War 2 and the role of the magnificent USS Houston, the *Galloping Ghost of the Java Coast*!

Chapter FIVE

The Sound of Reveille Pierces the Air

*****

As dawn heralded a new day, the first rays of the sun peeked over the distant horizon, bathing the USS Houston in a warm, golden light. The ship's deck, still damp with the morning dew, glistened under the early sun, reflecting a spectrum of light that danced across the sturdy metal surfaces. The calmness of the ocean at this hour, with its gentle, rhythmic waves, provided a serene backdrop to the awakening vessel.

The sharp, clear sound of reveille suddenly shattered the morning's tranquility. Echoing from bow to stern, the bugle call, a time-honored naval tradition, resonated actively throughout the ship. Its familiar notes signaled the start of a new day, reaching every corner and every sailor aboard.

In response to the call, the crew of the USS Houston began to stir. Bunks creaked as sailors rose, rubbing the sleep from their eyes, their movements a mixture of routine and reflex developed over months of life at sea.

The sounds of morning activity filled the air: boots thudded softly against the floor, uniforms zipped up swiftly, and a low murmur of voices rose as the crew greeted each other.

In the mess hall, the clatter of pots and pans heralded the preparation of the morning meal. The cooks, adept in their culinary ballet, worked efficiently, flipping pancakes, scrambling eggs, and brewing robust and aromatic coffee. The enticing smells wafted through the corridors, beckoning the sailors with the promise of a hearty breakfast to fuel the day's duties.

On the deck, the golden hue of the sunrise cast long shadows as the sailors began their daily tasks.

The crew neatly coiled the ropes, polished the brass to a shine, and swept the deck clean, performing each task with practiced precision. The officers, clutching their morning cups of coffee, reviewed their plans for the day, their voices a steady hum against the sound of the waves.

In the engine room, the mechanical heart of the ship, engineers, and mechanics checked the gauges and dials, ensuring that all systems were functioning optimally. The hum of the engines, a constant companion to the crew, was a reassuring sign of the ship's readiness for whatever the day might bring.

As the sun climbed higher, casting its light across the vast expanse of the ocean, the USS Houston came fully to life. Sailors moved about with purpose, each playing a vital role in the smooth operation of the ship. The sense of order and efficiency was a testament to their training and dedication, a well-oiled machine of men and metal united in their mission.

The morning routine aboard the Houston was more than just the start of a new day; it was a ritual that reinforced the unity and resilience of the crew. As they went about their tasks, there was a sense of camaraderie and shared purpose, a bond forged by life at sea and strengthened with each passing day. The sunrise brought light to the ship and symbolized its crew's enduring spirit and unwavering commitment, ready to face whatever challenges lay ahead.

In the bustling mess hall of the USS Houston, the air was rich with the smell of coffee and the sizzle of bacon. Johnny and his close-knit group of friends, their camaraderie a staple of their daily life, gathered around their usual table, a small oasis of familiarity in a world far from home.

Pete, his hair tousled from sleep, stretched his arms overhead with a yawn, the sound echoing slightly in the bustling space of the mess hall. "Another day in paradise, huh?" he joked, a twinkle in his eye, the early morning light casting a warm glow across his youthful face.

Johnny, leaning back in his chair with a relaxed smile, replied, his voice tinged with a hint of homesickness, "Better than shoveling snow back home in Iowa. At least here, the view changes every day. You wake up and never know what you'll see."

Sully, who always had a knack for lighting up the room, laughed heartily, his laughter resonating above the clatter of the mess hall. "I'd take your snow over my mom's cooking right now!" he said, his eyes crinkling with amusement. "You haven't lived until you've survived one of her 'experimental' meatloaf nights. The smell alone was enough to clear the house!"

The table erupted in laughter, a familiar and comforting sound amidst the ship's operations' constant hum and waves' distant crashing against the hull. The aroma of strong coffee mingled with the scent of bacon and eggs, creating a homely atmosphere in the otherwise utilitarian space.

Luis, joining the group with his tray, added with a grin, his voice filled with longing, "Your mom's cooking? Man, I miss my abuela's arroz con pollo. Nothing beats home cooking, especially when the sea air makes everything taste like salt."

Their banter was a daily ritual, a reminder of the diverse backgrounds from which they came. These light-hearted moments kept the morale high and provided a much-needed distraction from the constant undercurrent of tension that came with life at sea.

In the ship's cramped but cozy mess hall, Dave, known for his reserved demeanor, cradled a steaming mug of coffee between his hands. The rich aroma of the brew mingled with the briny scent of the sea and the faint, underlying odor of engine oil, typical of the ship's interior. He took a slow, thoughtful sip, the steam swirling up and momentarily fogging his glasses.

His distant and introspective gaze fixed on some unseen point in the middle distance. "You know, back at the farm, I'd be getting ready for the morning milking about now," he said, his voice soft and tinged with nostalgia. The words seemed to hang in the air, evoking images of a life far removed from the steel confines of their current reality. "The sound of the cows, the low, comforting moos, the smell of fresh hay... it feels like a different world."

Sitting across from him, Johnny peered over his mug, a smirk playing on his lips. "Fresh hay, huh? Beats the smell of diesel we wake up to every day," he quipped, but his tone was light, lacking any real edge.

Dave chuckled, a brief glimmer of amusement in his eyes. "You get used to it. There's something peaceful about the routine, you know? The cows depend on you, and the day has a rhythm. It's simple but... fulfilling in its own way."

Sully, who had been quietly listening, chimed in with a grin. "I can't imagine you, Dave, chasing cows around. Out here, you're the one who's always calm in the storm. Back there, were you the cow whisperer or something?"

The table erupted in light-hearted laughter, a welcome respite from the usual tension. Dave's smile broadened, his usual reticence giving way to the moment's warmth.

"Yeah, something like that," he replied, the distant look in his eyes replaced by a flicker of joy. "But believe me, cows can be stubborn. Not too different from some sergeants I know."

The soft hum of the ship's engines vibrated gently through the metal walls, a constant reminder of their ceaseless journey. Johnny sat at a weathered table, the surface scarred with the marks of countless meals and card games. His gaze drifted to the porthole, where the endless expanse of the ocean stretched out, a dark canvas under the starlit sky. He nodded slowly, his expression somber as he contemplated Dave's words.

"Yeah, it does," Johnny replied, his voice a low murmur that seemed to blend with the distant sound of waves against the ship's hull. "Sometimes I wonder what we'll find when we get back. The world's changing fast." He paused, running a hand through his hair. "You hear the news over the radio, and it's like we're in a different era now. Everything we knew, everything we took for granted... it's all different."

Across from him, Sully leaned back in his chair, a thoughtful look on his face. "It's hard to picture, isn't it? While we're out here, the world keeps spinning without us. Makes you feel disconnected in a way."

Luis, joining the conversation with a tray in his hands, chimed in as he sat. "You think the folks back home feel the same about us? Like we're the ones who've changed?"

Dave, still nursing his coffee, looked up. "Maybe. We're not the same people who left, that's for sure. War changes you in ways you don't expect."

Johnny's eyes met Dave's, a silent understanding passing between them. "I just hope we can find our place again when we return. Find some sense of normalcy, you know?"

Sully leaned in, his tone turning serious. "We all have something waiting for us back home. But right now, this," he gestured around the mess hall, its walls adorned with maps and a few personal mementos from home, "this is our world. We've got a job to do. And we've got to look out for each other."

Pete chimed in, his voice steady and resolute, "And we'll do it together. We're more than just a crew; we're brothers." He leaned forward, his elbows on the table, the early morning light catching the youthful eagerness in his eyes. "I'd be out on the boat with my dad, pulling in the crab pots back in Oregon. I miss the salt air, the sound of the gulls... But I know this is where I need to be."

Sipping his coffee, Johnny glanced around the mess hall, taking in the familiar faces and camaraderie. "This place, it's like a small town, isn't it? We've got our routines, our little jokes. It's not home, but it's something. It's ours."

Sully, with a mouthful of bacon, interjected, "And just like any small town, we've got the grumpy old-timers," he said with a nod towards a table of seasoned sailors, their faces etched with stories of the sea, "and the wide-eyed newcomers." He winked at Johnny.

While stirring his coffee, Luis added softly, "Back in Miami, I'd be waking up to the sound of the ocean and my mom's radio playing salsa music. It's funny the things you miss. The music, the vibrant streets, the warmth of the sun..."

Dave chimed in, his voice tinged with nostalgia. "I can almost hear the cows mooing back on the farm. Never thought I'd miss that sound. Or the smell of the earth after rain."

The group shared a collective chuckle, their laughter mingling with the clinks of cutlery and the distant hum of the ship's engines. The mess hall, with its worn but clean surfaces and the ever-present smell of diesel mixed with food, became a backdrop to their shared experiences and memories, a small floating piece of home in the ocean's vastness.

As the USS Houston cut through the Pacific, the vast expanse of the ocean around it seemed to merge with the azure sky at the horizon.

On the main deck, the air crackled with a palpable sense of purpose and anticipation.

Commander Paul H. Rice, the ship's Executive Officer, stood at the center of the controlled chaos unfolding on the deck, embodying a figure of composed authority amidst the flurry of activity. His posture was erect and commanding, starkly contrasting to the frenetic movement around him. With keen, observant eyes that missed no detail, he surveyed the gunnery crew as they scurried about, preparing for the upcoming drill.

Orders echoed across the deck, metal clanked, and boots thudded rhythmically on steel, creating the symphony of naval life he had intimately known throughout his years of service.

Paul Rice's journey to this moment blended rigorous discipline with a deep-seated passion for naval tradition. Growing up in a small coastal town in Maine, the sea drew him from an early age. His father, a decorated naval officer, had instilled in him a love for the ocean and a respect for the discipline of military life.

Stories of valiant naval battles and tales of strategic brilliance filled Paul's childhood, sowing the seeds of his future career. Graduating at the top of his class from the Naval Academy, Paul quickly distinguished himself as an officer of exceptional talent and unwavering commitment. His rise through the ranks was swift, marked by his attention to detail, strategic acumen, and ability to inspire respect and loyalty in his crew.

However, Paul's journey was not without its trials. He had faced personal losses that had deeply affected him, including the untimely death of his younger sister in a car accident, an event that had left a profound impact on his perspective on life and duty. This personal tragedy strengthened his resolve to protect those under his command, viewing each crew member almost like family.

As an Executive Officer, Paul was known for his calm demeanor under pressure and ability to make quick, decisive decisions. His leadership style balanced firmness and fairness, earning him the respect of his superiors and subordinates. He believed in leading by example, often working alongside his crew and sharing their tasks and hardships.

The current atmosphere on the ship was tense as the crew prepared for an important drill. It was an exercise designed to test their readiness for combat, a scenario that was becoming increasingly likely given the escalating global tensions. For Paul, these drills were not just about efficiency and precision; they were about ensuring the safety and preparedness of every person on board.

As Commander Rice watched the gunnery crew load and ready the artillery, his mind was in the present, reflecting on past experiences that had shaped him. Each decision he made, each order he gave, was a culmination of years of training, experience, and the lessons learned from those who had mentored him. In him resided the spirit of the naval tradition, a legacy he carried forward with pride and a deep sense of responsibility.

The sailors, a mix of seasoned veterans and eager young recruits, were at their stations, readying the ship's formidable armaments. The main deck was a hive of activity, with the crew checking and rechecking the heavy guns, ensuring that everything was in perfect working order.

"Alright, gentlemen, let's make every shot count today," Commander Rice called out, his voice ringing clear and authoritative over the din of the machinery. The deck vibrated subtly underfoot, a constant reminder of the ship's power. "Remember, precision and discipline are what set us apart."

His firm and resonant words elicited nods and murmurs of agreement from the listeners. Standing in neat rows, the crew respected Commander Rice for his rank and expertise and handled his responsibilities strictly and fairly.

At one of the gun stations, Seaman Johnny Thompson loaded the ammunition with his hands, slightly trembling with excitement and nerves. The metal shells were cold and heavy in his hands, starkly contrasting with the warm ocean breeze brushing his face. Beside him, his friend Pete Anderson checked the gun's alignment, his forehead creased in concentration.

Commander Rice approached the gun crew, his boots thudding solidly against the steel deck, each step resonating with authority. The rhythmic clank of his footsteps echoed in the narrow confines of the ship, merging with the distant hum of the engines and the occasional creak of the vessel's frame.

"How are we doing here, Thompson, Anderson?" His voice, clear and commanding, cut through the ambient noise of the ship. His gaze was sharp, like an eagle surveying its domain, missing no detail as his eyes swept over the gun setup.

Johnny, his uniform slightly damp with sweat under the unyielding sun, straightened up and saluted crisply. Wiping a bead of sweat from his brow with the back of his hand, he reported, "All set, sir. Just double-checking the alignments." His voice was steady, but the slight tension in his posture spoke of the respect Commander Rice commanded.

"Good, good. Remember, it's all about the details," Rice advised sternly and encouragingly. He stepped closer, inspecting the gun's alignment with a practiced eye. "A well-aimed shot is worth a dozen hurried ones."

Pete, his hands steady on the gun, nodded in agreement. "Understood, sir. We won't let you down." His words were few, but his determined expression and confident grip on the gun conveyed his commitment.

Captain Albert H. Rooks observed the proceedings through his binoculars from his vantage point on the bridge. The lenses brought the deck into sharp focus, allowing him to scrutinize every movement and interaction. His seasoned eyes, honed by years at sea, missed no detail. Watching Commander Rice's interaction with the crew, he turned to his navigator, a hint of pride in his voice. "Commander Rice has a good handle on the crew. They respond well to him."

"Indeed, Captain. He's got a way of bringing out the best in them," the navigator agreed, his eyes following the bustling activity below. He watched through the bridge's windows as the men moved with precision and purpose, each a cog in the ship's well-oiled machine.

Back on the deck, the air smelled of gunpowder and sea salt, a potent mixture almost synonymous with naval life. The sharp cries of seagulls mingled with the ship's sounds, creating a surreal chorus against the backdrop of the endless ocean. The relentless sun beat down, casting stark, angular shadows on the deck and etching the gunnery crew's faces with concentration and determination.

The gunnery drill was about to commence. Standing at a strategic vantage point, Commander Rice surveyed the target – a tiny speck against the vast, undulating canvas of the ocean. His voice, amplified by the ship's acoustics, rang out with clarity. "Gun crews, ready!"

The tension on the deck was palpable. Each man was acutely aware of the drill's importance, their bodies taut with anticipation.

Johnny and Pete exchanged a quick, nervous glance before focusing intently on their task. The ship's deck hummed with anticipation.

Upon receiving the command to fire, the deck erupted in a cacophony of noise as the guns roared to life. The ship shuddered slightly with the recoil, a testament to the sheer power of the armaments.

"Steady now, aim with purpose," Rice instructed, watching as the shells arced through the sky toward the target. The first rounds fell short, churning up the water in a spectacular display of power and precision.

Commander Rice, unflappable as ever, offered quick adjustments to the gun crews. "Adjust your elevation, Gun Three. Gun Four, delay your timing by half a second," he instructed his tone firm but encouraging. The crew worked quickly to make the necessary adjustments, their movements becoming more fluid and confident with each command.

The next volley was closer to the mark, the shells striking closer to the target. "Much better, much better!" Rice exclaimed, a hint of satisfaction in his voice. "Let's tighten it up even more. Concentrate on your training."

As the drill progressed, improvements were evident. The crew's coordination and accuracy increased with each round fired, a testament to their growing expertise and Commander Rice's practical guidance.

Captain Rooks, watching from the bridge, nodded in approval. "Commander, your training drills are shaping up quite the crew," he said over the intercom, his voice carrying a tone of respect and satisfaction.

Rice, his eyes still on the gun crews, responded with a hint of pride in his voice, "They're a good group, Captain. Eager to learn, eager to serve."

The booming sound of the guns echoed across the water, each round a symbol of the crew's dedication and skill. A sense of accomplishment rippled through the ship as the drill ended. The sailors, sweaty and tired but exhilarated, began cleaning and securing the guns.

Commander Rice made his way through the deck, offering praise and constructive feedback. Their attentive postures and earnest nods showed the crew's respect and admiration for him.

"Excellent work today, gentlemen," Rice said, addressing the crew. "Remember, what we do here is not just about firing guns. It's about working as a unit, being precise, and being ready for whatever comes our way."

Standing tall and proud, the sailors felt renewed purpose and camaraderie. They were more than just a crew; they were a finely tuned machine, ready to face any challenge that lay ahead.

As the sun began to set, casting a golden glow over the deck, the USS Houston sailed on, its crew united and prepared under the steady leadership of Commander Rice and Captain Rooks. The trials of war loomed on the horizon, but aboard the Houston, a collective strength promised resilience and heroism in the face of adversity.

As the evening settled over the USS Houston, the bustling activity of the day gave way to a more reflective atmosphere. The crew gathered around the ship in small groups and shared their intimate stories about their lives before their service on the Houston. In these moments, under the canopy of stars and the gentle ocean sway, the bonds of camaraderie deepened, transforming them into a family forged by shared dreams and fears.

In one such gathering, Dave, Johnny, Tommy, and Sergeant Davis sat on the deck, the vast ocean stretching endlessly before them. The soft glow of the ship's lights provided a cozy ambiance, and the distant hum of the engines was a soothing backdrop to their conversation.

Dave leaned against a coil of ropes, his gaze lost in the stars. "You know, back in Wisconsin, I used to spend nights like this watching the sky, dreaming of flying among those stars," he began, his voice tinged with nostalgia. "I thought I'd be a pilot, soaring above the clouds, free as a bird."

Johnny, sitting cross-legged on the deck, looked at Dave with interest. "So, what changed your mind?"

Dave chuckled softly, "Then my uncle took me to see the naval fleet at the Great Lakes one summer. I saw the Houston, her guns, her majesty... and I knew I belonged to the sea, not the sky."

Sergeant Davis, his usual stern demeanor softened in the dim light, joined the conversation. "It's funny how life takes us on paths we never expect," he mused. "I joined the Marines straight out of high school. Wanted to do something meaningful, stand for something greater than myself."

Tommy, the youngest of the group, shifted uncomfortably. "I guess I just wanted to escape the noise of New York, see the world beyond the skyscrapers and crowded streets. But now, with a war pending and on the horizon, everything..." His voice trailed off, revealing an undercurrent of anxiety.

Davis reached out, placing a reassuring hand on Tommy's shoulder. "Fear is a part of this life, son. It's what we do in the face of it that defines us. Remember, you're not alone in this."

Johnny nodded in agreement, "Yeah, we're all in this together. We've got each other's backs."

The group fell into a contemplative silence, each man lost in his thoughts. Around them, the subtle sounds of the sea filled the night airwaves gently lapping against the hull, night birds calling in the distance, and the ship occasionally creaking. After a moment, Sergeant Davis spoke again, his voice a low rumble. "Before the Marines, I thought I'd take over my dad's hardware store in Georgia. Never imagined I'd be here, in the middle of the Pacific, with you lot."

Johnny smiled, "And we wouldn't want it any other way, Sergeant. We're like a jigsaw puzzle; each of us fits in to make the picture whole."

As the evening settled over the USS Houston, the bustling activity of the day gave way to a more reflective atmosphere. The crew gathered around the ship in small groups and shared their intimate stories about their lives before their service on the Houston. In these moments, under the canopy of stars and the gentle ocean sway, the bonds of camaraderie deepened, transforming them into a family forged by shared dreams and fears.

The group chuckled, the tension easing as they shared a moment of lightheartedness. Their stories, dreams, and fears, shared under the starlit sky, wove them closer together. In these quiet hours, away from the demands of their duties, they found comfort in their shared humanity, a reminder that despite the uncertainty of their situation, they had found a family in each other.

As the night deepened, their conversation meandered from tales of childhood adventures to aspirations for the future. Each story, each shared dream and fear, strengthened the invisible thread that connected them, a thread woven from the fabric of their collective experiences aboard the Houston.

Chapter SIX

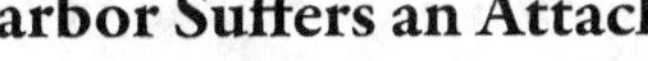

Pearl Harbor Suffers an Attack

The USS Houston, a formidable presence in the Pacific, glided through the waters with a sense of routine calm. Captain Albert H. Rooks, a figure of stoic leadership, stood on the bridge, his gaze fixed on the horizon. The crew, a blend of seasoned sailors and fresh recruits, went about their duties with the efficiency born of rigorous training. The atmosphere aboard was one of disciplined routine, the rhythm of naval life playing out in the hum of the engines and the creak of the ship's steel frame.

Suddenly, the crackle of the intercom pierced the steady hum of activity. " "All hands, this is not a drill. I repeat! This is not a drill.

"The enemy has attacked Pearl Harbor... The enemy has attacked Pearl Harbor!" Usually reserved for routine announcements, the voice now carried a substantial weight.

A stunned silence wrapped around the USS Houston as the grave announcement echoed through the ship, seemingly sucking the air out of its corridors and decks.

The rhythmic clanking of machinery and the distant hum of the engines, once the soundtrack of daily life aboard the vessel, now seemed to fade into a hushed stillness. The news of Pearl Harbor's attack was not just incomprehensible; it was a jolt of reality so profound that it momentarily froze time.

Sailors, engaged in their routine tasks just moments before, stopped in their tracks. Grease-stained hands holding tools hovered mid-air, and paperwork in the administration areas lay forgotten as fingers paused on typewriters. The clatter of pots and pans in the galley ceased abruptly, leaving only the sound of a lone pot boiling over unnoticed.

Faces, young and seasoned alike, turned towards the speakers, their expressions frozen in a tableau of shock and disbelief. Eyes widened, and mouths fell open, yet no words came out. The usual bustle of the ship, with sailors jostling, laughing, and shouting orders, gave way to an eerie stillness punctuated only by the distant lapping of waves against the hull.

On the deck, crew members stood like statues, gazes locked on the speakers that had delivered the unbelievable news. The bright sunlight seemed to cast harsher shadows than usual, accentuating the stunned expressions on their faces. Some slowly shook their heads as if trying to dispel a nightmare, while others clenched their jaws, the muscles in their necks standing out in sharp relief.

Below deck, in the dimly lit corridors, the news reverberated off the steel walls, enveloping sailors in a heavy cloak of uncertainty and fear. Hushed whispers began to ripple through the ranks, starkly contrasting the usual loud banter.

In the engine room, the engineers, usually absorbed in their work amid the heat and noise, stood motionless, their protective gear and tools now mere afterthoughts. Their faces, cast in the flickering glow of dials and gauges, bore expressions of worry. The news of Pearl Harbor's attack transformed the USS Houston from a vessel of war to a community in shock.

In this moment of disbelief, each sailor stood united regardless of rank or role. As the reality of their new world began to sink in, the silence was slowly, reluctantly broken by the resumption of movement. But the ship and the men aboard had irrevocably changed in those few, profound moments of silence.

In the USS Houston's command center, the heavy weight of silence lingered until Lieutenant Miller, standing beside Captain Rooks, broke it. His voice, usually steady and composed, carried an uncharacteristic tremor as he grappled with the gravity of the announcement. "Sir, could this be real?" he asked, his words trailing off as he struggled to comprehend what they just heard.

His eyes, broad with an expression of disbelief and dawning realization, met Captain Rooks's. The usually bustling command center, with its maps and strategic charts, felt eerily still as if time itself had paused in the wake of the news.

Captain Rooks, usually the epitome of naval composure, remained momentarily silent, allowing the weight of Miller's question to linger. The low hum of the ship's operations, once a comforting background noise, now seemed distant, overshadowed by the palpable sense of urgency that filled the room.

Finally, Captain Rooks replied, low and grave, "Yes, Miller, it's real. This changes everything." His gaze shifted back to the window, overlooking the vast expanse of ocean that suddenly felt more treacherous than ever.

Lieutenant Miller swallowed hard, the news settling in like a heavy anchor in his chest. "The implications... This means we're at war, doesn't it, sir? A full-scale conflict..."

Captain Rooks nodded solemnly, his eyes reflecting a well of experience and understanding of what lay ahead. "It does. We're now on the front lines of a battle that will test us all. Prepare the men, Miller. We have to be ready for what comes next."

As Miller turned to relay the orders, his mind raced with the enormity of the task ahead.

His words galvanized the crew into action, with the initial shock quickly giving way to a flurry of activity. Officers barked orders, and sailors rushed to their stations. The drill was no longer just a practice; it was preparation for the reality they now faced.

The air was thick with tension on the gun deck. The metallic scent of the guns mingled with the briny ocean air. His brow furrowed in concentration, Pete glanced at his fellow gunner, Johnny. A palpable sense of urgency now underscored the usual clatter of the deck. "Can you believe this? Pearl Harbor?" he called out, his voice rising over the din of hurried preparations.

Johnny, his hands moving with practiced efficiency as he checked and rechecked their equipment, felt a surge of adrenaline mixed with disbelief. "It's hard to believe," he replied, tightening a bolt with a precise turn. "But we've got to be ready for anything now. No more drills." His voice was steady, but his mind raced with the implications of their new reality.

Pete nodded, loading ammunition with more vigor than usual. "This is the real deal, Johnny. I never thought we'd see action like this." He paused, glancing up at the sky as if expecting enemy planes at any moment. "Do you think we're ready for what's coming?"

Johnny locked the ammunition in place and met Pete's gaze. "We have to be. Training's one thing, but this is... it's real." He took a deep breath, trying to steady his racing heart. "We'll do our jobs, Pete. It's what we trained for."

Around them, the gun deck was a flurry of activity. Sailors moved with a newfound urgency, the reality of war transforming routine tasks into matters of life and death. The heavy thud of boots on the deck, the clanking of metal, and the occasional shout of an officer created a symphony of war preparation.

Pete loaded another round, his movements automatic but his mind far away, picturing the scenes of destruction they had heard over the radio. "We're in this together, Johnny. We watch each other's backs."

Johnny nodded, checking the alignment one final time. "Together," he affirmed, the word bolstering his resolve. "Let's show them what the Houston is made of."

Captain Rooks' authoritative and resolute voice reverberated through the intercom, reaching every corner of the USS Houston. "We've trained for moments like these. We are a crew, a unit, and we will face whatever comes our way together. The Houston has never shied away from a challenge, and we won't start now. We will defend our country and each other. We will make history and do it as one team."

His words resonated with the crew, each member pausing to absorb the gravity of his message. Focus and determination now united the ship, a microcosm of a common purpose. But amidst this newfound resolve, there was an undercurrent of tension and grief, especially as thoughts turned to their friends and fellow sailors stationed in Hawaii.

Unspoken memories of comrades in Pearl Harbor filled the silence that followed the announcement. Faces of vibrant and full of life flashed in their minds - friends who had shared laughs, dreams, and the daily rigors of naval life. These were the men who stood shoulder to shoulder with them, who had become more than just fellow sailors but brothers.

The reality of their loss added a deep, personal dimension to the conflict. "I heard from Miller just last week," muttered a young sailor, his voice barely audible above the low hum of the ship. "He was stationed on the USS Arizona..."

Another sailor's eyes clouded with grief, added, "My brother, Sam, was at Hickam Field. Can't believe he's gone..." His words trailed off into a heavy silence.

The impact of the attack on Pearl Harbor was no longer just a strategic blow; it was a personal tragedy that had hit home for many aboard the Houston. The faces of their fallen comrades seemed to loom over them, a silent reminder of the stakes at hand.

Sensing the shift in mood, Captain Rooks added firmly, "We remember those we've lost. We honor them by doing our duty and fighting with everything we've got. They're with us in spirit, in every battle we face."

The tension aboard the ship was palpable. The threat of war had become real and immediate, but so, too, had the resolve to meet it head-on. As the Houston sailed forward, her crew stood united, not just in their mission, but in their shared loss and collective vow to avenge their fallen brethren.

Doctor Sullivan, the ship's medic, exchanged glances with his assistant. "Looks like we're going to be busier than we thought," he said, a note of determination in his voice. "Let's make sure the medical bay is ready for anything."

As Captain Rooks' speech ended, a renewed sense of purpose emerged. The crew moved with a sense of urgency, but their actions showed newfound determination. They were no longer just sailors on a ship; they were a crucial part of a conflict that would define their lives and their place in history.

The USS Houston, now more than just a ship, sailed forward, its course altered by the winds of war. Ahead lay challenges and trials that would test the crew to their limits. But under the leadership of Captain Rooks and with the unyielding spirit of its crew, the Houston was ready to make its mark in the annals of history, to take its place in the story of a world at war.

As the ship cut through the waters, heading towards an uncertain future, the sun dipped below the horizon, casting the sea in shades of crimson and gold. Even in the darkest times, a moment of beauty emerged amid the chaos, reminding everyone that they could still find light. The journey ahead would be fraught with danger and hardship, but the Houston and her crew were ready to face whatever lay beyond the setting sun.

As the USS Houston cut through the waters of the Pacific, a palpable tension enveloped the ship. An invisible yet unmistakable shroud seemed to affect every sailor aboard. The latest dispatches from headquarters, bearing news of escalating conflicts in the Pacific, had cast a solemn shadow over the vessel. The constant thrum of the engine mingled with the sound of waves crashing against the hull, a relentless reminder of their ceaseless journey through these contested waters.

A more serious tone took hold in the officers' mess, a room usually filled with the clink of cutlery and the hum of casual conversation. The air was thick with a mix of coffee aroma and the faint smell of sea salt, starkly contrasting the weighty atmosphere.

Captain Albert H. Rooks and Commander Paul H. Rice stood hunched over a large, worn map on the table, its edges curled from frequent use. The usually bright room was dim, lit only by a few overhead lamps that cast focused beams of light onto the map, highlighting the urgency of their discussion.

"Look here," Captain Rooks said, leaning over the large, detailed nautical chart on the table in the ship's dimly lit command center. He pointed to a cluster of red pins near the Philippine Sea, his voice low and steady, carrying the weight of experience and authority. "Enemy activity has increased in this region. We must adjust our course to avoid detection."

The soft humming of electronic equipment and the occasional crackle of radio communication filled the room, creating an undercurrent of tension. The subtle scent of coffee lingered in the air, a testament to the crew's long hours on watch.

Lieutenant Morrison, standing nearby, looked up from his charts, his brow furrowed in concentration. "Adjusting course, sir. What's our new heading?"

Captain Rooks, his eyes scanning the map, responded with precision. "Set a course to 45 degrees north-northeast. We'll skirt around the Palawan Passage. It's longer but safer."

Morrison nodded, quickly relaying the orders to the navigation team. "45 degrees north-northeast, aye, Captain."

Ensign Lee, monitoring the radar, interjected with a note of urgency in his voice. "Sir, I recommend we go to silent running. It'll reduce our chances of being picked up by enemy sonar."

Captain Rooks considered this, his gaze fixed on the map as if visualizing their path through the treacherous waters. "Agreed. All hands, prepare for silent running. Let's make ourselves as invisible as possible."

The command center's atmosphere grew even more focused, the crew moving swiftly. The seriousness of their situation hushed the usual sounds of activity as if it had permeated every corner of the room.

Commander Rice nodded, his eyes scanning the map intently. Standing beside Captain Rooks in the command center, he leaned in slightly, focusing on the chart that sprawled across the table. The dim overhead lights cast subtle shadows across his face, highlighting his determined expression.

"And our reconnaissance planes report suspicious movements near the Marshall Islands," he added, tracing an arc across the chart. The concern in his voice was evident, underlining the gravity of their strategic choices. As he moved, the slight rustle of his uniform was almost imperceptible against the low sound of the ship's operational systems.

Captain Rooks turned his attention to the area Rice indicated, his eyes narrowing as he assessed the new information. "That's troubling news," he murmured, his hands clasped behind his back. "It suggests they might be expanding their operational zone."

The command center was a hive of subdued activity; officers and crew members moved with purpose, their actions precise and methodical. The radar's soft beeps and computer fans' gentle whir created a background symphony of technology and vigilance.

Rice straightened up, crossing his arms as he considered their options. "We need to relay this to fleet command immediately. They need to be aware of these developments."

Captain Rooks nodded in agreement, the lines on his face deepening with the weight of responsibility. "Do it, Rice. And put our air patrols on high alert. I want eyes on every inch of that sector."

Commander Rice quickly turned to leave, his boots echoing softly on the metal floor as he moved with purposeful strides. The command center, a crucial nerve center of the USS Houston, continued its vigilant watch over the vast and unpredictable expanse of the Pacific.

The meticulously maintained and constantly updated map was a testament to the strategic intricacies of naval warfare.

An array of colored pins dotted the map, each signifying different information types - red for known enemy positions, blue for allied forces, and yellow for areas of interest. Around these pins, annotations in careful handwriting recorded dates, times, and observations, transforming the map into a living document of the war's progression.

The room, usually a sanctuary of solitude and thought for Captain Rooks, now resonated with the subtle sounds of the ship's operations - distant orders, the soft buzz of radio communications, and the occasional muffled footsteps outside. The captain, seated at his desk, leaned forward, his eyes moving meticulously over the chart. Each pin and notation represented a piece of the vast puzzle they were navigating.

"Commander, look at this," Captain Rooks called out, his voice breaking the silence. "If we reroute through this corridor," he gestured to a narrow passage between two clusters of yellow pins, "we can gather crucial intelligence and remain undetected."

Commander Rice leaned over the chart, his brow furrowed in concentration. "It's risky, but it might be our only chance to get the upper hand in this region," he replied with resolve and apprehension in his tone.

The room echoed with the sound of their strategic deliberations, a symphony of whispered conversations, and the rustling of maps interwoven with the ever-present backdrop of the ship's heartbeat.

Both men made decisions that could alter the war's course in this small, enclosed space, bearing this heavy responsibility steadfastly committed to their duty. The pins clustered more densely in certain areas, indicating regions of heightened tension and potential conflict. These hotspots were the focus of intense scrutiny, representing a puzzle of enemy movements and possible engagements. The areas around the Coral Sea and the Philippines were particularly congested, reflecting these waters' escalating confrontations and strategic significance.

As the light from the overhead lamp cast a warm glow on the map's surface, the etched lines of longitude and latitude, the meticulously drawn coastlines, and the marked archipelagos took on a heightened significance. This was more than just a map; it was a crucial tool in navigating the treacherous waters of wartime strategy. The sea, represented in varying shades of blue, seemed almost to ripple and move under the gaze of the officers, reminding them of the vast and unpredictable theater of war in which they were operating.

For the officers aboard the USS Houston, this map was not just a guide but a constant companion in their efforts to outmaneuver the enemy and protect their ship and crew. Each pin and annotation was a piece of a giant puzzle, a snapshot in the ever-changing landscape of war, and a reminder of their grave responsibility.

The air in the operations room aboard the USS Houston was thick with the scent of strong coffee, a stark contrast to the salty sea breeze that wafted in through the open porthole. The usual clatter and buzz of the ship seemed distant here as if the room had cocooned itself in its own world of strategy and planning. The faint sound of distant radio chatter and the occasional muffled order from the deck barely penetrated this sanctuary of tactical deliberation.

Captain Rooks had his eyes narrowed in concentration. They usually sparkled with a commanding presence, but now they reflected deep concern as he traced a route with his finger across the Pacific. "The Japanese fleet's movements are unpredictable. We need to anticipate their next step," he said, his voice low and steady, the weight of his words hanging in the air.

Commander Rice, standing beside him, nodded in agreement. His sharp features were set in a mask of concentration, a clear indication of the gravity of the situation. "Our reconnaissance suggests increased activity near the Coral Sea. It could be a diversion or the real deal," he replied, his hands clasped behind his back, his gaze fixed on the map.

The two officers leaned closer, their shadows merging on the parchment. The gentle creak of the ship's timbers filled the room, constantly reminding them of the vast ocean surrounding them.

The rustle of papers as they sifted through the latest intelligence reports was the only other sound, adding a sense of urgency to their task.

Lieutenant Jenkins, a young but capable officer, entered the room, his steps quick and purposeful. "Captain, Commander, we've intercepted encrypted communications. They're sparse, but our cryptologists are working on them," he reported, handing over a folder of transcripts.

Captain Rooks took the folder, his eyes quickly scanning the contents. "Good work, Jenkins. Keep me updated on any breakthroughs." His tone was firm yet appreciative.

Commander Rice interjected, "Let's increase our radio surveillance. If the Japanese are planning a major operation, they can't keep it hidden for long." His suggestion carried the expertise of years at sea, reflecting his deep understanding of naval warfare.

The seriousness of their task was evident in their focused expressions and the way they occasionally paused to consider their options. Every decision they made here, amidst the charts and reports, could alter the course of the ship and the lives of the men aboard. Strategic planning was in full swing in the room, charting the fate of the USS Houston and her crew one careful decision at a time.

As they continued to discuss their strategy, the sound of the sea against the ship's hull provided a rhythmic backdrop to their deliberations. The tension in the room was palpable, a reflection of the high stakes they faced in the vast expanse of the Pacific theater.

Outside, the sea stretched endlessly, its vastness a reminder of the opportunities and perils ahead. The sun cast a golden glow on the water, its beauty belying the tumultuous times. Inside, under the artificial light of the officers' mess, Captain Rooks and Commander Rice continued their deliberations, acutely aware that the fate of the Houston and her crew rested heavily on their shoulders.

Captain Rooks stood rigidly, his gaze fixed intently on the map sprawled before him. The dim light of the officers' mess cast deep shadows across his face, accentuating the worry lines etched into his forehead. As his finger traced the strategic points on the map of the Pacific, a sense of urgency underscored his movements.

"Looks like things are heating up faster than we anticipated," he remarked, his voice carrying a mix of concern and anticipation. The gravity of the situation was palpable in his tone, each word weighed down by the responsibility of command.

The operations room of the USS Houston was a scene of controlled urgency. Fluorescent lights flickered overhead, casting stark shadows across the room's utilitarian surfaces. Charts and electronic equipment adorned the walls, each screen and dial a testament to the technological prowess at their disposal. The low hum of the ship's advanced machinery mixed with the distant, muffled sound of the ocean, creating a reassuring and ominous soundtrack.

Standing across from Captain Rooks, Commander Rice mirrored the Captain's solemnity. His posture was rigid, the uniform crisp and impeccable, a sharp contrast to the seriousness etched on his face. His eyes, which usually shone with a bastion of resolve, now flickered with a hint of apprehension as he absorbed the implications of their discussion. He leaned in, his hand resting on the sturdy oak table for support, the wood worn smooth from years of strategic planning.

"The Japanese are making bold moves. We need to be prepared for any eventuality," he said, his voice tinged with fear and determination. His nod was firm, conveying a readiness to face the challenges ahead. The statement, though measured, carried an undercurrent of excitement - a testament to his commitment to duty even in the face of uncertainty.

Captain Rooks, his face a mask of stoicism, looked up from the array of charts and screens before him. "Agreed," he replied, his voice steady, betraying none of the tension he felt. "We need to adjust our tactics. Let's consider deploying additional surveillance drones in the critical zones. We can't afford any blind spots."

Commander Rice's eyes narrowed thoughtfully. "And what about the submarine patrols? If we reroute the SSNs to the northern flank, we might gain an edge in reconnaissance."

The Captain paused, considering the suggestion. "That's a solid plan. But we'll need to coordinate with the fleet at Midway. I don't want to stretch our resources too thin." His fingers drummed on the table, a physical manifestation of the strategic calculations racing through his mind.

Their focused conversation filled the room, interspersed with the occasional beep and whir of computers processing data. The air was tense, charged with the gravity of their decisions. Every word spoken here, every course of action plotted, could tip the balance in the vast and unforgiving theater of the Pacific.

As they continued strategizing, a young officer entered with a sheaf of papers. "Sir, latest intelligence reports from the South China Sea," he announced, handing the documents to Captain Rooks.

The Captain scanned the papers quickly, his brow furrowing. "This changes our calculations. Looks like we might have to fast-track those deployment plans."

Commander Rice stepped closer, peering over the Captain's shoulder at the report. "Time is not on our side, Captain. We need to act and act fast."

Their eyes met an unspoken understanding passing between them. Both men knew that the days ahead would test their mettle and that of their crew. In this quiet room, away from the hustle of the ship, the tension of impending conflict hung heavily in the air, a silent yet powerful presence that acknowledged the magnitude of what lay ahead.

In the officers' mess, where the palpable tension of the impending conflict hung like a dense fog, Captain Rooks and Commander Rice were deep in strategizing when the door swung open abruptly. A young ensign, his uniform crisp and his face etched with the urgency of his mission, stepped briskly into the room.

"Sir, new intelligence just came in," he announced, extending a folder towards Captain Rooks. Though steady, his voice betrayed a hint of the anxiety gripping the entire crew.

Captain Rooks turned, his eyes momentarily leaving the map to settle on the ensign. "Thank you, Ensign Harris," he said, nodding to the young officer. His hands, steady and experienced, reached for the folder, the action deliberate and measured.

Commander Rice leaned over as he opened the folder, the intensity in his eyes sharpening. The ensign stood at attention, his gaze shifting between the two senior officers, aware that the folder's contents could significantly alter their course of action.

Captain Rooks' eyes scanned the documents quickly but thoroughly. "This changes things," he muttered under his breath, a new wrinkle of concern appearing on his forehead.

"What's the update, Captain?" Commander Rice inquired, his tone laced with concern and a readiness to adapt to whatever challenge the new intelligence presented.

"It's the Japanese fleet," Captain Rooks began, his voice low. "They've been spotted much closer than we anticipated. Their trajectory suggests heading towards the Coral Sea sooner than expected."

Commander Rice's jaw tightened at the news. "That's aggressive positioning. It could mean an imminent engagement," he observed, the gears of strategy already turning in his mind.

Ensign Harris, sensing the gravity of the information he had delivered, remained silent but attentive. The room felt suddenly smaller, the weight of the impending conflict pressing down on them all.

"We'll need to adjust our patrol route," Captain Rooks decided, returning to the map. "And alert the crew. We must be ready for any engagement, possibly within days."

Commander Rice nodded in agreement, a resolute determination settling over him. "I'll start coordinating with the departments immediately. We'll make sure Houston is combat-ready."

As Ensign Harris excused himself to continue his duties, Captain Rooks and Commander Rice continued to pour over the map and intelligence reports, their minds racing with tactics and scenarios. The stakes had risen, and the USS Houston and her valiant crew were on the brink of finding themselves at the heart of a rapidly escalating conflict in the Pacific.

In the softly lit radio room of the USS Houston, a steady stream of encrypted messages crackled over the airwaves, each carrying vital information cloaked in secrecy. The room was alive with the sound of static and the rhythmic tapping of Morse code. Cryptographers, their eyes focused and fingers deft, worked tirelessly to decipher the incoming transmissions.

While overseeing the operation, Lieutenant Johnson moved among his team with a keen eye, ensuring they missed no detail. One of the cryptographers, a young sailor named Anderson, called out, "Lieutenant, I think we've got something significant here."

Johnson quickly made his way to Anderson's station. "Let's hear it, Anderson," he said, his voice a blend of urgency and anticipation.

Anderson read out the deciphered message, his voice steady despite the gravity of the contents. "It appears to be a reconnaissance report. The Japanese fleet has increased its activity near the Gilbert Islands."

Johnson's brow furrowed as he processed the information. "That could indicate they're planning a move in that region. We need to get this to the Captain immediately." He quickly scribbled a note to accompany the decoded message.

The radio room continued its buzz of activity, with other cryptographers diligently working through the backlog of transmissions. Another message came through this time from a cryptographer at the far end of the room.

"Sir, another message," the cryptographer announced. "It's a communication between two Japanese commanders discussing troop movements towards the Marshall Islands."

The Lieutenant took the message, his mind racing with the strategic implications. "This is vital intelligence. It's painting a clearer picture of their intentions in the Pacific." He grabbed the handset of the internal communication line. "Bridge, this is Johnson in the radio room. We've decoded messages indicating significant Japanese fleet and troop movements near the Gilbert and Marshall Islands."

On the bridge, Captain Rooks and Commander Rice listened intently. "Thank you, Lieutenant. Keep us updated on any new developments," Captain Rooks responded, a sense of urgency in his voice.

Commander Rice turned to the Captain, his expression tense with concern. The glow of the tactical screens illuminated his face, casting sharp shadows that underscored the gravity of the situation. "The Japanese are spreading their net wide, Captain," he said, his voice firm and laced with urgency. "We need to adjust our strategy accordingly."

Standing by the chart table with his arms crossed, Captain Rooks looked up at Rice, his eyes reflecting the moment's seriousness. "What do you propose, Commander?"

Rice leaned in, his hands planted firmly on the table, the maps and charts in front of him a tapestry of their current predicament. "We need to increase our reconnaissance patrols, for starters. And possibly reroute our supply lines to avoid their primary areas of operation," he suggested, his eyes scanning the chart, plotting potential courses and countermeasures.

"Rerouting could delay our supplies," the Captain pointed out, his brow furrowing in thought.

"Yes, but it's a necessary risk," Rice countered, meeting the Captain's gaze squarely. "It's better to face a delay than to walk into a trap. We should also consider sending false signals to mislead them about our position."

The Captain nodded slowly, absorbing Rice's suggestions. "Alright, implement the changes. But keep me updated on any potential impacts on our operations."

Rice acknowledged with a curt nod, a sense of resolve in his movements. "I'll coordinate with the departments right away, Captain. We'll stay one step ahead."

As Rice turned to leave, the weight of their decisions lingered in the air. The command center, usually a hub of controlled activity, now hummed with a heightened sense of alertness.

Back in the radio room, the cryptographers continued their vigilant work, aware that the information they were uncovering was crucial to the Houston's ability to navigate the increasingly dangerous waters of the Pacific. Lieutenant Johnson, proud of his team's efforts, remained focused on the task at hand, ready to relay any new intelligence that might give them an edge in the looming conflict.

"We've got another batch coming through. They're stepping up their communications," Johnson informed his team.

In the captain's quarters of the USS Houston, a room usually reserved for quiet contemplation and command decisions, the atmosphere was thick with the gravity of war.

The modestly sized space, steeped in naval tradition, bore adornments like a model of the ship, nautical charts, and the Captain's personal effects, all reflecting a life dedicated to the sea.

At the room's center, charts, maps, and various documents now covered a usually pristine, sturdy wooden table, each one marking crucial intelligence and strategic data. The table's surface, illuminated by the focused beam of a desk lamp, became the epicenter of a critical meeting.

Senior officers, their faces etched with the seriousness of their task, gathered around the table. Standing at the head, Captain Rooks projected a calm yet determined demeanor. His eyes, usually a well of stoic resolve, now flickered with a hint of concern as he addressed the group.

"We're in uncharted waters, gentlemen," he began, his voice steady but laden with the weight of responsibility. "The intelligence suggests the Japanese are making aggressive moves. We need to be ready for any kind of engagement."

Standing to his right, Commander Rice chimed in, his tone analytical yet tinged with urgency. "Our primary objective should be safeguarding our fleet and disrupting enemy movements. We'll need to consider every possible scenario."

A seasoned lieutenant, his brow furrowed in concentration, leaned over the table, pointing at a marked area on the map. "If we deploy our reconnaissance planes here, we can better understand their fleet's position."

Captain Rooks considered this, nodding slowly. "Good point, Lieutenant. We need all the intel we can get. But we must also be discreet. The last thing we want is to reveal our position."

Another officer, a grizzled commander with years of sea experience, added, "We should reinforce our anti-aircraft defenses. If they decide to strike, we'll be ready to warmly welcome them."

The room resonated with a sense of somber determination. Awareness of the stakes, each officer contributed thoughts and suggestions, weaving a complex tapestry of strategies and countermeasures. The discussion ebbed and flowed, with moments of heated debate followed by calm analysis.

Captain Rooks, listening intently, occasionally interjected with decisive commands, steered the conversation and ensured the consideration of every perspective. "Remember, we're not just defending the Houston," he said firmly. "We're protecting our nation and our loved ones back home. Let's make sure we do everything in our power to return to them."

The officers nodded in agreement, a silent pact forming among them. They were a crew, and a band of brothers united in a common cause. As the meeting drew close, each officer left the room with renewed purpose, ready to implement the plans and face the challenges ahead.

In the quiet that followed, Captain Rooks stood alone momentarily, gazing out the porthole at the vast ocean. The weight of command rested heavily on his shoulders, but his resolve was unwavering. He was prepared to lead his ship and crew through the trials of war, whatever they might be.

Chapter SEVEN

Battle of Makassar Strait

In the strategy room of the USS Houston, a soft glow illuminated the large nautical chart spread out before Captain Albert H. Rooks and his Executive Officer, Commander Paul H. Rice. The chart detailed the Makassar Strait, a crucial area soon to witness a significant naval engagement unfolding.

His brow furrowed in deep concentration, Captain Rooks broke the tense silence. "Commander, the latest intelligence is troubling. The Japanese are moving significant transport fleets through the Makassar Strait."

Commander Rice leaned over the chart, his eyes intense and focused, the dim light of the command room casting deep shadows across his stern face. "Yes, Captain. They're likely reinforcing their positions in the East Indies. Our orders are clear – we intercept," he said, his voice firm, echoing slightly in the hushed atmosphere of the room.

A shadow of concern passed over Captain Rooks' face, his eyes momentarily reflecting the deep blue of the strategic map before him. "This will be our first major engagement since Pearl Harbor six weeks ago. The crew is eager, but many are green. We'll need to be sharp," he voiced, the weight of responsibility evident in his tone.

With a determined nod, Rice assured him, his voice resonating with confidence. "Agreed, sir. We've been running drills non-stop. The men know their duties. They're ready, more than ready."

Rooks pointed to a specific location on the chart, his finger tracing potential routes, deliberate and calculated movement. "Our reconnaissance suggests the Japanese convoy will pass through here. We have the element of surprise on our side," he said, his words laced with a strategic edge.

"But we should expect air support from the enemy. Our anti-aircraft guns will need to be ready," Rice interjected, his tone underscored with a hint of caution, the stakes of their mission clear in his expression.

Rooks, rubbing his chin thoughtfully, added, "And let's not forget, this strait can be treacherous – narrow passages, unpredictable currents. We'll need to navigate carefully." His gaze drifted back to the map, considering each possible move like a chess player contemplating the board.

Rice's eyes, reflecting the seriousness of their situation, met Rooks'. "Our helmsmen are up to the task, Captain. And the engine room is ready to give us all she's got," he responded, his confidence in the crew unshakable.

A moment of contemplative silence filled the room, the air thick with the gravity of their forthcoming challenge. The distant hum of the ship's engines was a subtle reminder of the ever-present danger they faced.

Rooks then spoke with renewed determination, his voice resonating with resolve. "This battle... it's more than just intercepting a convoy. It's about showing the Japanese that we're still in the fight. That Pearl Harbor hasn't knocked us out."

Rice's eyes, alight with a rare blend of pride and steely resolve, conveyed the depth of his conviction. "The crew feels it too, sir. There's a fire in them," he said, his voice rising with a palpable intensity that filled the cramped quarters of the command center. "They're not just ready; they're eager. They want this — for the Houston, for the fallen at Pearl Harbor."

He paused, letting his words hang in the air for a moment. The usual ambient sounds of the ship seemed to fade into the background, overshadowed by the gravity of his statement.

Standing across from him, Captain Rooks remained silent, absorbing the weight of Rice's words. The tension in the room was palpable, a tangible force that seemed to underscore the significance of what lay ahead.

Rice continued, his tone now edged with a fierce determination that resonated through the room. "They're hungry for retribution, sir. Every man aboard knows what's at stake. We've lost friends, brothers..." His fists clenched involuntarily, a physical manifestation of the emotional turmoil within.

The captain's eyes narrowed, reflecting a similar fire. "And we will honor them," he replied, his voice firm. "We will make every sacrifice count. The Houston will not back down. We will meet this challenge head-on."

Rice nodded, a sense of solemn agreement passing between the two men. "We'll make history, sir," he affirmed, his words echoing a promise, a vow that extended beyond the ship's steel walls.

The room, charged with the energy of their exchange, seemed to pulse with a new purpose.

With a firm nod, Rooks concluded, "Let's ensure we hit them hard and fast. We must disrupt their plans, buy time for our forces to regroup."

"We'll be ready, Captain. The Houston won't let you down," Rice affirmed, his voice steady and confident.

A fierce resolve united them as they gazed at the map, standing side by side. The USS Houston, a bastion of American naval strength, was embarking on a critical mission, a testament to the bravery and determination of her crew, ready to face the imminent confrontation in the Makassar Strait, their first confrontation of the war.

As the USS Houston sliced through the choppy waters of the Makassar Strait, a palpable tension settled over the ship. The vast expanse of blue water stretched endlessly around them, the choppy waves slapping against the hull, but the knowledge of what lay ahead transformed the serene seascape into an arena of imminent conflict.

On the bridge, Captain Rooks stood with an unwavering gaze, peering through his binoculars. The lines on his face seemed more pronounced under the moment's weight, each wrinkle telling a story of battles past and the burden of command. "Any sign of the convoy yet?" he asked, his voice cutting through the silence like a knife.

The lookout at the ship's highest point scanned the horizon intensely, his eyes squinting against the sun's glare off the water. "Nothing yet, Captain," he replied, his voice steady but tinged with anticipation, the binoculars held firmly in his hands.

The crew of the USS Houston was on high alert. Each man was prepared for the battle on the horizon, ready to defend their ship, their country, and each other.

Below, on the main deck, the crew moved with purpose and urgency. The gunners, positioned at their stations, were a picture of focused intensity.

As they checked and rechecked their weapons, the heavy artillery gleamed under the unforgiving sun, its surface scorching to the touch. The men moved with a sense of urgency, aware of the immense responsibility that rested on their shoulders.

"Hey, Thompson, ensure those breech blocks are properly greased!" Sergeant Davis's voice cut through the din of activity. He wiped the sweat from his brow, the heat bearing on them like an oppressive weight.

Thompson, hunched intently over his gun, responded without looking up. "Got it, Sarge! Wouldn't want these babies jamming up when we need them most." His hands, coated in grease, moved with practiced expertise honed by countless hours of training and drills.

Nearby, Private Martinez, another gunner, meticulously checked the ammunition feed. "Ammo's all set here," he called out, trying to keep his voice steady as adrenaline coursed through his veins. "These rounds are ready to sing." He patted the ammunition box, a small gesture of reassurance to himself.

The metallic clinks and clanks of their preparations provided a rhythmic backdrop to the building tension. Each sound was a deliberate note in the symphony of war preparations, each movement a calculated step in the dance of readiness.

Lieutenant Harris surveyed the scene from the upper deck with a keen eye. "Check the traverse on Gun Two!" he shouted, his voice echoing across the deck.

"Traverse checked, Lieutenant. Smooth as silk," Gunner's Mate Lee responded, giving a thumbs up from his station. He adjusted his helmet, his face a mask of grim determination. "We're ready for whatever comes our way," he muttered, more a vow than a statement.

The crew worked with a silent understanding, each man acutely aware of the gravity of the situation. They were bound by a shared knowledge, a common purpose that transcended their roles. They were guardians of the sea, each a vital piece in defense of their ship, their home on the water.

As the moments ticked by, the anticipation grew.

Each man lost in his own thoughts, remained united in their resolve and poised at the brink of battle, ready to defend their vessel and each other against the looming threat. The air was thick with the scent of gunpowder and sea salt, a tangible reminder of the imminent challenge.

"We've got this, guys," Thompson said, breaking the silence. "We're the Houston's best. Let's show them what we're made of."

His words, simple yet powerful, resonated with the crew. A nod here, a determined look there – the ship's gunners were ready. As they waited for the first sign of the enemy, they stood together, a band of brothers forged in the crucible of impending battle.

As the crew completed the last checks, a sense of readiness settled over the deck. The gunners stood by their stations, eyes fixed on the horizon, waiting for the command to engage.

Walking briskly among the men on the main deck, Commander Rice exuded a sense of calm determination. He offered encouragement, his voice cutting through the tension like a beacon of confidence. "Stay sharp, everyone. Remember, our success today depends on each of you," he said, making eye contact with the crew members as he passed by them.

Captain Rooks' presence on the deck was like a beacon of calm in the rising tide of tension.

He moved among his crew with measured steps, assessing the readiness of each sailor with his gaze. The air was heavy with the smell of the sea, mingled with the faint odor of oil and metal, the lifeblood of the ship. The distant rumble of the engines provided a constant backdrop to the heightened activity on board.

He observed them closely while stopping beside a group of young sailors as they attentively checked their equipment. Each movement was deliberate, a dance of preparation they had rehearsed countless times, yet now it carried a weight far more significant than any drill.

"You've trained for this," Captain Rooks said, his voice firm yet reassuring. He clapped one sailor, a young man barely out of his teens, on the shoulder. The gesture was firm, conveying both encouragement and the seriousness of the situation. "Trust your instincts and your training. We're all counting on you."

The young sailor, Private Jenkins, looked up, his eyes meeting the captain's. "Yes, sir. We won't let you down." His voice was a mix of resolve and the unmistakable edge of nerves.

Nearby, Gunner's Mate Lee, a more seasoned crew member, overheard the exchange. "You hear that, boys? The captain's got faith in us. Let's show him what we're made of," he called out to his fellow sailors.

His words seemed to bolster the younger sailors, a small flame of determination kindling in their expressions. "We've got this," another sailor, Rodriguez, added, checking the load on his gun. "We're the Houston's shield. No one's breaking through on our watch."

The metal clanking, the shuffling of feet, and the occasional murmur of voices created a symphony of readiness. Each sailor was acutely aware of the enormity of the task ahead. They were the first line of defense, the protectors of the ship and each other.

As Captain Rooks continued his rounds, he could feel the resolve of his crew. Their determination was palpable, a tangible force that seemed to infuse the air. The ship, a fortress on the sea, bristled with anticipation.

"Positions, everyone!" Lieutenant Harris's voice rang out clear and authoritative. "Eyes on the horizon. Remember, steady and focused."

The sailors took their positions, eyes straining against the vast expanse of ocean, searching for the first sign of the enemy. The sun glinted off the water, starkly contrasting the looming grim reality.

With each word, Rice instilled a sense of purpose and unity among the sailors. They straightened their backs, their grips tightening on their tools and weapons, ready to face the challenge ahead. Commander Rice's presence and words had kindled a fire of resolve in their hearts, preparing them for the battle on the horizon.

Among the crew was Johnny, his hands gripping the railing as he gazed out at the open sea. His heart pounded in his chest with fear and adrenaline coursing through him. "It's really happening, isn't it?" he muttered to Pete, who stood beside him.

Pete, usually quick with a joke, now wore a serious expression. "Yeah, we're about to make history here. Let's just hope it's on the right side."

Above the sound of the waves crashing against the hull and the ship's steady propulsion cutting through the deep blue waters, the air on the USS Houston was thick with the low hum of anticipation. This palpable tension mingled with the muted conversations of the sailors, each exchanging a mixture of strategy, concern, and steely resolve.

Near the stern, two seasoned sailors, Jenkins and Carter, leaned against the railings, their voices low. "We've seen action before, but this feels different, eh, Jenkins?" Carter said, his eyes scanning the horizon.

Jenkins nodded, his face set in a grim line. "Different indeed. Bigger stakes this time. But we're ready. Just have to keep our heads in the game."

On the other side of the deck, a group of younger sailors huddled together, their voices a mix of nervous excitement and quiet determination. "Can't believe we're actually going into battle," murmured one, a young man named Rodriguez. "Feels surreal."

His friend, a slightly older and more experienced sailor named Bishop, clapped him on the back. "Just stick to the drills, Rodriguez. We've trained for this. We'll watch each other's backs."

Nearby, the ship's medic, Lieutenant Grace, spoke softly to his assistant, his voice calm yet firm. "Double-check the medical supplies. I want everything ready for any scenario. We need to be prepared to act fast."

Above them, in the crow's nest, the lookout whispered into his radio, his eyes never leaving the vast expanse before them. "All clear for now," he reported, his voice barely more than a breath. "But I've got a feeling that's about to change."

Each conversation whispered strategy and word of encouragement wove together into a tapestry of camaraderie and readiness.

Near the bow of the ship, Johnny leaned against the railing, his gaze fixed on the distant horizon. The ocean stretched beyond him, vast and unending, starkly contrasting with the small, familiar world he left behind. He turned to Pete, who was methodically checking his equipment beside him.

"You know, back in Iowa, my folks run a small grocery store," Johnny began, his voice tinged with nostalgia. "It's one of those places where everyone knows everyone. I used to help out there after school."

Pete paused his work, looking up at Johnny. "Yeah?" he asked, interest piqued by this glimpse into his friend's life.

Johnny nodded, a small smile playing on his lips. "Every Sunday, we'd have a big family dinner. Mom's pot roast... I miss that. She had a way of making it that... felt like home, you know?" His voice trailed off, lost in the memory.

Pete leaned in closer, resting his equipment on the deck. "Sounds nice, man. Family dinners are something special. What else did you guys do?"

"Ah, the usual small-town stuff," Johnny continued, his eyes momentarily brightening. "Summer fairs, baseball games. I played shortstop for the high school team. And every Fourth of July, the whole town would come together for a barbecue and fireworks. It feels like a different world now."

Pete chuckled, "Sure does sound different from this," he gestured around them to the vastness of the sea and the ship's business. "But hey, we've got our own kind of family here, right?"

Johnny's smile widened, and he nodded. "Yeah, we do. It's different, but it's good. We're all in this together, after all. I guess that's what counts in the end."

As they shared this quiet moment, the bond between them strengthened. The world they once knew seemed far away, but in the camaraderie, they found aboard the Houston, there was a new sense of belonging, a new kind of family forged in the crucible of shared duty and looming battle.

Pete, pausing in his task, nodded once more. "Yeah, I get that. My little brother in Oregon is probably out fishing right now. Taught him everything he knows." A faint smile crossed his face at the memory.

Elsewhere, a group of sailors gathered around a gun turret. "My wife's expecting our first child," one sailor, Mark, said with pride and worry in his voice. "I left her a letter, just in case... You know."

His friend, Sam, clapped him on the back. "You'll be home before you know it, Mark. Holding that baby in your arms."

A young lookout spoke softly into his headset in the crow's nest, "Wish my dad could see me now. He always wanted to join the Navy, but life got in the way."

A few off-duty sailors shared photos and letters from home in the mess hall. "This is my girl, Mary," one sailor, Luis, said, holding a crinkled photograph. "Promised her I'd come back. Can't break a promise to her."

These exchanges, filled with memories of home and hopes for the future, wove a rich tapestry of personal stories against the stark backdrop of the upcoming battle. They served as reminders of what each man was fighting for, anchoring them to the world beyond the ship's steel hull.

As the USS Houston drew closer to the confrontation, these stories of home and loved ones lingered in the air, a poignant counterpoint to the sounds of the ship and the sea, fortifying the crew with the strength and resolve

As the vessel advanced more profoundly into the strait, every sailor and officer stood ready for the battle looming on the horizon. Their eyes fixed forward, each person acutely aware they were moments away from confronting the enemy as the sun rose above the horizon on February 4, 1942.

Chapter EIGHT

The Japanese Convoy Appears

Captain Rooks surveyed the horizon with a hardened gaze. "All stations, battle readiness!" he commanded over the intercom. The ship buzzed into action, the crew efficiently manning their posts.

As the USS Houston cut through the waters, its course set towards the enemy, Captain Albert H. Rooks stood at the helm, embodying the essence of naval command. His eyes, honed by years at sea, fixed intently on the horizon.

The early morning light cast a pale, ominous glow over the ocean, turning the sea into a vast, undulating expanse of gray and blue.

Ahead, the Japanese convoy appeared as a collection of dark silhouettes against the lighter sky backdrop, a menacing presence in the vastness of the Pacific. The ships, moving in a disciplined formation, seemed like predatory shadows, each one a threat looming more prominent as the Houston closed the distance.

Captain Rooks, his jaw set and his gaze unwavering, issued a series of commands, his voice resonating with authority and urgency. "Steady as she goes," he ordered his hand firm on the wheel. "Prepare to adjust course, fifteen degrees starboard on my mark."

The air on the bridge was thick with tension, the crew members poised and alert, ready to respond to each of the captain's commands. The ship's strategic prowess, a culmination of design, weaponry, and human skill, was now at the forefront, every piece essential in the intricate dance of naval warfare.

"Mark!" Rooks called out, and the Houston began its calculated maneuver, its massive frame responding with surprising agility.

The tactical move positioned the ship advantageously, allowing for optimal use of its firepower while minimizing exposure to enemy attack.

As they approached the enemy convoy, the sounds of the Houston's readiness were palpable - the low hum of the engines at full throttle, the distant clanking of machinery, and the murmurs of the crew. The smell of saltwater and the faint scent of diesel fuel constantly reminded everyone of the ship's ceaseless vitality.

Captain Rooks's experienced eye assessed the formation of the enemy ships, calculating angles and distances. His mind worked through scenarios, strategies forming and reforming with each passing second.

The Houston, a formidable force under his command, was more than just a ship; it was a statement of power and intent, cutting through the water toward a confrontation that would test the mettle of every sailor aboard.

A palpable mix of anticipation and apprehension hung in the charged atmosphere aboard the USS Houston. For Captain Rooks and his crew, the impending battle loomed as a formidable test of their mettle. It wasn't just about strategy and skill but their collective resolve, the culmination of their rigorous training, and their unity as a cohesive fighting unit. Tension was taut like a bowstring, each man acutely aware of the gravity of the situation. Eyes were steely, hearts beat in unison – they were a team forged by shared purpose and unwavering dedication. The moment was upon them, and history awaited their response.

"Helmsman, bring us to thirty degrees starboard. Steady... steady as she goes," Captain Rooks ordered, his voice calm yet authoritative, resonating across the bridge.

"Ahead full, increase speed gradually. Let's close the gap but remain undetected," he continued, his eyes fixed on the navigational charts, plotting each move with precision.

"Communications, keep the lines open but secure. I want updates on their position every two minutes," he directed, ensuring they were constantly aware of the enemy's movements.

"Gunnery crew, stand by. Prepare to engage on my command. I want those guns ready to fire the moment we're in range," he stated, his tone underscored by the situation's urgency.

The crew responded to each command swiftly, their movements a well-rehearsed dance of naval discipline.

The ship, a massive structure of steel and power, responded with surprising grace. Her hull pivoted smoothly through the water, leaving a churning wake behind as she maneuvered into an optimal firing position.

The sensation on the deck was one of controlled urgency. Sailors felt the deck tilt beneath their feet as the ship turned, the motion a visceral reminder of the Houston's agility and speed.

The scent of the sea, tinged with the acrid tang of engine exhaust and gunpowder, filled the air. The sound of water slapping against the hull punctuated the tense atmosphere, waves crashing more intensely as the ship picked up speed.

Above, seagulls, disturbed by the commotion below, swooped and dived around the ship, their cries adding to the discord of sounds that enveloped the crew. The sun, shining brightly above, cast a shimmering path across the water, starkly contrasting the grim task.

As the enemy ships edged closer and closer into view on the distant horizon, a tangible shift occurred aboard the USS Houston. The main guns, impressive 8-inch cannons that were the ship's pride, swiveled with mechanical precision, guided by the expert hands of the gunnery crew. These massive barrels, glinting metallic under the sun's harsh glare, turned slowly, aligning with the approaching targets with deliberate, ominous intent.

The gun crews, clad in their battle gear, worked in perfect unison. Their movements were a choreographed dance, each step a result of relentless training and unwavering discipline. They loaded and primed the cannons, handling the heavy ammunition with a mix of respect and familiarity. The clanking of shells being set into place, the clicking of mechanisms locking into position, and the shouts of coordination among the crew melded into a rhythm of war readiness.

The sound of the heavy artillery gearing up reverberated through the ship's steel structure, sending vibrations underfoot. A deep, resonating hum, almost like the growl of a giant beast awakening, underscoring the impending engagement. This sound, both daunting and exhilarating, coursed through the ship, setting nerves on edge and heightening the senses of every sailor aboard.

The deck of the USS Houston was alive with the sharp tang of gunpowder, a vivid prelude to the might it was about to unleash. In a scene reminiscent of a Tom Clancy thriller, the air was heavy with tense anticipation, the stillness before the storm of battle. Sailors and officers, their expressions a mask of focus and resolve, stood poised, ready for the conflict's onset.

The crew fixed their eyes on the distant enemy ships, once mere dots against the vast ocean, now growing more prominent as the Houston surged forward. The moment of confrontation was imminent, each second stretching out, laden with the weight of impending action.

In these moments, the USS Houston was not just a ship; it was a living entity, pulsating with the collective heartbeat of its crew, each member ready to play their part in the imminent clash of naval might.

The atmosphere aboard the USS Houston was palpably electric, a potent blend of fear, determination, and a deep-rooted sense of duty. For the crew, this culminated in their rigorous training – a moment that would put their skills and ship to the ultimate test. The air was thick with anticipation, every sailor acutely aware that the hour to demonstrate their readiness for battle had finally arrived.

The anticipation was tense as the crew awaited the command to fire, their hearts pounding ninety miles an hour in their chest. Eyes fixed on the distant shapes of the Japanese transports, the crew held their breaths as the Houston lined up her shots. The moment culminated with skill, strategy, and sheer naval might, a testament to the ship's prowess and her crew.

Commander Rice stood resolutely on the bridge, his eyes narrowing as he observed the approaching enemy through his binoculars. He turned to his crew, the moment's gravity etched on his face. "Prepare to engage," he commanded in a steady, determined voice. The crew members tensed, readying themselves for the imminent battle. Seconds later, with a steely resolve, Commander Rice gave the order to unleash Houston's firepower. "Fire at will!" he barked, his voice echoing with authority and urgency across the deck.

With a sudden burst of sound that shattered the tense silence, the Houston's eight-inch guns fired. The explosion of the cannons sent shockwaves through the ship, vibrating the deck and reverberating in the sailors' chests. The smell of gunpowder filled the air, and the sight of shells arcing through the sky toward their target was awe-inspiring and terrifying.

At this moment, the USS Houston was not just a ship; she was a formidable instrument of war, her crew united in their mission, her guns a declaration of their readiness to fight. The tactical maneuvers and the interplay of natural and mechanical elements coalesced into a singular, powerful force as the Houston engaged the enemy in the vast expanse of the Pacific.

"Target their lead ship!" Captain Rooks ordered, his voice booming over the ship's intercom, cutting through the chaos with clarity and command. His words acted as a catalyst, setting into motion a precise and deadly response from the crew of the USS Houston.

The ship shuddered violently, a visceral response to her guns unleashing their fury. It was a coordinated ballet of destruction, each movement meticulously planned yet executed ferociously. The main cannons, massive and unyielding, recoiled with each discharge, sending shockwaves through the ship's structure. The sound was deafening. A series of earth-shattering roars echoed across the open sea, punctuated by the sharp, staccato reports of the smaller guns joining the fray.

As the USS Houston thundered its wrath upon the enemy, smoke erupted from the gun barrels, engulfing the deck in a haze of acrid fumes. The stinging smoke clouded the sailors' vision, searing their eyes and throats, yet they remained undeterred, fixated on their grim task. The pervasive smell of gunpowder, thick and overwhelming, was a constant reminder of the deadly earnestness of their mission.

The gun crews, their faces streaked with a mix of sweat and soot, moved with a frantic yet precise rhythm. The physical exertion of reloading the heavy artillery was immense, but they operated with the efficiency of a well-oiled machine, their actions honed by relentless training.

"Shells ready!" shouted Private Martinez, his voice strained but resolute as he hefted an ammunition round into position. His arms ached from the effort, but the adrenaline coursing through his veins fueled his resolve.

"Fire in three... two... one... Fire!" Gunner's Mate Lee commanded, his hand gesturing in sync with his count. The gun roared to life, its recoil sending vibrations through the deck, a raw display of the ship's might.

"Reload! Keep them coming!" barked Sergeant Davis, overseeing the operation. His gaze darted from one crew member to another, making sure to waste no second and spare no effort. Thompson, positioned at a nearby gun, responded to the call. "On it, Sarge! These guns aren't going to rest tonight!" He grunted as he slid another round into the breech, his movements deft despite the exhaustion that threatened to overtake him.

Amid the thunderous booms of the guns and the shrieks of passing shells, the sailors' shouted instructions and encouragements melded into the chaos of battle. Yet, each command and response was crucial, a testament to the unspoken bond and understanding among the crew.

As they loaded, aimed, and fired, time seemed to warp, the minutes stretching and blurring under the relentless pace of combat. The gun deck, shrouded in smoke and reverberating with the sounds of warfare, became a world unto itself, where every action and decision could tip the balance of the battle.

"Steady, lads! Keep it focused!" yelled Sergeant Davis to his gun crew, his voice raw with the strain of command. He moved along the line of cannons, ensuring each was operating at its peak.

At around eleven in the morning, as if on cue, the Japanese planes appeared. "Here they come," announced Captain Rooks, his voice echoing through the ship's intercom. The Dutch admiral in charge ordered a scatter maneuver as the bombers descended upon them, unleashing their deadly cargo.

The atmosphere aboard the USS Houston was tense as the crew braced for the approaching Japanese aircraft. The ominous drone of enemy planes filled the skies, a sound that seemed to vibrate through the very bones of the ship. The air was thick with the smell of oil and sea salt, mixed with the acrid tang of gunpowder from the ship's guns firing in defense.

The approaching aircraft released a deadly bomb, a projectile glinting in the sunlight. Its menacing silhouette stood stark against the sky as it descended with terrifying speed, watched intently by the crew members. The seconds stretched into an eternity as the bomb hurtled towards the Houston, its shadow growing larger and larger.

Captain Rooks, standing on the bridge, watched with a steely gaze. His voice was tense but composed as he issued commands. "Brace for impact! All hands, brace!" he ordered, gripping the railing tightly, his knuckles white with tension.

The bomb struck with a deafening roar, the sound reverberating through the ship like the angry roar of some great beast. The impact near the number three turret on the stern was catastrophic. The explosion was a hellish symphony of noise: the screeching of tearing metal, the shattering of glass, and the thunderous blast of the bomb itself.

An instant obliteration reduced the crew's washroom to a tangled mess of metal and debris. Shrapnel flew through the turret with lethal force, turning the confined space into a deadly trap.

Dust and smoke filled the air, making it difficult to see or breathe. The smell of explosives mixed with the sharp, metallic scent of blood and the burning remnants of the destroyed area.

Sergeant Davis, who had been close to the turret, felt the shockwave hit him like a physical blow. Staggered, he stumbled back, his ears ringing, his mind struggling to process what had just happened. "We've been hit!" he shouted, his voice a mix of panic and disbelief. "We've been hit hard!"

Chaos threw the crew around him into disarray. Men shouted orders and called for help, their voices tinged with fear and urgency. Some rushed to the damaged area to fight fires and rescue trapped comrades, while others manned their stations, determined to keep the ship fighting despite the severe damage.

Captain Rooks, amid the turmoil, maintained his composure. His voice, though strained, carried the weight of command. "Damage control teams to the stern, now!" he ordered. "Medical team, prepare for casualties! We need to stay afloat and keep fighting!"

The Houston, wounded but still defiant, continued its battle against overwhelming odds. Despite the shock and devastation, the crew rallied under their captain's orders, each man doing his part in the desperate struggle to survive and fight on.

Miller, stationed at gun eight, had just returned from inspecting a magazine issue when the bomb hit. "I couldn't believe it," he said, the shock still evident in his voice. "One minute, we were fine. The next, chaos."

In the wake of the devastating explosion, the Houston was a scene of utter ruin and despair. The blistering inferno transformed the steel turret's once orderly and disciplined interior.

Conflict dramatically transformed the once robust gray walls. They now stood seared and blackened, coated in thick soot and ash, vividly showcasing the intense heat and turmoil they had withstood.

Flames leaped and danced with a voracious appetite, consuming everything in their path, turning dials, controls, and machinery into twisted, molten wreckage. The intense heat created shimmering waves, distorting the horrific scene into a nightmarish tableau.

The air inside the turret was a toxic brew of smoke and fumes, thick and cloying. It filled the lungs with a burning sensation, each breath a painful struggle. The acrid stench of burning metal, electrical fires, and charred fabric was overwhelming, mingling with the faint, sickly sweet odor of burned flesh. The smoke swirled in dense clouds, obscuring vision and turning the space into a labyrinth of confusion and danger.

The turret, now an embodiment of Hell itself, echoed with the desperate, haunting cries of the trapped crew. Their voices, filled with pain and fear, cut through the roar of the flames, creating a chilling disharmony of human anguish. "Help! Someone, please! Help us!" a voice screamed from somewhere in the smoke, its owner unseen but clearly close.

Another crew member, strained with terror, shouted, "It's too hot! I can't see a way out!" The panic in his voice was palpable, a clear indication of the dire situation they were all in.

From the depths of the turret came a guttural, pained groan. "My leg... I can't feel my leg!" a young sailor cried, his voice breaking in despair. The sound of his agony was a stark reminder of the brutality of their predicament.

Above the din, the crackling and popping of the fire added a menacing undertone, a constant reminder of the relentless destruction around them. The metallic groan of the turret's structure, warped and stressed by the heat, added a sinister note to the chaos, hinting at the possibility of a total collapse.

Through the haze, the flickering light from the flames cast eerie, dancing shadows across the faces of the men, highlighting their expressions of fear, pain, and determination. Their eyes, wide with terror and glistening from the heat, reflected the inferno surrounding them.

In this Hellish landscape, the crew fought against the physical flames but also against the rising tide of panic and despair. Each shout, each cry for help, was a testament to their desperate struggle for survival in the face of overwhelming odds.

The chaos within the turret was tense, a maelstrom of destruction and pain. Amidst this turmoil, Sergeant Davis found himself in a dire predicament. A heavy steel beam, dislodged by the force of the explosion, had trapped him beneath its oppressive weight. The beam, searing hot from the intense heat of the surrounding flames, lay across his lower body, pinning him helplessly to the charred floor.

"Sergeant Davis!" cried a nearby sailor, struggling to navigate through the smoke and debris to reach him. "Hold on, we're coming!"

Davis's face was a mask of sheer agony, his features twisted in a grimace of pain. Sweat mixed with soot streaked down his face, dripping onto the floor beneath him.

The intense heat scorched and smoldered his once crisp and immaculate uniform, causing the fabric to stick to his skin in places. "Help! Someone, please!" Davis screamed, his voice hoarse and cracking under the strain. He coughed violently, the acrid smoke filling his lungs, making each breath a torturous endeavor. A relentless assault on his senses made the heat unbearable as if he were inches away from the flames' consumption. The superheated air around him shimmered with the intensity of the blaze. The burning fabric and metal smell was suffocating, mingling with charred flesh's faint, distressing scent. The roar of the fire filled his ears, a constant, deafening presence that seemed to drown out all hope.

His fellow sailors fought through the smoke and debris to reach him. "Hang in there, Sergeant!" one of them shouted, his voice barely audible over the din of the inferno. They worked frantically to lift the beam, their hands blistering from the heat, their muscles straining with the effort.

Despite the excruciating pain, Davis tried to offer words of encouragement, his voice a strained whisper. "You can do it, boys... Lift it off..." But even as he spoke, his consciousness wavered, the edges of his vision blurring as the pain and smoke threatened to overwhelm him.

The desperate attempt to free him was a race against time, each second a battle against the spreading flames and the suffocating smoke.

"Can't... get out!" Corporal Lee shouted from the other side, his words almost lost in the cacophony. He was frantically clawing at a jammed hatch, the metal too hot to touch, his hands red and blistered.

Young and terrified, Private Jenkins was barely audible over the crackling flames. "Mom... Mom, I'm scared!" he sobbed, curled up in a corner, his body shaking uncontrollably. The words were a heartbreaking testament to his youth and the overwhelming terror he felt.

The screams melded together, a chorus of despair and pain, each cry a stark reminder of the horror unfolding. The relentless roar of the fire seemed to mock their plight, growing louder and more intense as if to drown out their pleas for salvation.

"Stay down! Cover your face!" Miller tried to shout orders, his voice hoarse from smoke inhalation. But his attempts to organize an escape or rescue were futile against the might of the blaze.

In this chaos, the screams of pain and fear, the shouts for help, and the desperate commands of a leader trying to save his men all clashed against the backdrop of the merciless fire.

Miller stood at the threshold, his heart pounding in his chest, his eyes wide with horror. He could hardly believe the scene unfolding before him. The interior was a chaotic blur of orange and red, the heat so intense it felt as if it were peeling the skin from his bones. In the middle of all the chaos, he caught sight of one of the gunners, young Thompson, a boy barely out of his teens. The poor lad was still at his post, his hands gruesomely fused to the control wheels, his eyes wide open in a silent scream. The image was so horrifying, so heart-wrenching, that Miller felt a surge of nausea.

"No! Thompson!" Lieutenant Miller cried out, his voice cracking with emotion. But it was too late. The flames had claimed the young gunner and the rest of the crew. Tears streamed down Miller's face, mixing with the soot and sweat. He had trained with these men, laughed with them, and shared stories of home. Now... they were gone, their lives extinguished in an instant.

The sight of Thompson's charred figure, still clinging to his post, would haunt Miller for the rest of his days. It was a stark reminder of the cruel and unforgiving nature of war, a memory that would burn in his mind just as fiercely as the flames that ravaged the turret.

Clearing the smoldering remains of the turret revealed the grim toll of the battle, becoming painfully evident. The medics, a team of dedicated and battle-hardened professionals, worked with a sense of urgency that was both awe-inspiring and heart-wrenching. The ground around them had transformed into a makeshift triage area, littered with the injured and the lifeless, a stark representation of war's brutal reality.

Private Johnson, his uniform stained with soot and his face smeared with ash, stood nearby, a look of shock and disbelief etched across his youthful features. "I never imagined it would be like this," he muttered, his voice barely above a whisper, his eyes wide as they followed the frenzied movements of the medics.

One of the medics, a young sailor with short red hair, moved swiftly from one injured soldier to another, his hands steady as he administered first aid. His face was set in a mask of concentration, betraying no emotion despite the chaos around her.

Nearby, the lead doctor, a middle-aged man with streaks of grey in his hair and a look of determined resolve was knee-deep in the crisis. "We need more bandages here!" he barked, his voice cutting through the din. "And get me another IV stand, quickly!"

A medic, his uniform drenched in sweat, hurried to comply, weaving through the maze of injured bodies. "Doctor, we've got another one with severe burns!" he called out, guiding a stretcher towards a cleared space.

The doctor moved efficiently, his hands working deftly as he assessed the new arrival. "Keep him stable. Monitor his breathing," he instructed with a firm yet calm tone. "Let's get some morphine for the pain."

Private Johnson, watching this scene unfold, felt a surge of emotions. Fear, sadness, and respect for the medics' bravery and skill mingled in a tumultuous mix. He overheard snippets of their conversations - urgent requests for medical supplies, quick assessments of injuries, comforting words to the wounded - and it struck him just how critical their role was in this hellish landscape.

The medics' faces, streaked with dirt and sweat, were portraits of focus and dedication. They moved like a well-oiled machine, their actions a testament to their training and commitment to saving lives, even amid such overwhelming devastation.

For Private Johnson, this scene was a visceral reminder of the harsh realities of war.

The Houston, though wounded, continued to fight. Captain Rooks's skillful maneuvering helped the ship evade further bombings, but the damage had already occurred. "We were lucky to get out of there," Rooks admitted, the weight of the experience etched in his expression.

The deck of the USS Houston was a dissonance of noise and activity, a stark contrast to the hellish scene within the turret. Despite the overwhelming chaos that had engulfed them, the crew rallied with remarkable resilience, their training taking over in the face of imminent danger.

Above, the Japanese planes swooped down like predatory birds, their engines screaming as they dove toward the ship. They cut through the sky with lethal grace, their silhouettes ominous against the backdrop of the cloudy sky. Each descent brought a new wave of terror as the planes released their deadly payloads, aiming for the beleaguered ship below.

On the Houston, the anti-aircraft guns continued to roar, a thunderous response to the aerial assault. Their faces were set in grim determination. Gunners worked with feverish speed, loading and firing with practiced efficiency. The guns recoiled with each shot, the sound of their firing a constant staccato that echoed over the water.

"Keep firing, men! Don't let them get a clean run!" bellowed Lieutenant Harris, overseeing the gun crews. His voice, laced with urgency, cut through the din of battle.

Nearby, a young gunner, trembling slightly with adrenaline, shouted back, "I've got one in my sights, Lieutenant!" His fingers worked quickly, adjusting the aim of his gun, trying to track the fast-moving target above.

The smell of gunpowder and the salty tang of the sea filled the air, mingling with the faint trace of engine fuel from the enemy planes.

Bullets and shells whizzing through the air created a deadly symphony, punctuated by the occasional explosion as a shell found its mark on a plane.

"Steady, steady..." another sailor muttered to himself, squinting through the sights of his gun, his focus unwavering despite the chaos around him.

The deck vibrated with each discharge of the guns, the whole ship seeming to shudder under the strain of the battle. Sailors moved about with purpose, some assisting the gunners, others attending to damage control, all working in unison to keep the Houston fighting.

It was uncertain whether their fire was hitting the intended targets amid this frenzy. The Japanese planes were agile, darting through the sky quickly, making them difficult targets.

As the battle raged on, the crew of the USS Houston, weary but resolute, kept their eyes trained on the skies. They had stood their ground against the relentless assault, their guns firing continuously despite the overwhelming odds. Then, as abruptly as it had begun, there was a noticeable shift in the tide of the aerial attack.

Through the haze of smoke and the occasional burst of anti-aircraft fire, the sailors noticed the Japanese planes beginning to change their trajectory. One by one, the enemy aircraft, which had been swooping down in menacing dives, started to turn away, their dark silhouettes pivoting against the sky. The engines' whine, a constant and ominous drone throughout the attack, began to fade, growing fainter as the planes distanced themselves from the Houston.

"Look! They're turning back!" shouted a young sailor, pointing towards the receding planes. His voice tinged with a mix of surprise and relief, carried over the noise of the deck.

Others on the ship quickly picked up on the change. "They're retreating!" another crew member called out, his words sparking a ripple of reactions among his shipmates.

Standing on the bridge, Captain Rooks observed the scene through his binoculars, a deep frown on his face. "Keep your guard up, men," he cautioned, his voice steady. "They might be regrouping for another attack. Stay alert."

But as the minutes ticked by, it became increasingly apparent that the Japanese planes were withdrawing, their formations growing smaller in the distance, eventually disappearing over the horizon. The relative quiet replaced the relentless hum of their engines, a stark contrast to the chaos that had engulfed the ship moments before. On the deck, the crew members slowly lowered their weapons, their bodies tense with the adrenaline of the fight. Some collapsed against the railings, their chests heaving with exertion, while others exchanged weary yet relieved glances.

"We held them off," murmured a seasoned sailor, his voice a mix of pride and exhaustion. "We actually held them off."

The crew experienced a collective sense of relief as the immediate threat subsided. However, their awareness of the sustained damage and suffered losses tempered this feeling. The Houston, scarred and battered, had survived this encounter, but the cost was evident in the destruction around them and in the eyes of the crew.

Chapter NINE

Protect the Marblehead at All Costs

"We did our job. That's all that matters," Lieutenant John Miller would say later, reflecting on the fierce determination of his crew.

Smack dap in the middle of the tumultuous seas, the USS Marblehead, grievously wounded by the enemy's relentless assault, was in a perilous situation. The ship, a proud vessel of the allied fleet, had taken a devastating hit that rendered it nearly helpless. The impact of the attack had jammed its steering gear, essential for navigation, causing the ship to circle uncontrollably. The once mighty warship, now reduced to a drifting target, was a stark image of vulnerability amidst the chaos of war.

The sea around the Marblehead was a swirling maelstrom, the waves crashing against its hull with relentless force. The sound of creaking metal and groaning structures filled the air, a haunting reminder of the damage sustained. Crew members scrambled across the deck, their faces etched with urgency and fear, as they tried desperately to regain control of their ship. The smell of burning fuel and electrical fires hung heavy, a pungent reminder of the recent attack.

Meanwhile, the USS Houston, having witnessed the plight of its ally, made a decisive and courageous move. The Houston bravely circled back towards the Marblehead with a sense of duty that transcended the dangers they faced. The ship cut through the water with determination, its engines roaring, defying the risks of exposing itself to further enemy fire.

On the bridge of the USS Houston, Captain Rooks stood with a gaze as hard as tempered steel, scanning the chaotic aftermath. "We can't just leave them out there," he declared, his voice resonating with a commanding resolve. He turned to his crew, his eyes burning with determination. "All hands, prepare to cover the Marblehead. We're going back in." Sensing the gravity in their captain's voice, the crew sprang into action, ready to follow his lead into the fray. The tension on the bridge was palpable.

The crew of the Houston sprang into action, galvanized by their captain's command. Gunners manned their stations, peering intently into the distance, ready to defend their ally against any further attacks. Sailors on deck secured equipment and braced for potential combat, their faces grimly determined.

As the Houston maneuvered closer to the Marblehead, the tension was substantial. Every crew member knew the gravity of the situation - they were fighting for their own survival and the lives of their fellow sailors on the stricken ship.

Circling back to protect the Marblehead was a powerful testament to the solidarity among the allied forces. It was a moment that transcended the chaos of battle, a demonstration of unwavering commitment to their comrades-in-arms.

As the Houston neared Tjilatjap, the crew, shaken from their first actual combat, tried to process their experiences. Miller, his gaze lost in the distance, broke the silence among his friends. "It changes you," he said softly. "You never forget your first action. It stays with you forever."

One of his friends, a young sailor with eyes still wide from the battle, responded, "I never imagined it would be like this. It's... overwhelming."

"Yeah," another chimed in, his voice tinged with a newfound solemnity. "It's one thing to train for it, another to live it. But we did it together, and that's what counts."

Their conversation, a mix of reflection and quiet understanding, continued as they stood side by side, bonded by the shared ordeal of battle.

However, Houston found itself in a precarious situation as it entered the shallow waters of the port at Tjilatjap. The ship's propellers churned up mud, leaving a telltale trail in the water.

"We're practically sitting on the bottom," Miller remarked to Sergeant Davis as they observed the muddy wake. "We're vulnerable here."

On the deck of the USS Houston, the sun cast a melancholic glow over the solemn assembly of sailors. Captain Rook stood at the forefront, his gaze steady yet filled with a feeling of deep, unspoken sorrow. The ocean breeze carried a hush over the crew as they prepared to take their fallen comrades ashore for a final farewell.

"Alright, gentlemen," Captain Rook's voice broke the silence, steadier than his wavering heart. "Today, we honor those who've given their all for their country, for us. We're not just sailors; we're a family, and today, we say goodbye to our brothers."

Lieutenant John Miller, a young officer with a somber expression, stepped forward, carrying the flag that draped one of the coffins.

His resolve was unbreakable despite his eyes being rimmed red. "Aye, Captain. They'll be remembered, always."

The procession moved solemnly towards the shore, the sound of the rolling waves a somber accompaniment.

Grief and respect painted each face, and everyone measured their steps. The shore party, led by Captain Rook, carried their fallen with the utmost dignity under the watchful eyes of the sea that had been both their home and their adversary.

Once ashore, Captain Rooks stood by the graves, his heart heavy. "We're gathered here not just in grief but in gratitude," he began, his voice carrying across the assembled sailors. "These brave souls stood by us through storms and calms alike. They've sailed their final voyage, and we must continue ours without them. But let's carry them in our hearts, in every mission, every challenge. Their legacy will steer us forward."

Tears glistened in the eyes of many as they listened, feeling the weight of his words. One by one, the sailors paid their respects, a silent promise to uphold the legacy of their fallen brethren.

The return to the USS Houston was a quiet affair. Once bustling with life, the ship seemed to understand the depth of its crew's loss. Captain Rooks stood at the helm, his gaze fixed on the horizon. "Set course," he ordered, his voice firm yet layered with a profound sense of loss and determination.

The crew worked in unison, a testament to their bond, strengthened by the trials they had faced together. The engines hummed to life, and the USS Houston began its steady journey forward, cutting through the waves with renewed purpose.

"Remember, men," Captain Rooks addressed his crew, his eyes reflecting the vast ocean, "we sail not just on water but on the legacy of those who've sailed before us. Let's do them proud."

As the ship sailed into the embrace of the open sea once more, there was a sense of unity, of shared resolve. The faces of the men, though marked by loss, also bore the determination to continue the legacy of their fallen comrades.

The Houston soon returned to its convoying duty with no time for repairs. The eight-inch turret, destroyed in the attack, remained a gaping wound on the ship, a constant reminder of their vulnerability.

Their next significant encounter, a pivotal moment in the early stages of the Pacific War, found the USS Houston embarking on a critical mission: escorting a vital convoy from Port Darwin,

Australia, to Koepang, on the island of Timor. This convoy, carrying a contingent of Australian and American troops, was of paramount importance. The significance of this mission lay not only in its military necessity but also in the burgeoning camaraderie and cooperation between the Australian and American forces, a bond that would only strengthen as the war progressed.

The troops aboard were crucial reinforcements intended to bolster the Allied presence in the region, particularly in Timor, where Japanese advances threatened the stability and security of the Allied positions. This reinforcement mission was part of the larger strategic effort to maintain control over the sea lanes and key territories in the Pacific, which were crucial for both sides in the broader context of the war.

However, a new challenge emerged as the convoy entered the treacherous waters. A Japanese reconnaissance plane, likely dispatched from one of the nearby bases established by the rapidly expanding Japanese Empire, soon spotted the convoy. The plane, a symbol of the far-reaching eye of the Japanese military, ominously circled above, staying just out of range of the convoy's anti-aircraft guns. This was a common tactic employed by Japanese reconnaissance aircraft, gathering crucial intelligence while avoiding engagement.

The sighting of the Japanese plane starkly reminded everyone that the enemy maintained unrelenting watchfulness, escalating the risk of a more significant and deadly confrontation due to the constant threat of tracking.

The crew of the Houston and the convoy acutely realized that they had compromised their position, and they must proceed with even greater caution. The possibility of a Japanese ambush or an attack from lurking submarines added a layer of tension to the already perilous journey.

This encounter illustrated the constant game of cat and mouse played in the Pacific theater, where information was as critical as firepower. The ability of the Japanese to spot and monitor Allied movements was a significant challenge, one that the Allies had to constantly adapt to.

"We've been made," Captain Rooks announced urgently. "Expect company soon! All hands, stay sharp and get ready for engagement. This isn't a drill – we're in the thick of it now. We need to be prepared for anything they throw at us." His voice carried a tense mix of caution and readiness, rallying his crew for the imminent confrontation. The air on the bridge crackled with a heightened sense of alertness as they embraced the inevitable.

True to his prediction, a squadron of Japanese bombers appeared the next day around eleven o'clock... always at eleven o'clock! The Houston and the destroyer USS Perry quickly drew away from the convoy, drawing the bombers' focus. "They're trying to isolate us," Lieutenant Miller realized, gripping his weapon tightly.

Despite multiple bombing runs, the Houston miraculously evaded direct hits, thanks in part to Captain Rook's daring maneuvers. "Did you see that turn?" Miller exclaimed, amazed as the ship leaned sharply, the sea washing over the stern.

"That's Captain Rooks for you," Private Johnson replied, his voice mixed with awe and fear.

In a twist of fate, the convoy suffered only one casualty, a soldier hit by shrapnel. The Houston's surgeons worked tirelessly, but the soldier died that night. "We did our best," the ship's doctor said wearily, a sentiment echoed by the crew.

The Houston's anti-aircraft guns blazed away at the Japanese bombers, which eventually withdrew. "We gave them a run for their money," Lieutenant Miller said with grim satisfaction.

However, the victory was short-lived. Upon learning that Koepang had fallen to the Japanese, the convoy turned back, arriving in Port Darwin the next day. The Houston left Port Darwin that evening, dodging potential submarine threats.

In a cruel twist of fate, the Japanese launched a massive assault on Port Darwin the following day, destroying many of the ships the Houston escorted to this port.

Returning to Soerabaja a few days later, the Houston crew witnessed the aftermath of a Japanese raid. A burning merchant ship loaded with rubber lit up the port, a stark beacon for further attacks.

As the Japanese planes returned for their regular raids, the Houston's crew immediately sprang into action, disregarding the Dutch restrictions on firing directions. "We can't let them have a free run at us," Captain Rooks declared as the guns thundered in response.

Miller couldn't help but contrast the Dutch sailors' rush to air raid shelters with their stance on the ship. He stated resolutely, "We stay and fight," a sentiment shared among his American crewmates. The Houston and its crew stood their ground in Soerabaja, firing at the Japanese planes with determination and courage despite the frequent air raids. This was a testament to their resolve in the face of overwhelming odds.

In the shallow waters of the port at Tjilatjap, the Houston faced one of its most intense and harrowing experiences. Captain Rooks, along with some of his crew, had to navigate not only the threats from enemy planes but also the dangers posed by their own shrapnel falling back onto the ship.

"It's like we're sitting ducks here," Rooks said to Commander Rice as they watched the American submarine nearby dive during air raids. "These Japanese pilots know exactly where to find us."

The constant bombing raids took a toll on everyone, but Rooks noticed how it affected different people in various ways.

The Chinese mess boys on the Houston, particularly Tsao, a towering figure usually full of energy, showed immense stress, now visibly shaken by the relentless attacks.

"You never really get used to this," Captain Rooks admitted to Sergeant Davis. "It's about staying focused and doing your job despite the fear."

One particularly intense day of bombing left a vivid memory in everyone's mind. After firing at the Japanese planes for over an hour, they returned to their quarters to find water leaking from under a pile of mattresses. Hidden beneath them was one of the Chinese mess boys, terrified and almost dehydrated from fear.

"This poor guy," Lieutenant Miller remarked, shaking his head. "He couldn't believe the planes were gone. Said he'd rather jump overboard next time."

Despite the constant threat of bombings, the Houston and its crew remained steadfast. Each day brought new challenges, but Rooks and his crew were determined to do their duty, no matter how exhausting or dangerous.

As they patrolled Madoera again that night, the crew was on high alert, aware of the ever-present danger. Additional allied ships, including the HMS Exeter, HMAS Perth, and several English destroyers, joined the next day.

"The more, the merrier," Commander Rice commented wryly to his crew. "Looks like we've got company for our next dance with the Japanese."

Together, this formidable group of ships represented a significant force, ready to face whatever challenges lay ahead. For Rooks and the crew of the Houston, it was another day in their relentless struggle, marked by courage, resilience, and an unyielding commitment to their mission.

In the thick of battle, the Houston, alongside the Exeter and other allied ships, faced a formidable Japanese fleet. Lieutenant John

Miller, who had taken on increased responsibilities due to the injuries of his fellow crew members, was at the heart of this intense confrontation with the gun crews.

"It's like we're facing the entire Japanese Navy," Miller said to Private Johnson, as they prepared for the looming battle.

The Houston opened fire at extreme range, engaging the enemy with remarkable accuracy. "We've got them in our sights," Miller called out as the ship's guns roared to life. The Japanese responded with their own precise and relentless bombardment.

During the battle, the Exeter weakened from a previous engagement, suffered further damage, and had to withdraw under a smoke screen laid by the destroyers. "They're taking a beating," Rooks observed, watching the Exeter fall back.

The Houston, though hit by Japanese fire, sustained minimal damage. One shell entered the ship's port side and exited through the bottom, causing flooding in some storage spaces. Another shell struck near Miller's gun position, briefly cutting the electrical power and plunging them into darkness. "That was too close for comfort," Miller shouted, feeling the ship shudder under the impact.

As night enveloped the seas around Port Darwin, the darkness brought an ominous silence, a stark contrast to the chaos and destruction of the day. A new and deadly threat soon shattered this deceptive calm. The USS Houston and its allied vessels, still reeling from the aerial assault, now found themselves in the crosshairs of a hidden enemy: Japanese submarines.

Captain Rooks, ever vigilant, paced the deck of the Houston, his eyes scanning the dark waters. He knew that beneath the deceptive calm of the ocean's surface lurked a formidable adversary.

Renowned for their stealth and precision, Japanese submarines exploited the cover of darkness, masterfully turning the night into a strategic ally for their campaign. The dark skies and sea became their realm, where they maneuvered with eerie silence and deadly accuracy, heightening the sense of terror under the cloak of night.

The first indication of the lurking danger came in the form of a distant, muffled explosion. A torpedo struck a merchant ship that was part of the convoy escorted by the Houston. The impact was devastating; a water column shot up into the air, illuminated by the ensuing fireball as the ship's fuel ignited. The sound of twisting metal and cries of the crew carried across the water, a harrowing reminder of the ruthlessness of submarine warfare.

Captain Rooks immediately ordered his crew to battle stations. "Sound general quarters! Prepare for underwater threats!" he bellowed.

The crew, already battle-weary, sprang into action, their training taking over in the face of imminent danger. The anti-submarine warfare team manned the sonar equipment, desperately scanning the depths for any sign of the enemy, while others prepared the depth charges, their only real weapon against the submerged threat.

The Houston, along with its allied ships, began evasive maneuvers. They zigzagged across the water, making their course unpredictable to throw off the enemy's aim. The tension on board was palpable; each sailor understood that a single well-placed torpedo could spell disaster for their ship.

Another explosion rocked the night during the high-stakes cat-and-mouse game. This time, it was a destroyer, part of the escort fleet, hit squarely by a torpedo. The ship, its stern nearly obliterated, listed heavily in the churning waters. Crew members launched into frantic, coordinated efforts to save the vessel, their actions a blend of desperation and determination.

Amid the chaos, they also tirelessly worked to rescue their fellow sailors, fighting against time and the unforgiving sea to bring everyone to safety. The scene was of intense urgency, underscored by the ship's critical state and its crew's perilous situation. His face set in grim determination, Captain Rooks continued to issue orders. "Keep changing course! Watch for their periscopes!" he commanded.

The sailors obeyed, their eyes peeled for the slightest sign of the enemy's presence. The anti-submarine team worked feverishly, their ears straining to interpret every ping and echo from the sonar.

Suddenly, a faint blip appeared on the sonar screen, a whisper of sound that set every heart on the Houston racing. "Bearing two-four-zero, range one thousand yards!" shouted the sonar operator. Desperate to neutralize the unseen adversary, the crew swiftly rolled depth charges off the stern, causing them to explode underwater.

Throughout the night, this tense game of hide and seek continued. Taking advantage of their stealth and the cover of darkness, the Japanese submarines launched several more torpedoes, each a deadly messenger of destruction. The Houston and its allies responded with every tool and tactic at their disposal, fighting an enemy they could not see in a battle where the stakes could not be higher.

As dawn broke, revealing the aftermath of the night's harrowing encounters, the actual cost of the battle became evident. Debris littered the sea, and several ships were either damaged or sunk.

The exhausted but resolute crew of the Houston continued their vigil, knowing that the threat of submarine attack remained as long as the enemy lurked beneath the waves. As the day passed and nightfall again came, the Houston and its allies faced a threat once more... more torpedoes. Japanese submarines had joined the fray again, adding another layer of danger to the already chaotic and exhaustive battle.

"I've never seen anything like this," Private Johnson exclaimed as they narrowly avoided torpedo tracks in the water.

Miller, through his binoculars, witnessed a scene of utter devastation. The Java was torn asunder by the force of the impact, its midsection erupting into a fiery inferno. The shockwave from the explosion was so intense that it visibly hurled crew members off the ship, their figures silhouetted against the fiery backdrop, tossed helplessly into the air like ragdolls.

"They've hit the Java! Dear God, they've hit her!" Miller cried out, his voice echoing with horror and disbelief. The shock in his tone was palpable, mirroring the helplessness and dismay that gripped everyone on board. "How could this happen?" he stammered, struggling to comprehend the scale of the disaster unfolding before their eyes. His words, filled with raw emotion, resonated with the crew, each grappling with the harsh reality of their situation. The air was heavy with a sense of dread as the grim consequences of the attack became increasingly apparent.

Hearing Miller's shout, Captain Rooks rushed to his side, his eyes widening as he took in the horrific scene. "Man the rescue stations! We need to get survivors out of the water now!" he ordered, his voice urgent, commanding action amid the chaos.

The crew of the Houston sprang into action, the grim reality of their situation setting in.

The sounds of their hurried movements and the distant cries of the survivors struggling in the water filled the air as they scrambled to launch lifeboats and deploy rescue teams.

The night once shrouded in a deceptive quietness, erupted into chaos with the piercing screams of the wounded and the desperate shouts of men struggling for survival. The sea around the Java transformed into a fiery hellscape, burning oil spreading like a sinister blanket over the water's surface. Its eerie glow cast a haunting light on the frantic rescue efforts.

"Help over here!" a sailor yelled, his voice strangled by smoke and fear as he fought against the oily grip of the sea.

Another cried out in panic, "I can't swim with this oil! It's everywhere!"

As they flailed in the water, the inferno reflected in their eyes. The scene was a harrowing dance of life and death. The desperation of the survivors, coupled with the relentless spread of the fiery oil, created a nail-biting tableau of survival against all odds.

In the heart of chaos, Miller stood petrified, the destruction of the Java etching a permanent image in his mind. Around him, the explosion's raw force sent men flying through the air like ragdolls, their screams piercing the night. Amidst the cacophony of anguished cries and roaring flames, Miller watched in horror as the fiery waters hurled his comrades into them, leaving their fates uncertain.

The devastating power of the blast and the sight of his fellow sailors' plight would forever haunt his memories, marking a moment of profound shock and helplessness.

The battle continued into the night, with both sides demonstrating skill and determination. For Rooks and his crew, it was a stark reminder of the prowess and professionalism of the Japanese navy. Despite the challenges, they remained steadfast, their training and resilience shining through in these dire moments.

As the Houston navigated through the flares and hazards of battle, Miller and his gun crew were acutely aware of the stakes. Each moment brought new dangers, but they faced them with courage, ready to do whatever it took to fulfill their duty and protect their allies.

As the USS Houston navigated the treacherous waters amid a fierce battle with the Japanese, Lieutenant John Miller and others witnessed the stark reality of war. They saw the Java and the DeRuyter, two Dutch cruisers, hit by torpedoes, their crew members visibly blown off the decks amid fire and chaos.

"Those submarines are ruthless," Miller muttered to Private Johnson, his eyes fixed on the horrific scene unfolding before them. "We're in deep waters now, literally and figuratively."

The Houston narrowly escaped a similar fate, thanks to quick action by Captain Rooks.

"That was too close," Miller exclaimed as torpedo tracks passed harmlessly behind them. "Captain Rooks's quick thinking saved us there."

The loss of the Dutch cruisers was a harsh blow, and it was a stark reminder to sailors and Marines of the precariousness of their situation. "We're really up against it now," Sergeant Davis said, shaking his head in disbelief.

Exhaustion was setting in for the crew, including Captain Rooks, who hadn't rested properly in days. "I just need some sleep," he confided to Commander Rice. "Just a few hours to shut my eyes."

The discussion turned to the possibility of capture. "Capture is the last thing on our minds," Rooks said. "Survival is our only focus."

The crew knew their chances of survival were slim, but they were determined to fight to the end!

Chapter TEN

Japanese Submarines Back Off

As the Japanese submarines backed off, the Houston and others navigated through rain squalls toward Batavia. During their trek, they encountered a Japanese float plane patrolling the minefields. "Why aren't they taking that plane down?" Miller wondered aloud while standing near his gun crews, frustration evident in his voice.

Upon reaching Tanjong Priok, the port facility of Batavia, Captain Rooks went ashore for a brief meeting. Upon his return, rumors circulated that they might head to Australia and possibly back to the States. "

It wasn't long, and a shout came from the ship's top!

"Fire control, report!" Captain Rooks demanded, gripping the bridge's railing as he stared intently through his binoculars at the distant enemy fleet, now shrouded in the smoke of battle.

"Direct hit on the lead ship, sir! They're taking on water!" came the crackled response from the fire control team, their excitement palpable even through the static of the communication line.

The Houston, once a silent predator stalking its prey, the hiding submarines, was now fully engaged in a symphony of violence and strategy. The crew moved as one entity, bound by duty and a fierce determination to protect their ship and cripple their enemy.

As the Houston continued her relentless assault, the enemy fleet scrambled to respond, their silhouettes illuminated by the flashes of exploding artillery.

Amid the deafening roar of battle, the gun deck of the Houston was a maelstrom of fury and chaos. The air was thick with the acrid stench of gunpowder, and the overwhelming heat from the guns stifled the atmosphere. Sweat poured down the sailors' faces, mixing with the black soot that coated their skin, creating streaks of grime that marked them like war paint.

The gun crews worked feverishly, their movements a blur of practiced efficiency. "Shells incoming!" one sailor shouted over the din, his voice hoarse with exertion as he hoisted a heavy artillery shell into position.

"Fire!" bellowed Miller, his command slicing through the cacophony. The guns recoiled with a thunderous blast, the shockwaves rattling the very bones of the ship. Each discharge was a physical force, felt as much as heard, that jolted the crew to their core.

Around the guns, the deck was a frenzy of activity. "Reload! Reload!" yelled another crewman, wiping sweat and grime from his brow with a grimy sleeve. The sailors heaved the massive shells into the breeches of the cannons, their muscles straining under the weight.

The sharp commands of the officers punctuated the air, along with the shouted responses of the gun crews. "Aim two degrees starboard!" "Ready to fire!" The dialogue was a rapid-fire exchange, each word critical amid the tumult.

The battle raged with unrelenting fury as the USS Houston, a sea leviathan, cut through the waves, her guns blazing. The sky was a tapestry of chaos, streaked with the fiery trails of shells and the ominous shapes of enemy planes. Amid this maelstrom, the crew of the Houston remained steadfast, their focus unwavering despite the pandemonium that enveloped them.

Suddenly, a high-pitched whine, different from the usual cacophony of battle, pierced the air. The sound grew louder, more insistent, a harbinger of imminent danger. The crew's trained ears recognized it instantly - an incoming shell, its trajectory zeroing in on the Houston.

"Brace!" The warning shout barely had time to leave the lips of Captain Rooks before the shell made its impact. It landed mere feet from the Houston's starboard side, the ocean erupting in a colossal explosion. Like a monstrous geyser, water surged upwards, a towering wall of frothing, churning sea.

The concussion of the blast was a physical force, a shockwave that rattled the very bones of the ship and those aboard her. The deck trembled violently underfoot, throwing off the balance of the sailors. The sound was deafening, a thunderous roar that seemed to consume all other noises, leaving a ringing silence in its wake.

AGAIN, THE AIRWAYS were alive, with the Japanese celebrating the sinking of the USS Houston. The entire deck was ablaze, and smoke billowed from different parts. This news reached the Houston's allies and, from there, reached back to the mainland. But, oh, how wrong the Japs and Tokyo Rose were in their premature celebration...

Chapter ELEVEN

The Battle of Sunda Strait

In the tense hours leading up to what would become a pivotal moment in their struggle, the crews of the USS Houston and the Australian light cruiser HMAS Perth braced themselves for the daunting challenge ahead.

They had just endured a day of relentless battle, each explosion and burst of gunfire etching a permanent mark on their memories. With their bodies and spirits weighed down by total exhaustion, they sought a brief respite in the calm of smooth sailing as they attempted a daring escape through the Sunda Strait.

The atmosphere aboard the Houston was one of grim determination mixed with an undercurrent of anxiety. The crew, though battle-hardened, could not shake off the fatigue that clung to them like a heavy shroud. John Miller, his eyes heavy with weariness, reviewed the readiness of his gun crew, his voice steady but betraying the strain of the continuous fighting.

The raw power of the explosion, the sight of men flung from the ship, and the anguished cries of the wounded will haunt him for the rest of his life. The blurred sunlight cast a ghostly glow over the deck, illuminating the faces of the crew, each etched with the same mix of resolve and apprehension. Standing by his post, Private Johnson scanned the dark horizon, his thoughts a tangled blend of fear and hope.

The brief period of calm shattered suddenly when the lookout sounded the alarm again on February 27, 1942.

The crew spotted enemy ships and realized their safe path through the Sunda Strait had ended. The news rippled through the ship like an electric shock, snapping everyone back to heightened alertness. "Battle stations!" bellowed Captain Rooks as the crew scrambled into action, their exhaustion momentarily forgotten in the face of imminent danger.

The Houston and the Perth, side by side, prepared to face their adversaries.

With its pastel skies and calm waters, the tranquil dawn at sea immediately transformed into a scene of urgent activity and rising alarm. The previously still morning air, which had carried only the soft sounds of waves and the distant call of seabirds, now vibrated with the energy of a ship bracing for action.

"Battle stations! Battle stations!" the alarm blared over the ship's loudspeakers, jolting the crew of the Houston from their morning routines. The urgency of Rooks's voice echoing through the corridors and across the decks was unmistakable, a clear signal that the threat they faced was immediate and real.

"All hands, man your positions!" Captain Rook's commanding voice cut through the growing tumult, his words sharp and decisive. He stood on the bridge, his eyes scanning the horizon, the weight of command etched in his stern expression.

The crew members, seasoned by their experiences yet constantly aware of war's unpredictable nature, responded swiftly. They knew that every second counted. "Torpedo crew, ready the launchers!" shouted Lieutenant Johnson as he raced to the forward deck, his voice carrying over the din of running feet and clanging metal.

"Engine room, full speed ahead!" Chief Engineer Thompson's voice crackled over the radio, laden with tension yet unwavering. Below deck, the engineers sprang into action, the heart of the USS

Houston roaring to life. The massive engines vibrated intensely, their rhythmic thrumming echoing through the hull as the ship surged forward with renewed urgency, slicing through the churning waters. Amid the clatter and hiss of machinery, shouts of coordination and determination filled the engine room, each crew member keenly aware of their critical role.

"Aircraft on the starboard bow! Get those guns up!" cried Gunner's Mate Peters, pointing towards a distant speck in the sky that was rapidly growing larger.

As the anti-aircraft gun crews scrambled into position, the deck became a hive of intense activity. "Ammo up, let's move!" shouted a gunner, his voice cutting through the din. With practiced hands, crew members loaded ammunition swiftly and precisely, the urgency palpable in their every move. "On target, stay sharp!" another called out as they prepared to face the imminent aerial threat. The air was thick with focus and determination, each crew member acutely aware of the stakes at hand.

"Signal the convoy, evasive maneuvers!" ordered Captain Rooks, his hand gripping the bridge's railing tightly. Around them, the water churned as the allied ships responded, turning and weaving in a desperate dance to avoid the unseen dangers that lurked beneath the surface and the threats swooping down from above.

In the middle of this orchestrated chaos, the ship's sounds created a symphony of survival: the engines rumbled deeply, machinery whirred, guns emitted sharp reports as crews tested them, and above all, the voices of men, united in a common purpose, rose.

"Battle stations! Man the guns!" the captain's voice thundered across the deck, each word commanding urgent action. "Acknowledge your orders!" came another shout, ensuring every crew member knew their role in this synchronized dance of defense. The air crackled with tension as sailors moved with purpose and precision, a living embodiment of the ship's will to survive. The sound of boots pounding on metal, orders echoing, and the rhythmic clanking of machinery underscored the scene – a ship bracing for battle, its crew united in a singular, vital effort to protect their vessel and each other.

The tension was palpable, a living thing that gripped every sailor on board. Eyes scanned the skies and the sea, every sense heightened, every muscle tensed for action. The USS Houston, a mere speck in the ocean's vastness, was a hive of activity.

Earlier in the day, the chaos and destruction around him visibly shook Tsao, the young Chinese mess boy. But as the situation intensified, a transformation overtook him. His usual timid demeanor became a steely resolve, his face set in a determined scowl. He understood the gravity of the moment, the need for every hand on deck, regardless of their usual duties.

Tsao made his way to his assigned emergency station, his steps firm, his jaw clenched. "I'm ready," he muttered to himself, a quiet affirmation of his newfound courage.

Meanwhile, on the deck, the crew of the Houston was a picture of focused readiness. "Alright, boys, this is it! Check your stations!" barked Miller as he oversaw his gun crew. The men around him, faces smeared with sweat and grime, nodded their understanding, each man acutely aware of the looming confrontation.

The Australian cruiser Perth, a steadfast ally in the Pacific theater, signaled their readiness to engage. The flashing of their signal lights in the distance was a silent yet powerful testament to the unity and resolve of the Allied forces.

"Perth is with us. We're not alone in this," Miller shouted to his crew, a statement that bolstered the spirits of those who heard him. In response, the men around him tightened their grip on their weapons, their eyes fixed on the horizon.

Standing on the bridge, Captain Rooks surveyed the scene with apprehension and determination. "Positions, everyone. Stay sharp.

We need to be ready for anything," he commanded, his voice a steady beacon in the rising tide of tension.

A sense of impending conflict filled the vast, seemingly endless ocean as the enemy ships drew nearer. The once calm blue waters now served as a battleground, where the fate of many hung in the balance.

In these crucial moments, the cumulative weight of their experiences came to bear. The fatigue from previous sea-to-air battles lingered in their muscles; the uncertainty of escape clouded their thoughts, but their unyielding spirit shone brightest. Each man on board the Houston and the Perth, from seasoned officers to young sailors like Tsao, understood the magnitude of what was to come.

"Remember what we're fighting for, men!" Captain Rooks called out, his voice carrying over the ship. "For our homes, for our families, for each other!"

The response was a chorus of affirmations, a collective expression of their readiness to face whatever the enemy brought their way.

The air was electric with anticipation, every eye scanning the horizon, every ear listening for the sound of the first shot. It was a climax that had been building since their last significant encounter on February 4th... a moment that would indeed test their mettle and shape their fate.

The stage was now set for a confrontation of monumental proportions, a clash etched with suspense and tension. Each member of the Houston's crew braced for the impending battle, a battle that would stand as a testament to their unyielding bravery and resilience. Amid the overwhelming odds, they prepared to engage, their resolve as solid as the steel of the ship they served on. This imminent encounter, under the shadow of looming adversity, promised to etch their names in the annals of history for their courageous stand against a formidable foe.

FOR A MOMENT, TIME seemed to stand still. Sailors were momentarily frozen, caught in the awe and terror of the explosion's proximity. Then, as the shockwave dissipated, reality snapped back into focus. The colossal column of water crashed down upon the deck and the ocean around, drenching the sailors in a salty, cold deluge. The force of the water was a stinging slap against their skin, a chilling reminder of their vulnerability in this vast, hostile ocean.

The near miss left a tangible mark on the crew. Faces, already grim with determination, now bore the added weight of a narrowly escaped catastrophe. Eyes wide with the adrenaline rush of the close call, they exchanged glances that spoke volumes - they had survived, but the battle raged on.

The explosion was deafening, a thunderous roar reverberating through the USS Houston, sending shockwaves across the deck. As the water settled and the ringing in their ears began to subside, the sailors, momentarily disoriented, quickly shook off their stupor and regained their composure. The near miss was a jarring reminder of their precarious situation.

"Back on your feet, men! We're not done yet!" Captain Rook's voice boomed across the deck, cutting through the lingering dissonance. Standing resolutely against the backdrop of chaos, his figure was a rallying point for the crew.

Commander Rice's uniform, stained with sweat and soot, echoed the captain's urgency. "All hands, man your stations! Stay sharp!" he shouted, moving swiftly among the crew, his eyes assessing the state of his ship and men.

The gun crews, momentarily shaken by the blast, sprang back to life at the sound of their leaders' voices. Miller, a veteran of the gun deck, barked orders to his team with a renewed sense of determination. "Reload! Check those barrels! We can't afford a misfire now!" he yelled, his voice barely audible over the cacophony of battle.

The sailors around him responded instantly, their movements quick and precise. The gunners loaded shells, the lookouts scanned the horizon, and the damage control teams assessed and addressed the impacts of the explosion. Each man knew his role, and the moment's urgency lent a frenetic pace to their actions.

"Torpedo crew, ready on the left! We've got incoming!" one of the sailors called out, his eyes fixed on the ominous shapes approaching in the water.

"Engine room, give me everything you've got! We need to maneuver now!" Captain Rooks commanded through his radio, his voice a blend of command and urgency.

Operating like a well-oiled machine, the crew responded to each command efficiently. The sense of camaraderie and shared purpose was palpable, each man driven by a desire to protect his ship and his brothers-in-arms.

"Stay focused, boys! We've been through worse!" yelled a seasoned sailor, his words offering a brief moment of morale amidst the storm of battle.

The crew's actions were a testament to their training and resolve as the Houston maneuvered through the water, dodging the deadly threats that lurked beneath the surface and in the skies. The air was thick with the smell of gunpowder and sea spray, the sounds of battle echoing around them.

From his vantage point on the bridge, Captain Rooks witnessed the unfolding battle with an intensity that matched the pounding of his heart. His eyes, sharp and unblinking, darted across the chaotic panorama before him. Once a tranquil expanse of blue, the sea was now a tumultuous battlefield, streaked with the white froth of churning waves and marred by the dark silhouettes of enemy ships.

The recent close call sent a visceral jolt through his body. He felt the ship shudder under the impact of the near miss, the vibration reverberating through the soles of his boots and into his very core.

It was a stark, unyielding reminder of the high stakes of this deadly game – a game where the currency was the lives of his men and the integrity of his ship.

Captain Rooks's hands, weathered and strong, gripped the railing of the bridge with a firmness that belied his inner turmoil. His knuckles whitened under the strain, a physical manifestation of the immense pressure he bore. He stood like a statue, his gaze fixed on the horizon, the lines on his face etched deeper by the gravity of the situation.

Around him, the bridge was a hive of activity. Officers barked orders, relaying information received from the deck below and from the lookouts perched in the crow's nest. The air was thick with tension, punctuated by the crackle of the radio and the occasional shout of a new sighting or status report.

But for Captain Rooks, the world narrowed to the immediate challenge. He watched as his crew, dots against the ocean's vastness, worked with a frenetic energy. The gun crews adjusted their aim, the engineers coaxed more engine power, and the medical team stood by for the inevitable casualties.

As he watched, another volley of enemy fire streaked across the sky, its deadly intent clear. Captain Rooks's jaw tightened, his eyes tracking the trajectory of the incoming threat. Time seemed to slow as he braced for impact, his mind racing through the myriad of decisions and orders that might follow.

"Hold on tight!" he shouted, his voice carrying the weight of his command, a beacon of leadership in the storm of uncertainty. Another shell landed only feet away with another gusher of white water fifty feet high mushroomed from the sea's surface.

Captain Rooks looked down at his wristwatch and said, "Well, I don't have to look at my watch to tell what time it is. The incoming Zero's are telling me it must be near eleven hundred hours, once again on cue."

The Japanese planes appeared. "Here they come," announced Captain Anderson, who shouted over the radio from the Perth, his voice echoing through the ship's intercom. The Dutch admiral in charge ordered a scatter maneuver as the bombers descended upon them, unleashing their deadly cargo.

A bomb struck the Houston, landing near the number three turret on the stern, causing catastrophic damage.

Shrapnel savagely tore through the turret, utterly obliterating the crew's washroom in its path. "We've been hit!" shouted Sergeant Davis, panic and disbelief in his voice.

Miller, stationed at gun eight on the USS Houston, had just returned from resolving a magazine issue when the bomb struck. "I couldn't believe it," he recalled later, the disbelief still evident in his voice. "One minute, everything was routine; the next, it was total chaos."

He remembered the moments before the impact, hearing a fellow sailor's warning shout, "Incoming!" The sky was clear except for the menacing silhouette of a Japanese aircraft, its deadly cargo visible against the sun.

The bomb's descent was swift and terrifying. "Brace yourselves!" Miller had yelled instinctively, even as the reality of the imminent explosion set in.

Fear and adrenaline-charged the air as everyone braced for impact.

The explosion was deafening. A massive upheaval shook the ship to its core. Shrapnel flew, metal screamed, and the deck trembled under their feet. "Man down!" someone cried out amidst the chaos, the urgency in his voice mirroring the pandemonium around them.

In the aftermath, the scene was one of devastation. "Medic!" calls echoed, mixed with groans of pain and the continuing battle sounds. Amidst it all, Miller stood dazed, his ears ringing, as the magnitude of what had just happened slowly sank in.

The aftermath of the explosion was a scene of unimaginable devastation. The interior of the gun turret, once a hub of coordinated, precise activity, was now an inferno, its insides engulfed in merciless flames. The acrid smell of burning metal and charred flesh filled the air, a pungent reminder of the tragedy that unfolded within those steel walls.

Standing a short distance away, Miller witnessed the horrifying sight with a sense of disbelief and profound sorrow. The explosion had been so intense, so absolute, that it had trapped and killed the entire crew inside the turret. These were men he had known, trained with, and shared meals and laughter with. Now, all that remained were the twisted, scorched remnants of their existence.

"My God, they're gone... all of them," Miller muttered to himself, his voice barely a whisper, choked with emotion. His eyes, wide with shock, took in the grisly scene – the scattered remains of his comrades, once full of life and vigor, now reduced to unrecognizable fragments.

The heat from the still-burning turret was intense, a scorching wave that hit him in the face, singeing his eyebrows and making his eyes water. The metal groaned and creaked as it succumbed to the relentless assault of the flames, a haunting symphony to the tragedy.

"Miller! Miller!" The shout snapped him out of his daze. It was Lieutenant Johnson, his face smeared with soot, his expression a fusion of urgency and compassion. "We need to move! There could be secondary explosions! Hurry! Get out of here!"

Miller nodded, his body moving on instinct despite the shock that gripped him. He took one last look at the ruin of the turret, a silent vow forming in his mind to remember the fallen, to honor their sacrifice.

As they quickly moved away, the sounds of the continuing battle seemed distant, muffled by the ringing in his ears. The image of the turret, a tomb for his fellow sailors, seared into his memory.

The smell of smoke and burnt metal followed him, a lingering ghost of the tragedy, as he rejoined the fray, his heart heavy with loss but steadfast in his duty.

The Houston, though wounded, continued to fight. Captain Rooks's skillful maneuvering evaded further bombings, but the damage had already occurred. "We're lucky to get out of there," Miller admitted, the weight of the experience etched in his expression.

The deck of the Houston transformed into a realm where death and bravery danced in unison. Amid the harshness of war, men darted with purpose, a ballet of urgency under the iron-gray sky.

Crew members loaded shells, manned guns, and shouted coordinates, all while relentless Japanese planes sliced through the sky, their machine guns unleashing torrents of fire and death.

Commander Rice, eyes fixed on the menacing dance of a Japanese Zero lining up for a strafing run, bellowed, "Starboard, 45 degrees!" His voice cut through the chaos, a beacon of command in the madness. The gun crew swiveled to follow his direction, the deck vibrating under the rhythm of their 5-inch guns. Each blast was a chorus of defiance, the recoil jarring Lieutenant Miller's frame, who stood near the anti-aircraft guns.

"Keep it steady!" Miller shouted to Private Johnson, who was gritting his teeth against the recoil. "We can take this bastard down!"

Johnson, eyes squinted against the smoke and sweat, nodded, his hands steady despite the tremor of fear. "Got it, Lieutenant!" he yelled back, the words almost lost in the roar of gunfire and explosions.

Above them, the sky was alight with the surreal beauty of destruction. Explosions painted the heavens in bursts of orange and crimson, a macabre display of deadly fireworks. Shrapnel sang a lethal melody as it whistled through the air, a metallic rain threatening to shred flesh and metal.

The crew of the Houston, a tight-knit tapestry of sailors and Marines, moved with an almost preternatural synergy. Each man knew his role, fighting not just for personal survival but for the brother beside him. This unspoken bond, forged in the heat of battle, was their anchor amid the storm.

"Cover me! I'm reloading!" yelled a sailor to his mate as they worked in tandem to keep their guns firing.

"Got your back!" came the determined reply, punctuated by the clang of a spent shell hitting the deck.

Captain Rooks, a figure of calm authority at the helm, deftly maneuvered the Houston. His hands were steady on the wheel, guiding the wounded ship with a finesse that belied her size. Each turn and evasion he orchestrated was a masterful dance step away from annihilation.

In the middle of the bedlam, a moment of lucidity struck Miller. The realization that they were part of something far greater than the sum of their fears and adrenaline gave him a sense of profound purpose. "We're doing our job. That's all that matters," he thought to himself, a silent oath to the fallen and the fighting.

Amid the deafening roar of battle, the gun deck of the USS Houston continued to be a maelstrom of fury and chaos. The air was thick with the acrid stench of gunpowder, and the overwhelming heat from the guns stifled the atmosphere. Sweat poured down the sailors' faces, mixing with the black soot that coated their skin, creating streaks of grime that marked them like war paint.

The USS Houston's deck was a symphony of war. The guns boomed with a deafening roar, each blast sending tremors through the ship as if the metal were crying out. Amid the chaos, the sharp clank of ammunition rang out, a constant, urgent rhythm in the background.

"The jam's cleared!" shouted a young sailor, his voice barely audible over the cacophony. Drenched in sweat, with streaks of grease painting his face, he wrestled with the machinery of the gun. "Keep it up, boys!" bellowed Sergeant Davis, his voice rough like gravel, cutting through the noise. He moved among his crew, a pillar of strength, his eyes as sharp as the shards of sunlight piercing the smoke-filled air.

The air was full of the smell of gunpowder, a bitter, choking scent that mingled with the salty tang of the sea. The pungent odor of engine exhaust hung heavy, a reminder of the ship's ceaseless effort.

"Fire!" commanded the gun captain, his arm extending towards the enemy. Each time he gave the order, the ship responded with a thunderous reply, the guns recoiling as they spat fire and fury into the distance.

The sailors operated in a state of heightened focus, the tension in their bodies evident in every swift, deliberate movement. "Ammo coming through!" yelled a sailor, his voice laced with urgency as he maneuvered a heavy shell through the cramped space.

Above the relentless barrage of their guns, the distant whine of enemy aircraft wove an ominous melody. The sound of shells splashing perilously close sent shivers down the spine, a visceral reminder of the enemy's presence.

"Two degrees to starboard, now!" shouted Commander Rice, his eyes fixed on the murky shapes of the enemy through his binoculars. His command was precise, a lifeline amid the uncertainty of battle.

The crew responded like a well-oiled machine, each member playing their part in this deadly dance. Sweat and sea spray mixed on their skin, the physical evidence of their exertion and the ocean's proximity.

As the Houston bore down on its adversaries, the scene was one of controlled chaos. Smoke billowed around the gunners, obscuring their view but not their resolve. They moved like shadows in a dance with danger, each step, each action a testament to their training and bravery.

As the battle raged on, the crew of the Houston operated as a single, cohesive unit. Their faces, etched with determination and fatigue, were a testament to their resilience and commitment. In this moment of intense combat, they were more than just sailors; they were guardians of their ship, standing defiant against the onslaught, united in their resolve to fight and survive. The fury of the battle, the relentless pace of the gunnery, and the sheer will of the men who manned them were the lifeblood of the USS Houston in her valiant stand in the Pacific.

The Houston was fiercely engaged in a naval skirmish when the sudden appearance of dozens more Japanese bombers descending from the clouds escalated the chaos of battle. The menacing silhouettes of the enemy aircraft, cutting sharply against the overcast sky, cast a new shadow of dread over the ship.

"Airborne targets incoming!" screamed a lookout from his perch atop the bridge. His eyes, wide with alarm, scanned the skies as he clutched the railing, his voice laced with tension carrying across the deck. The warning rippled through the crew, igniting a flurry of activity as sailors scrambled to man the anti-aircraft guns.

"Positions, now! Bring those birds down!" Commander Rice shouted, his authoritative voice resonating over the ship's din. Standing on the bridge, he pointed to the sky, his face a mask of determination. The gunners, their uniforms soaked with sweat from the intense heat of battle and the pressure of their task, adjusted their weapons skyward with quick and precise movements.

The drone of the approaching bombers filled the air, a guttural sound that sent a chill down the sailors' spines. "Here they come! Brace yourselves!" yelled a gun captain stationed at one of the anti-aircraft guns. His hands were steady on the weapon as his eyes narrowed, focusing on the diving aircraft.

"Steady... steady..." muttered Sergeant Davis, a veteran gunner, as he calibrated the aim of his gun. His fingers danced over the controls with the expertise of countless drills, his gaze never wavering from the approaching threat.

The bombers swooped lower, releasing their deadly cargo. The Houston's anti-aircraft guns roared to life in response. "Fire! Fire!" chanted the crews in unison, a chorus melding desperation and defiance. The sky above the Houston erupted into a deadly ballet of tracer fire and explosions. Each burst from the ship's guns was a blazing arc, a determined attempt to protect their vessel.

The sky above the Houston had transformed into a deadly arena, where the whine of engines and the crackle of gunfire composed a symphony of war. Japanese Zero fighters, sleek and lethal, swooped in with predatory precision, their engines screaming like banshees in the wind. The sun glinted off their metallic fuselages, making them appear as sinister specters against the vast, cloud-speckled sky.

Aboard the Houston, the response was immediate and fierce. The crew, their faces set in grim determination, manned their stations with a ferocity born of necessity. Anti-aircraft guns roared to life, sending a hail of lead skyward. The booming of the large-caliber guns melded with the rapid thud of the smaller AA fire, creating a wall of resistance against the aerial assault.

Gunpowder filled the air, its acrid scent mingling with the salty tang of the sea. The deck vibrated with the recoil of the guns, a constant reminder of the ship's might. Sailors shouted commands and status updates, their voices almost lost in the cacophony of battle.

One Zero, caught in the relentless barrage, erupted into a ball of fire. Its demise was violent and spectacular, a vivid explosion of orange and red that lit up the sky. A cheer erupted from the crew of the Houston, a momentary release of tension in the unyielding stress of combat.

But the battle raged on. More Zeros dived, their pilots skilled and relentless. The Houston's guns tracked their movements, the gunners' eyes squinting through the sights, fingers tensed on the triggers.

The crew hit another Zero, its wing erupting in flames and sending it spiraling toward the ocean in a plume of smoke. His eyes scanning the skies, Captain Rooks issued orders with a calm that belied the chaos around him. "Keep firing! Protect the ship at all costs!" His voice, though steady, carried the weight of their dire situation.

The Houston, a lone sentinel in the vast Pacific, stood her ground against the aerial onslaught. Each fallen Zero was a testament to the skill and bravery of her crew; each burst of anti-aircraft fire was defiance against the enemies that swarmed above.

As the battle continued, the sky became a tapestry of desperation and valor, of attackers seeking to destroy and defenders resolute in their protection. The USS Houston, amid the smoke, the fire, and the relentless noise of war, held her own in a dance as old as warfare itself.

"Keep it up! We can take them!" encouraged Lieutenant Morris, overseeing the gun crews. His voice was firm, rallying his men amid the cacophony of battle.

The deck vibrated with each discharge, the air thick with the smell of cordite and the metallic tang of spent shells. The gunners' faces, smeared with soot, worked tirelessly, feeding ammunition, adjusting angles, firing, and repeating. Their actions were a testament to their training and their unyielding spirit.

In the middle of this aerial onslaught, the Houston stood resilient, her crew a unified force against both the sea's perils and the threats from above. Each explosion in the sky, each determined response from her guns, underscored the fierce resolve of the men who manned her.

The deck continued to vibrate with the force of the anti-aircraft fire, the smell of cordite mixing with the salt air. "Reload faster!" a sailor barked to his companion as they worked in tandem to feed ammunition into the starving maws of the guns.

A young Marine named Corporal James Henderson, stationed at one of the smaller caliber anti-aircraft guns, stood as a pillar of concentration and resolve. Henderson's focus never wavered among the relentless vibrations of the Houston's deck and the dense cloud of gunpowder smoke hanging in the air.

"Got one in my sights!" he barked, his voice slicing through the tumultuous roar of gunfire. His hands, surprisingly steady in the chaos of his first combat, were firmly on the gun. With a deep breath, he squeezed the trigger, the recoil jolting through his body.

As the gun thundered, another crew member, Petty Officer Mark Simmons, stationed nearby, glanced over and saw the aircraft falter in the sky, a victim of Henderson's precise shot. "You got it, Henderson!" Simmons yelled over the din, a wide grin breaking through the grime on his face.

"Yeah! That's how we do it!" Henderson shouted back, exhilaration mixed with disbelief in his voice. His heart pounded in his chest, adrenaline coursing through his veins as he realized the impact of his actions.

Simmons quickly turned back to his station, reinvigorated by Henderson's success. "Keep firing, boys. They're not done yet!" he called out to his fellow sailors, his own determination reignited.

Henderson, meanwhile, wiped sweat and soot from his brow with the back of his hand and squinted through the smoke, searching the sky for his next target. "There's more where that came from," he muttered under his breath, the weight of the moment grounding him in his duty.

In those intense minutes of battle, Henderson, Simmons, and the rest of the USS Houston's crew embodied the unyielding spirit and bravery that defined their service. Each successful hit against the enemy, each moment of heroism, no matter how small, reinforced their collective resolve to stand firm against the onslaught.

On the bridge of the USS Houston, the atmosphere was electric with suspense and tension. The ship's officers, stationed at their posts, barked orders and encouragement, orchestrating the battle with intense focus. During the tumultuous storm of combat, their voices rang out, guiding the crew through the chaos.

"Keep it up, Houston! We can do this!" Captain Rooks called out, standing steadfast at the helm. His robust, unwavering voice cut through fear and chaos, a beacon of hope and determination. His eyes, seasoned by years at sea and countless battles, remained fixed on the unfolding scene outside the bridge's windows.

"Engineering, I need more speed!" he shouted into the intercom, his command urgent but controlled. "Push the engines to their limit. Every knot counts!"

Lieutenant Morrison, the ship's navigator, responded with equal urgency. "Adjusting course, Captain. We're maximizing maneuverability to evade their fire."

The bridge crew worked with a sense of desperate purpose, their hands moving swiftly over the controls and instruments. The tension was palpable, each officer acutely aware of the stakes of their actions.

Sensing the growing anxiety among his crew, Captain Rooks raised his voice to rally them. "This is what we've trained for, people! Stay sharp, stay focused! We've faced tough odds before, and we've come through. We'll do it again!"

Outside, the guns of the Houston roared in response, the ship jolting slightly with each recoil. The relentless boom of the artillery was a testament to the crew's tenacity.

Lieutenant Harris, a gunnery officer, relayed targeting adjustments. "Captain, adjusting fire for maximum impact. We're giving them all we've got."

The sky continued to be in a frenzy of activity, with enemy bombers weaving through the barrage of anti-aircraft fire. The sound of near and far explosions added to the cacophony of battle.

"Stay vigilant!" Captain Rooks commanded, his gaze scanning the horizon. "They're not backing down, and neither are we. This ship and her crew are the pride of the Navy. Let's show them why!"

As bombs continued to splash dangerously close, sending geysers of water onto the deck, the crew of the Houston remained steadfast, their faces set in grim determination. Each explosion from the enemy and counter-response from the ship created a symphony of survival, a testament to the bravery and resilience of the crew.

"Anti-aircraft crews, take aim!" Commander Rice's voice was a steady beacon in all the chaos.

The Houston shuddered as bombs exploded nearby, water and shrapnel spraying the deck. The anti-aircraft guns answered back, a relentless chorus of thunderous retorts, as sailors fought to protect their ship against the aerial onslaught.

Captain Rooks stood tall and unflinching on the bridge in the raging heart of the battle aboard the USS Houston. His seasoned eyes surveyed the unfolding chaos, his voice cutting through the din of warfare with a commanding presence. "Keep steady, men! We can do this!" he bellowed, his words slicing through the air like a sharp blade. His firm stance and unwavering voice were a beacon of strength, rallying the sailors amid the storm of battle.

The deck of the USS Houston was alive with a whirlwind of frenzied action, a scene of controlled chaos under the unforgiving sun. Sailors, their faces streaked with sweat and soot, darted to and fro, each moving with practiced skill and raw urgency. The tension was palpable, almost as tangible as the thick, salty sea air that enveloped them.

As the ship's massive guns continued to roar, their deafening booms resonated across the deck, sending shockwaves that the sailors could feel in the very marrow of their bones. With each volley fired toward the enemy, the guns recoiled with a powerful force, their mechanisms clanking and groaning under the strain. The sound was overwhelming, a relentless thunder that dominated the soundscape of war.

Plumes of smoke from the continuous gunfire marred the sky above them, with black and gray clouds swirling against the blue canvas, intermittently obscuring the sun. The heat was oppressive, adding to the physical exertion of the crew as they loaded and reloaded the guns, their movements a dance of grim determination.

With each blast, the deck vibrated, the wooden planks and metal surfaces shuddering as if the ship was voicing its might. The sailors' ears rang, and their voices were hoarse from shouting orders and status updates over the cacophony.

Meanwhile, the atmosphere below deck in the engine room was a discord of mechanical roars and human endeavor. Marine engineer Robert Smith, a veteran of many battles, had to shout over the roar of the engines to make himself heard. "We need more power! The Captain wants more power!" His seasoned and authoritative voice cut through the noise as he coordinated his crew.

His team, a group of men with faces streaked with sweat and grease, worked intensely. The air was hot and heavy, filled with the smell of oil and metal.

Wrenches turned with urgent precision, and crew members adjusted valves desperately to coax every ounce of strength from the ship's heart. The engines thrummed louder, a testament to the crew's skill and the old engineer's experience.

In the engine room of the USS Houston, the air was thick with the heat and noise of machinery working at its limit. The symphony of mechanical sounds was almost deafening - steam hissed from valves under pressure, metal groaned as it bore the strain of high speed, and the relentless thrum of the engines provided a constant, vibrating backdrop.

"More steam to the turbines!" yelled Lieutenant Commander George Morris, the chief engineer, over the din. His voice carried an urgent tone, commanding immediate action.

His crew, a team of dedicated engineers and mechanics, moved with frantic yet focused energy amidst the clanging and hissing of the engine room. "Opening valve three!" shouted Ensign Michael Harris, a young but talented engineer aboard the USS Houston. His hands moved deftly over the controls, a dance of precision under pressure. The hiss of steam grew louder, almost a roar, as more power surged through the engines, signaling their increased output.

Engineer Mate First Class James Thompson, stationed near a large pressure gauge in the bowels of the USS Houston, called out, "Pressure's rising fast, chief! We're pushing her hard! She's gonna blow!" His voice echoed in the cramped engine room, reflecting the strain they were all under.

The chief engineer glanced at the gauge, his eyes calculating. "Keep an eye on it! We can't afford a blowout, and we sure can't afford not to get a bit more power!" he barked back, his voice laced with tension.

Nearby, two mechanics on the USS Houston, Motor Machinist's Mate Second Class Robert Johnson, and Electrician's Mate Third Class Samuel Lee, worked feverishly to tighten a series of bolts that had vibrated loose. "We've got to keep these secure!" Johnson shouted, straining against the wrench. "She's shaking like a leaf!" echoed Lee, his hands working swiftly alongside his mate to stabilize the critical components.

The entire room was a blur of motion as each crew member played their part in the intricate dance of keeping the engines running at peak performance. Sweat poured down their faces, mixing with the grease and grime that coated their skin, but their focus never wavered.

"Chief, we're at full capacity!" another engineer called out, his hands gripping a lever tightly. "She's running hot, but she's holding together!"

Lieutenant Commander George Morris nodded, a look of fierce determination etched on his face in the middle of the chaos of the engine room. "Good! Keep her steady! The ship and everyone on it are counting on us!" His voice, seasoned and commanding, resonated with authority and conviction, inspiring his team amid the heat and noise.

Each man knew that the outcome of the battle above hinged on their ability to keep the engines running smoothly. The weight of this responsibility hung heavily in the air, but the resolve and skill of the engine room crew were unwavering. They were the unsung heroes, the heartbeat of the ship, driving her forward through the perilous waters of combat.

Back on the bridge of the Houston, Captain Rooks stood with a commanding presence, his eyes intensely scanning the shifting seascape of battle. The panoramic view from the bridge offered a vivid tableau of the conflict unfolding before him.

Captain Rooks could see the distant enemy ships maneuvering for a position through his binoculars, their gray silhouettes stark against the churning sea. Plumes of smoke rose from their decks, evidence of their own furious gunnery.

Around them, the white froth of shell impacts marred the water, with each explosion sending up towering geysers that briefly obscured the vessels from view. The sky above was tumultuous, with dark clouds of smoke from the continuous gunfire smudging the horizon. Occasional bursts of bright orange and red punctuated the scene as shells found their mark, contrasting starkly against the gray clouds.

Captain Rooks could see his crew in action - a coordinated flurry of activity. The gunners were relentless, their cannons thundering in response to the enemy's fire, the recoil sending vibrations through the ship. Sailors scurried across the deck, delivering ammunition, relaying messages, and performing crucial repairs.

Despite the situation's intensity, there was a sense of order in the chaos, a testament to the crew's training and discipline. Captain Rooks felt a surge of pride as he observed their efficiency and resolve.

"Hard to port! Take us into their blind spot!" he commanded, his voice resounding with the clarity of a seasoned leader. The helmsman, a young but adept sailor named Petty Officer Jameson, responded with immediate precision, the wheel turning swiftly under his hands. The ship responded with impressive agility, veering sharply to the left, the force of the turn causing the crew to brace themselves against the sudden shift.

Below deck, Lieutenant Commander George Morris monitored the engines' response to the maneuver. "Keep those engines steady! She needs all we've got right now... max her out!" he yelled over the roar.

The seasoned veterans and eager young mechanics worked feverishly, their faces illuminated by the flickering lights of the engine room.

As the Houston maneuvered, her guns continued their deadly dance. Gunners stationed at their posts fired with relentless determination. Shells streaked across the sky, leaving trails of smoke in their wake. "Another round, load it up!" barked Sergeant Davis at the artillery deck, his voice cutting through the noise as he oversaw the gunners' synchronized efforts.

Ensign Michael Harris, stationed in the engine room, shouted updates to Morris. "Pressure's holding, sir! She's giving all she can!" His hands, blackened with grease, moved deftly over the valves and gauges, his youthful energy a vital force in the engine room's frenetic activity.

The ship shuddered with each discharge, the vibrations running through her like a living entity engaged in a deadly struggle for survival. Every thud of the guns, every creak of the timbers, echoed the intensity of the moment.

Despite being outgunned and facing relentless attack, the Houston's resilience shone through.

"She's barely clinging on!" exclaimed a sailor on the deck, pride ringing in his voice over the din of battle. His comrades, standing shoulder to shoulder, nodded in agreement, their faces set in grim determination.

As the battle drew to a close, the Houston, battered but unbroken, emerged from the smoke and chaos. The crew, exhausted yet exhilarated, shared glances of relief and camaraderie. They had faced overwhelming odds and emerged valiantly, a testament to their bravery and the indomitable spirit of the USS Houston.

The deck was a scene of weary but triumphant faces in the aftermath. The crew, understanding the weight of what they had just achieved, shared stories and pats on the back, their bond strengthened by the ordeal.

However, as they would find out, the war was far from over. Three weeks later, the USS Houston would face another challenge, a testament to the relentless nature of war and the unyielding courage of her crew.

The Battle of Java Sea, fought fiercely on February 28, 1942, between the islands of Borneo and Sulawesi in Indonesia, was a harrowing encounter that tested the mettle of every soul aboard the Houston. As the ship steamed away from the battlefield, it knew there was another day ahead of battle. The Japanese convoy was close but rested its attacks temporarily to regroup.

On the bridge of the Houston, Captain Rooks stood gazing out at the horizon, his hands clasped behind his back, a contemplative expression on his face. The sea around them was calm now, starkly contrasting to the chaos that had reigned just hours before. The setting sun cast a golden hue over the deck, bathing the ship in a warm light that belied the intensity of the day's events.

Commander Rice approached him, his footsteps echoing softly on the metal floor. "Captain, we held our ground," he said, his voice tinged with fatigue and satisfaction.

Captain Rooks turned to face him, a faint smile on his lips. "Yes, we did, Commander. Thanks to the bravery of our crew and your tactical acumen." He paused, looking out at the crew on the deck, busy with post-battle responsibilities, their movements slower, weighed down by the day's exertions.

"The crew showed extraordinary heroism today," Rooks continued, his voice filled with admiration. "They're more than just sailors – they're heroes, every single one of them."

Commander Rice nodded in agreement, his gaze following Rooks'. "It's battles like these that forge a crew into something stronger. We faced another test today, but I'm afraid the convoy will be on us soon," expressed Rice with growing apprehension, drawing a historical parallel: "Looks like we're in for it, just like those guys at the Alamo, up against Santa Anna and his thousands."

Captain Rooks, acknowledging the gravity of their situation, responded with a sense of foreboding that mirrored a historic last stand. "I know what you're saying, Paul... I know exactly how Jim Travis felt that morning at the Alamo... the eerie calm before the storm of battle." His voice carried a weight of understanding, recognizing their dire circumstances, reminiscent of a pivotal moment in Texas history. The tension was palpable, as history seemed to echo their present struggle.

The two leaders, Captain Rooks and Commander Rice stood side by side in silence on the bridge, each lost in thought as they reflected on the day's harrowing events. The first day in the Battle of the Java Sea, now etching its final strokes into the annals of history, had been a crucible that tested every fiber of the USS Houston and her valiant crew.

Captain Rooks finally broke the silence, his voice tinged with pride and solemnity. "Today, we've written another chapter in the Houston's history. Surely, Tokyo Rose will taunt our soldiers with their sinking of us once more. Our crew showed what they're made of – true grit and bravery."

Commander Rice nodded, eyes scanning the deck below where the crew was methodically attending to post-battle duties. "They did indeed, Captain. It's an honor to serve with such resilient men and women. The ship held her own, and so did they. We will keep watch, but try to get some rest because I'm afraid tomorrow morning will come early."

As the last light of the day ebbed away, casting the sky in hues of purple and gold, the USS Houston, scarred yet steadfast, sailed on through the calm waters. Her crew, a mosaic of individuals united by a singular experience, moved with a renewed sense of purpose. The bond forged in the heat of battle was palpable – a bond that had transformed them from a crew into a family.

Below deck, the sailors and Marines shared quiet conversations, recounting moments of fear, acts of heroism, and the relief of survival in their last battle. "We did it, didn't we?" a young sailor said to his comrade, a small smile breaking through his exhaustion.

"We sure did. But I'm afraid today was only the tip of the iceberg. There's more to come. We'll be ready," his friend replied, clapping him on the shoulder, their camaraderie shining through the fatigue.

As the Houston continued her journey, the crew, though weary, stood tall and proud. They were more than survivors of another fierce naval battle; they were symbols of courage and determination, a testament to the enduring spirit of those who serve at sea.

The battle was indeed over, for now, but the war raged on. Little did the sailors know it would rage on so quickly!

Chapter TWELVE

The Fading Green of the Java Coast

On the evening of February 28, 1942, as the sun began its slow descent towards the horizon, casting long shadows and painting the sky in hues of orange and pink, Captain Rooks stood solemnly on the quarterdeck of the USS Houston. His eyes, tired yet unyielding, fixed on the distant Java Coast, shrouded in the dimming light of the evening.

The Java Coast, with its lush greenery and swaying coconut and banana palms, had once been a symbol of exotic beauty and solace, a reminder of the world beyond the confines of war. But now, as Captain Rooks gazed upon it, it seemed nothing more than a distant, meaningless blur, its beauty lost amidst the chaos and uncertainty that engulfed them.

The weight of exhaustion now marked his usually upright and commanding posture. His shoulders were slightly slumped, bearing the burden of command and the responsibility for the lives of his men. The lines on his face, etched by stress and sleepless nights, told the story of the grueling campaign they had endured.

The fading light of the day cast a somber glow on his features, reflecting the internal turmoil that plagued him. His mind was a whirlwind of strategy and concern, wrestling with the pressing question that haunted him and every man aboard the Houston: "Would we make it through Sunda Strait?"

The Sunda Strait, a narrow passage between the islands of Java and Sumatra, was their intended escape route, but it was fraught with danger. The threat of enemy ships and hidden submarines loomed large in his thoughts, each possibility a grim reminder of their challenges.

He turned slightly, looking back at his ship. Unaware of his quiet vigil, the crew continued their duties with diligence, their faces set in expressions of determination and resolve. They, too, felt the weight of the situation, each man grappling with his own fears and hopes for the journey ahead.

Captain Rooks took a deep breath, the salty sea air filling his lungs, bringing a brief moment of clarity amid the storm of his thoughts. He knew the hours ahead would test them all, demanding every ounce of their skill, bravery, and endurance.

As the last light of the day slipped below the horizon, the Java Coast became little more than a silhouette, a fading memory of a world that seemed increasingly distant. Captain Rooks turned away, his gaze now fixed on the path ahead, his mind set on the challenges that lay in the dark waters of the Sunda Strait. The night ahead would be long, and the fate of the Houston and her crew hung in the balance, a reality that Captain Rooks faced with a grim yet unwavering determination, wondering just how much more the ship could endure.

Captain Rook's mind wrestled with the pressing question that haunted every man aboard: *"Will we make it through Sunda Strait? What will we do with our ship in chaos and our ammunition low?"*

Around him, the crew shared a sense of foreboding. Across the ship, a sense of foreboding had settled among the crew as they discussed their situation. In the mess hall, a group of sailors huddled around a table, their voices low but filled with concern.

Amid the clinking of cutlery and the low hum of the ship's engines, Seaman First Class Thompson sat hunched over his meal, expressing deep concern. He spoke softly, almost conspiratorially, to the sailor beside him. "I tell ya, we've been lucky so far, but it feels like we're pushing our luck too far this time," he said, his eyes darting around the room, reflecting the worry that was a common thread among the crew. "Both of our big gun turrets are gone... we're low on ammunition and—-"

"Those Japanese cruiser planes have been tailing us all afternoon," Thompson continued, his voice tinged with unease. "They've got eyes on us, no doubt about it. It's like we're never out of their sight."

Passing by with his own tray of food, Lieutenant Harris caught snippets of the conversation and felt compelled to weigh in. He set his tray down on a nearby table and leaned against a bulkhead, his posture relaxed but his expression serious. "You're right about the planes, Thompson," he said, acknowledging the seaman's concerns. "Our movements are no secret to the enemy. They've been shadowing us with a more than a little unnerving persistence."

He folded his arms across his chest, his gaze drifting to the porthole where the endless sea stretched beyond. "And I wouldn't be surprised if there are subs in the Sunda Strait, lying in wait for us," he added, his voice low but clear. "It's a strategic point for them; they know it's our most likely route. Besides, the entire Japanese Fleet appears to be begging us to continue. There's no turning around now."

Meanwhile, a group of junior officers was discussing similarly at another corner of the mess hall. Ensign Davis, a young officer with a furrowed brow, voiced his concerns to the group. "The Strait is a chokepoint, a perfect spot for an ambush," he said, his voice tinged with anxiety. "If there are subs out there, and I bet there are, they'll be looking to pick us off as we try to make it to the Indian Ocean. It's like navigating through a minefield, except we can't see the mines."

Petty Officer Martinez, who had been quietly listening, chimed in, his expression grim. "It's like we're heading into a trap," he said, echoing the sentiment of his fellow sailors. "Those waters are dangerous, crawling with threats. And if the subs don't get us, the planes will. They keep coming like there's no end. We're like sitting ducks out here in the middle of the ocean."

The conversations around the mess hall reflected the palpable tension and unease permeating the ship. Each man aboard the Houston knew the risks they faced, understood the strategic importance of their mission, and grappled with the reality of their precarious situation. Everyone's expressions easily showed the tension.

Having entered the mess hall for a brief respite, Captain Rooks overheard the murmurs of concern. Approaching the sailors, he addressed them with a steady voice. "I know you're all concerned, and rightly so. But remember, the Houston has faced tough situations before. We're not out of options yet. Our job is to navigate these challenges as best we can."

His words offered little comfort, but they served as a reminder of the resilience and strength that had carried the crew thus far. As the sailors returned to their duties, the weight of the situation hung heavily in the air.

Suddenly, the intercom in the USS Houston's mess hall crackled to life with the unmistakable voice of Tokyo Rose. "Attention, American sailors," she proclaimed with mock gravity, "your beloved 'Galloping Ghost of the Java Coast' has finally been sunk by the mighty Imperial Japanese Navy!"

A brief, stunned silence fell over the sailors, which they quickly replaced with roars of laughter. One sailor quipped, "Well, fellas, looks like we're broadcasting live from the bottom of the sea!" While they were very much afloat and in action, the absurdity of her claim brought a moment of levity to the tense atmosphere, reminding them of the psychological tactics at play in warfare.

Commander Rice walked in alongside Captain Rooks as the tense conversations continued in the mess hall. The crew, noticing their arrival, shifted their attention to the higher-ranking officers, sensing that their input could offer a new perspective on the situation.

Aware of the room's heavy atmosphere, Commander Rice injected a bit of humor to lighten the mood. "Evening, gentlemen," he began with a slight smile. "I couldn't help but overhear some of your concerns. But remember, we're the 'Galloping Ghost of the Java Coast.' We just heard her words of wisdom," he said lightly, laughing. "For all the enemy knows, we might just be a phantom ship, a ghost they can't catch."

Standing beside Rice, Captain Rooks nodded with a slight chuckle at Tokyo Rose's announcement. "That's right, Commander. According to legend, ghosts can pass through obstacles unscathed. Maybe we'll just glide through the Sunda Strait like a specter in the night," he joked lightly. The humor in his voice was evident, aiming to ease the tension among the crew. Catching on to the jest, Commander Rice replied with a grin, "In that case, Captain, let's hope our ghostly ship can spook the enemy as well." Their light-hearted banter brought a few chuckles from the crew, a welcome relief amid the stress of war.

A few sailors exchanged amused glances, the tension in their shoulders easing slightly at the officers' attempt to lighten the mood.

Trying to add a bit of levity to the conversation, one sailor quipped with a grin, "You know, at this rate, Tokyo Rose will probably be on the air bragging about sinking the Houston for the fourth time!" He chuckled lightly at his own joke. The others around him couldn't help but join in, their laughter mingling in a moment of shared humor amidst the tension.

Commander Rice continued, leaning against a table with a casual air. "Who knows, maybe the Japs are scratching their heads right now, wondering if they're chasing a real ship or just chasing shadows. We've been dodging them so well, they might start thinking we're just a figment of their imagination."

Captain Rooks added, "And let's not forget, ghosts are notoriously hard to hit. We've got some of the best evasive maneuvers up our sleeves. The Houston isn't about to make it easy for anyone trying to pin us down."

The crew members couldn't help but smile at the banter between their commanding officers. Ensign Davis, joining in the lighter mood, joked, "So, what you're saying, sir, is that we should start spreading rumors that the Houston is haunted? That might just keep the enemy at bay."

Petty Officer Martinez piped up, "Yeah, and if you see a ghost, report it to the bridge. We'll log it as an unofficial crew member."

The laughter that followed these remarks rippled through the mess hall, providing a brief respite from the otherwise somber mood. Moments like these, where humor and camaraderie shone through, reminded the men of their shared humanity amid the uncertainties of war.

Pleased to see some cheer return to the crew, Commander Rice concluded, "All jokes aside, stay sharp and keep the faith. The Houston has made it through tough spots before, and we'll do it again. Let's show them why they call us the Galloping Ghost of the Java Coast."

Despite the dire situation, a flicker of hope persisted. The Houston had defied the odds before, fighting through situations heavily favoring the Japanese. Captain Rooks, known for his naval aviator's philosophical outlook, couldn't believe this would be the end for the Houston. Clutching onto a shaky confidence, he turned from the railing and headed towards his stateroom, relieved from his duties as Officer-of-the-Deck and yearning for a few hours of rest.

Darkness enveloped the ship's interior, with the heavy metal battle ports bolted shut and lights forbidden within the darkened vessel. Only the eerie blue beams of battle lights, placed close to the deck, illuminated his path. Captain Rooks navigated the narrow companionway, briefly flicking on his flashlight to find the opening of his stateroom door.

He paused to survey his surroundings as he stepped into the small space that served as his room. Everything was unchanged for the past two and a half months except for one addition – a beautiful Bali head named Gus, a silent companion he acquired in Surabaya. Turning off the light, Captain Rooks settled into the darkness of his quarters, the ship's gentle rocking starkly contrasting with their turbulent journey. In the quiet of his room, he braced for the uncertain night ahead, the Houston continuing its perilous course through dangerous waters.

In the faintly lit stateroom of Captain Rooks, the atmosphere was heavy with anticipation and unease. The polished wooden statue sat atop the desk. Its presence was almost blatant in the cramped quarters, a silent, almost lifelike observer in the room. The faint light cast eerie shadows across its carved features, giving it an almost otherworldly appearance.

Captain Rooks, his face etched with the weight of command, stood by the desk, his gaze resting on Gus. The ship creaked and groaned around him, a constant reminder of the precarious situation outside. He let out a long, weary sigh before speaking to the statue, seeking a momentary escape from this unusual ritual.

"We'll get through this, won't we, Gus?" he murmured, the stress in his voice betraying his attempt at lightness. His eyes reflected hope and fear, half-expecting the inanimate object to respond.

As the weight of fatigue began to press heavily upon Captain Rooks, he slowly succumbed to the grasp of a much-needed but ill-timed slumber. His eyelids grew heavy as he leaned back in his chair in the quiet of his cabin. The events of the day, the relentless pressure, and the unending responsibilities had taken their toll, and despite his best efforts, he drifted towards sleep.

In this half-awake, half-asleep state, the cabin around him seemed to blur, and the boundaries between reality and dreams began to fade. He heard a smooth and surprisingly friendly voice in this twilight of consciousness.

"Rough day at sea, eh, Captain?" The voice seemed to come from nearby. Startled, Captain Rooks's eyes snapped open, and he looked around, trying to locate the source.

His gaze landed on Gus, the polished wooden head that had long been a silent fixture in his cabin. To his amazement and fatigue-fueled disbelief, it seemed as if the statue was speaking to him. Who knows, maybe it was?

"Ah, you can hear me. I thought you might need someone to talk to," Gus continued, his wooden features unchanged but his tone warm and oddly comforting.

Captain Rooks, aware that he was dreaming yet playing along with the whimsy of his tired mind, replied, "Yes, it's been quite a day. Never a dull moment in these waters."

Gus chuckled, a sound that resonated with the ship's creaking. "You're doing a fine job, Captain. These waters would test the mettle of any man. But remember, even the steadiest ship needs its captain to be well-rested. A call to arms can come at any moment!"

The captain, amused and oddly reassured by this imaginary conversation, nodded. "I suppose you're right. But there's little time for rest when danger lurks around every corner."

"True, but even the sharpest eye can't spot danger if it's blurred by weariness," Gus advised, his voice echoing like a wise old sailor recounting tales of the sea.

Captain Rooks couldn't help but smile, the situation's absurdity oddly soothing. "I'll take that advice to heart, Gus. Maybe a few minutes of shut-eye won't hurt."

"That's the spirit, Captain. I'll keep watching for a while," Gus replied, his tone playful.

With a light heart and a chuckle at the surreal nature of his dream, Captain Rooks closed his eyes, allowing himself to drift into a brief but restorative sleep under the watchful, imaginary gaze of Gus, the talking wooden head.

THE SHIP'S CREAKING seemed to grow louder in response to his words. Captain Rooks let out a soft chuckle, a brief respite from the gravity of his thoughts.

"Alright, Gus, keep your secrets," he said, finally breaking the tension with a small smile. "We've been through tough spots before. Just have to navigate this one, too."

Turning away from the statue, Captain Rooks gazed out the small porthole into the dark waters beyond. The deep black of the ocean mirrored his uncertainties, but his conversation with Gus, however fanciful, had provided a much-needed respite.

Rooks slipped off his shoes and placed them methodically at the base of the chair by his desk, next to his tin hat and life jacket.

He arranged them with the precision of a ritual, positioning them for quick access, a precaution years of naval service and the ever-present threat of emergency had ingrained in him.

He then eased himself into his bunk, his movements slow and deliberate. His exhausted body sank into the relative comfort it offered, starkly contrasting with the steel decks where many of his men had resigned themselves to rest near their battle stations. As an aviator with the remnants of their last airplane aboard, Rooks had the privilege of his own quarters, though these days, rest was a luxury seldom afforded.

Turning to the statue of Gus, Rooks found a semblance of solace in the inanimate figure. "Well, Gus, thanks for the pep talk," he said softly, his voice tinged with weariness. "I sometimes wonder—-."

The statue of Gus, bathed in the faint glow from a small lamp, seemed to continue listening intently. In the quiet of the stateroom, Rooks' words filled the air, seeking comfort in the one-sided conversation.

The captain turned over, fluffed his pillow, and said, "Do you ever pray, Gus?" Rooks continued, his voice dropping to a whisper. "I find myself doing it more often these days. Not sure who's listening, but it helps, somehow."

He closed his eyes briefly, collecting his thoughts. "Dear Lord, guide us through these troubled waters. Protect this ship and her brave crew. Give us the strength to face what comes our way."

In the stillness that followed, it was almost as if Gus offered silent support, an unwavering presence in a time of need. Rooks opened his eyes and looked at the statue again. A faint smile played on his lips.

"Thanks again for the chat, my friend. I needed that," he said, a sense of calm washing over him. "We'll get through this. Together."

With that, Captain Rooks turned off the lamp, enveloping the room in darkness. The only sound was the ship's engines' distant thrum and the ocean's gentle lapping against the hull.

The past four days had been a relentless blur, offering little opportunity for sleep. Now, lying in the oppressive tropical heat of his room, Captain Rooks tossed and turned, sleep eluding him despite his fatigue.

The constant hum of the blowers, pushing air into the ship's depths, mingled with the gentle rolling of the Houston as she moved through the quartering sea. The occasional groan of her steel plates added to the symphony of sounds surrounding him. Rather than being comforting, these noises served as reminders of the tumultuous events that had beset the ship in recent weeks.

His mind raced, replaying the frantic pace of their recent engagements, the near misses, and the relentless pressure they were under. Each creak and whisper of the ship seemed to echo the uncertainty of their situation, a testament to the trials they had faced and those that lay ahead. In his small, faintly lit room, surrounded by the mementos of his journey and the ever-present Gus, Captain Rooks lay awake, caught in the grip of the restless night, as the Houston continued her course through perilous waters.

The memory of that harrowing day in the Flores Sea in the Battle of Makassar Strait, twenty-four days ago, refused to leave Captain Rooks as he paced the deck of the USS Houston. Each step seemed to echo with the remnants of the battle, the images as vivid as if they had happened moments ago. Then, the day-long battle yesterday with the Jap Zeros. They continued to pass through his mind and the 15 gunnery crewmen who perished in the last turret explosion.

COMMANDER RICE'S GAZE lingered on the deck of the Houston, scarred and battered from the relentless battle the day before. The deck bore the marks of warfare - pockmarks from shrapnel, burn marks from explosions, and the stark, jarring emptiness where both turrets once stood. "I remember that bomb... the stray one. It was like watching a nightmare unfold in broad daylight," he said, his voice barely more than a whisper, each word laced with the vivid memory of the explosion.

Captain Rooks stood beside him, his hands clenched behind his back, a posture of controlled composure. "The whole turret... gone in an instant," he murmured, his voice steady but tinged with an undercurrent of sorrow. "And then the other one only yesterday." The haunting image of a blinding flash and deafening roar obliterating those turrets, symbols of the ship's might and resilience, etched itself in his memory. "Good men, all of them," he continued, "and the repair party below... we lost far too many."

Rooks turned his head, looking out of a nearby porthole as if the vast expanse of the ocean could wash away the vivid images that haunted him. "I still hear the hammers at night, building the coffins. Ninety-one of our shipmates..." His voice trailed off, choked by emotion. The sound of hammering, a grim rhythm in the stillness of the night, was a reminder of the price they had paid.

The captain placed a hand on Rice's shoulder, a gesture of shared grief and understanding. "We did everything we could, Commander. War takes its toll, and we bear its weight as best we can."

Commander Rice nodded, swallowing hard against the lump in his throat. "Yes, Captain. But it's the sounds that stay with you—the blasts, the screams, the relentless pounding of the guns. It's like a music of destruction that never quite leaves your ears."

Rooks's gaze turned inward, reflecting on the battle around them. "I remember the moment they came into view," he said, his voice taking on a distant quality. "The enemy planes, diving out of the sun, their guns blazing. We were caught off-guard, but the crew responded with everything they had."

The memories of the last two battles played out in his mind - the sudden, chaotic scramble as men rushed to their battle stations, the roar of the guns as they returned fire, and the acrid smell of gunpowder filling the air. "Our guns blazed back, a relentless barrage against their assault. The deck was alive with gunfire, shouts, and orders. Men ran to and fro, some manning the guns, others tending to the wounded."

Rice interjected, his voice a mix of admiration and grief. "The medics were everywhere, patching injuries and dragging the wounded to safety. Amid all the chaos, they were a beacon of hope, a reminder that we were still fighting, still alive."

Rooks nodded in agreement. "And then there was the explosion," he said, the words heavy with the weight of the memory. "That bomb, it came out of nowhere, a streak of death from the sky. The impact was like nothing I'd ever felt. The ship shuddered, metal twisted and tore, and then there was a terrible, ringing silence."

"The aftermath was... indescribable," Lieutenant Miller began, his voice barely more than a whisper, trembling with the vivid recall of the horror. His eyes, distant and haunted, seemed to focus on something far beyond the confines of the room.

He continued his words, painting a vivid and harrowing picture. "Smoke and debris were everywhere, clouding the air, choking us. The acrid smell of burning metal was overpowering, mixing with the sickening scent of charred flesh. It clung to everything, a constant, gruesome reminder of the destruction."

Miller paused, swallowing hard, as if speaking brought the smells and the sounds back to him. "You could hear the men crying out for help, their voices filled with pain and fear. And then there were the others, those in stunned silence, just staring into nothing, unable to comprehend the chaos around them. Their faces... they were ghostly, etched with shock and disbelief."

He shook his head slowly, the memories clearly overwhelming. "It was like a scene from Hell itself. The flames seemed to dance with a life of their own, consuming everything and casting eerie shadows that flickered across the devastated deck. The heat was intense, almost suffocating. And the sounds... the groaning of twisted metal, the crackle of fire, the sporadic bursts of orders being shouted over the din... it all merged into a cacophony of disaster."

Miller's voice trailed off, and he looked down, his fists clenched as if holding onto the moment would somehow make sense of it. "I've seen a lot in this war," he murmured, "but nothing quite like that." His words hung in the air, a stark testimony to the brutal reality of the conflict they were all engulfed in.

Hardened by the scenes he had witnessed, Rooks' eyes held a distant, pained look. "We gathered the fallen and gave them the honors they deserved. But no ceremony can erase the loss, the void left by their passing."

The three men stood in silence, lost in their memories of the battle, the losses, and the unrelenting cruelty of war. The USS Houston, though victorious in their three earlier battles and still afloat, bore the scars of conflict, a testament to the bravery and sacrifice of her crew.

Rooks continued, breaking the silence. "We'll carry on, Lieutenant. For them, for the Houston, for the fight ahead. We owe them that much."

Rice turned to Captain Rooks and added, with a determined glint in his eyes. "Yes, Captain, we carry on. We fight, we endure, and we remember. That's our duty to them and to all who sail with us."

The two stood in silence, the hum of the blowers and the gentle rocking of the ship starkly contrast to the turmoil in their hearts.

The memory of the battle, the loss of their comrades, and the solemn ceremony in Tjilatjap and the day before the Java Sea battles had deeply etched into their souls, reminding them of the brutal reality of war and the sacrifice it demanded.

Captain Rooks stood on the deck as the USS Houston steamed through the minefields protecting Surabaya's port, observing the chaos that unfolded. The city was under siege, air raid sirens filling the air with a haunting wail. In the distance, lookouts reported bombers dotting the sky, an ominous sign of the continued assault.

The rampant conflagration consuming everything in its path transformed the night at the docks into a Hellish tableau, eerily illuminated by the flames. Voracious flames now engulfed large warehouses, which once stood as stoic sentinels of commerce and trade. The unrelenting inferno devoured their massive structures, housing goods from distant lands for decades. The fire licked the night sky with its malevolent tongues, painting it in sinister shades of orange and red, casting an ominous glow over the entire area.

A merchant ship, a casualty of this ruthless assault, lay on its side like a defeated giant. Its once proud hull, designed to navigate the vast oceans, now succumbed to the blaze, surrendering to the fiery onslaught. The ship emitted dense, black smoke that billowed into the sky, forming a thick, dark cloud that obscured the stars. The smoke spiraled upwards, signaling distress and destruction visible from miles away.

The acrid smell of burning wood and melting metal filled the air, stinging the nostrils and making breathing laborious. The crackling of the fire mixed with the occasional groan and creak of the yielding structures, creating a work of destruction that echoed hauntingly through the night.

Amid the chaos, the docks, usually bustling with activity, lay eerily deserted. The only movement came from the occasional flicker of shadows as firefighters battled bravely against the overwhelming flames, their silhouettes ghostly against the backdrop of the fire's fury. Their hoses spewed water in futile attempts to quell the blaze, but the fire seemed insatiable, consuming everything with a ravenous appetite.

The scene was a stark reminder of the enemy's destructive visit – a brutal, unprovoked attack that had transformed a place of industry and life into a nightmarish landscape. The destruction was total, a testament to the merciless nature of war, leaving nothing but ash and ruin in its wake.

As the fire raged on, unchecked and unrepentant, its baleful glow continued to light the night sky, becoming a beacon of devastation that would burn itself into the memory of all who witnessed it.

"We've anchored, Captain," Lieutenant Miller reported, his voice barely audible over the din. "But those docks... it's a grim sight."

Captain Rooks nodded grimly. "The enemy has made his mark here. They are surely all around us. We need to stay vigilant."

For two grueling days, the USS Houston became the focal point of a relentless aerial onslaught. Anchored and unable to maneuver, she felt like a sitting duck in the vast expanse of the ocean, a stationary target for the enemy's merciless air raids.

Chapter THIRTEEN

The Battle of Java Sea

The hastily assembled force of allied ships, a small yet determined fleet, had never operated together before. But on that fateful day, a singular, daunting purpose united them, known to every man on board: to confront and disrupt a formidable enemy task force advancing on Java, even at the cost of their own vessels and lives. In this dire moment, they represented the last hope for the Netherlands East Indies.

Through the night, the allied ships scoured the sea for signs of the enemy convoy, which had seemingly vanished from their last known positions. Tension mounted as day broke, with the crew still at battle stations. The afternoon two days after their previous battle, air reconnaissance reports came in at 1415 hours, revealing the enemy's location south of Bowen Island, heading south. The two forces were a mere fifty miles apart.

A tense conference followed in the wardroom. Commander Rice, the gunnery officer, laid out their mission sternly. "Our objective is clear," he said. "Sink or disperse the enemy's fleet units, then destroy the convoy." His words sent a thrill of excitement mixed with apprehension through Captain Rooks. The imminent Java Sea Battle, a confrontation destined to etch itself in history, approached.

Little did Captain Rooks or Commander Rice know it wasn't just a convoy... it was The Convoy. They would outnumber the ships by at least 50 to 1. Captain Rooks couldn't help but wonder if this was the final chapter for the USS Houston and her brave crew. However, he only kept his thoughts between him and Sam in his quarters.

Haunted by memories, Captain Rooks imagined the bridge scene again: a vast sea brimming with enemy silhouettes. The horizon teemed with the masts of ten destroyers arrayed in two columns led by light cruisers. Behind them, an imposing fleet of four light cruisers loomed, flanked by two heavy aircraft carriers. They were dauntingly outnumbered, facing a formidable armada.

The sharp call over the intercom, "All Hands on Deck!" abruptly shattered this tense reflection. Rooks shot up from his reverie, instantly alert and ready for action. The urgency in the call echoed the gravity of their situation, catapulting him back into the present challenge and back up on the Houston bridge.

THE JAPANESE FLEET was the first to open fire. Flashes of copper-colored flame erupted along their line, momentarily shrouding their ships in black smoke. Captain Rooks felt his heart pounding violently, a cold sweat breaking out as he realized the first salvo was coming. To him, it felt personal, as if someone aimed each shell directly at him.

"Why aren't we firing back?" he muttered under his breath, a sense of urgency gripping him. But as the enemy shells fell short by a thousand yards, he understood - the range was still too great for effective engagement, and his crew knew better to not waste the ammunition.

Finally, at twenty-eight thousand yards, the British cruiser Exeter took the lead, its guns roaring to life. Moments later, the Houston followed suit. The sound was deafening, a fierce cry of defiance that swept across the deck. Captain Rooks felt the shockwave from the gun blasts, strong enough to rip his steel helmet off and send it clattering across the deck.

At that moment, as their guns thundered and the battle unfolded with no possibility of retreat, the crew of the Houston stood ready to face their fate, united in their resolve to fight against overwhelming odds. The Java Sea Battle began! The Houston and her allies braced for a confrontation that would test the limits of their courage and determination.

On the bridge of the Houston, Captain Rooks stood with his eyes intently fixed on the chaotic ballet of war unfolding before him. The sea around them was a maelstrom of danger, with shells slicing through the air and the water churned by the maneuvers of ships and the impact of artillery.

"Steady, men," Captain Rooks called out to his crew, his voice a firm anchor amid the turmoil. "Keep your focus. Every shot counts!"

Standing beside him, his executive officer relayed orders with crisp precision, "Gunnery stations, maintain fire! Target their main batteries!"

Below on the deck, the gun crews worked feverishly. The booming of the Houston's guns was a constant thunder, each salvo a testament to the crew's determination and skill. The air was thick with the smell of gunpowder and the metallic tang of spent shells.

"Reload! Keep the pressure on them!" shouted a gunnery officer as the crew efficiently operated the massive guns, sweat, and grime streaking their faces.

The Houston maneuvered nimbly, despite its size, dodging incoming fire while maintaining its own offensive. Captain Rooks, a veteran of naval strategy, anticipated the enemy's movements, issuing commands to adjust their course and angle of attack.

"Hard to starboard! Bring us around for another pass!" he ordered, his eyes never leaving the view of the battle through his binoculars.

The crew responded to his commands with practiced efficiency, the ship responding like a living, breathing entity under their collective control. The tension on the bridge was palpable, a mix of focus, fear, and an unspoken understanding of the battle's significance.

As the ships drew closer, the risk of damage and casualties increased exponentially. The Houston, alongside its counterparts, engaged in a deadly dance where any misstep could lead to disaster.

"This is it, men! Hold the line!" Captain Rooks shouted, his voice cutting through the noise of battle, inspiring his men to fight with every ounce of their strength.

The intensity of the battle in the Java Sea had reached a crescendo, with salvos of enemy shells cutting through the air, each a harbinger of destruction. The shells splashed into the sea ever closer to the USS Houston, creating towering fountains of water that crashed back down with a thunderous roar. Each eruption sent a spray of salty water over the deck, leaving a lingering chill in the air that mingled with the fear and adrenaline coursing through the veins of the crew.

"Port side, watch out!" bellowed a lookout from his high vantage point, his voice strained with urgency. His warning came just in time as a shell landed perilously close to the ship's port side, sending a massive geyser of water skyward. The crew on deck flinched instinctively, feeling the shockwave and the spray of cold seawater.

Almost immediately, another cry rang out, "Starboard, incoming!" This time, the shell landed with a deafening crash near the starboard side, so close that the ship seemed to shudder under the force of the near miss. The crew tensed, their hearts pounding in their chests, as they braced for what felt like the inevitable impact.

Standing firmly on the bridge, Captain Rooks kept his eyes fixed on the looming threat, his jaw set in determination. "They've got our range!" he yelled to his officers. "Adjust heading! Full speed ahead, and zigzag pattern! Throw off their aim! Hurry!"

The helmsman responded instantly, his hands moving swiftly over the controls. "Changing course, full speed!" he confirmed, his voice steady despite the chaos around him.

Below deck, the engine room was a frenzy of activity. "Captain wants more speed! Let's give it all she's got!" shouted the chief engineer, his team working furiously to squeeze every ounce of power from the engines.

The men operated the artillery on the gun decks with renewed urgency. "Keep firing! Don't let up!" commanded the gunnery officer, his face smeared with sweat and soot. The gun crews responded with a volley of their own, the thunderous booms of their guns a defiant answer to the enemy's assault.

Despite the danger, the Houston maneuvered with impressive agility, its crew working as one to evade the deadly accuracy of the Japanese artillery. Each near miss was a reminder of the razor-thin margin between survival and catastrophe in this relentless exchange of fire.

In these moments, the USS Houston was not just a ship but a living entity, pulsing with its crew's collective will and determination. They united in a singular purpose: to endure the fierce onslaught and retaliate with every available resource. Their collective resolve was unshakable, each member ready to do whatever it took to hold their ground and fight back.

The next salvo enveloped the Houston in a deadly embrace with a terrifying scream of shells, but miraculously, not a single hit registered.

"It's a straddle, but we're still afloat!" yelled Lieutenant Miller, relief evident in his voice.

The crew's confidence surged as four more salvos straddled the Houston without causing damage.

Following close behind the Houston, the HMAS Perth also miraculously avoided damage despite enemy fire straddling it eight times. This remarkable evasion highlighted the ship's agility and the crew's adept maneuvering under intense pressure. "Our luck's holding," murmured a sailor, his knuckles white as he gripped his station.

Amid the chaos, the Houston's guns found their mark. "Direct hit on the last Jap heavy!" Commander Rice reported from his station, his voice crackling over the phone to Captain Rooks. Cheers erupted from the crew as they witnessed black smoke and debris erupt from the enemy cruiser.

Meanwhile, three enemy cruisers focused their fire on the Exeter. Captain Rooks, observing the situation, ordered, "Shift targets! Give Exeter some cover!" Soon after, Exeter's shells struck an enemy light cruiser, forcing it out of line, ablaze and smoking.

Despite the USS Houston's remarkable resilience and the skill of its crew, the ship wasn't impervious to the relentless barrage from the enemy. Amid the chaos of battle, the Houston sustained significant damage, a testament to the ferocity of the engagement.

With a shrieking whistle that cut through the din of battle, one enemy shell tore a jagged path through the ship's bow. The force of the shell's passage flung the crew members nearest to the impact off their feet, sending a shudder through the entire ship structure. Metal groaned and screeched as the shell carved its way through the steel, leaving a trail of twisted and torn bulkheads in its wake. It narrowly missed vital parts of the ship, such as the ammunition magazine and critical machinery, by mere inches.

The breach in the hull was a grim reminder of their vulnerability, the ocean's waters visible through the gaping hole.

Almost simultaneously, another shell screamed towards the aft of the ship. It struck with a thunderous impact, the sound resonating through the decks. This shell grazed the ship's exterior, tearing through layers of metal before impacting a small oil tank. The collision resulted in a minor but ominous rupture, from which oil began to seep, creating a slick, dark stain on the water. Smoke billowed from the point of impact, adding to the already thick haze that enveloped the ship.

Miraculously, both shells failed to explode upon impact, a stroke of luck that didn't go unnoticed in the middle of the onslaught. Upon realizing this, the crew felt a fleeting sense of relief during the terror of the event. "Those shells didn't blow!" shouted a sailor, his voice a mix of disbelief and gratitude. "We're still in this!"

Upon hearing the report of the damage, Captain Rooks clenched his jaw. "Damage control teams to the bow and aft, immediately!" he ordered, his voice cutting through the noise. "Seal off any breaches and contain that oil spill before it ignites!"

The crew sprang into action, rushing to address the damage. The sound of hasty repairs filled the air, the clang of metal on metal as sailors worked to patch the wounded ship. The smell of the sea mingled with the acrid scent of burning oil and hot metal, creating a potent reminder of the dangers they faced.

Despite these harrowing moments, the spirit of the Houston's crew remained unbroken. They moved with a sense of purpose and urgency.

The tide of battle in the Java Sea, already a maelstrom of chaos and destruction, took a dramatic turn when the HMS Exeter, a key vessel in the Allied fleet, suffered a devastating hit. The ship, renowned for its previous engagements, including the Battle of the River Plate, was a critical component of the Allied naval force in the region.

The shell that struck the Exeter did so with a ferocious intensity. It slammed into the ship with a deafening roar, the impact sending shockwaves through the vessel. Flames erupted from the point of impact, belching thick, black smoke into the sky.

The sudden devastation sent the ship's crew reeling, scrambling to maintain balance and function.

On the bridge of the Exeter, alarms blared, and the smell of burning metal and electrical fires filled the air. The ship's captain, his face set in a grimace of resolve, shouted orders to his crew, "Damage control teams, to your stations! We need to keep her afloat!"

Captain Rooks watched with a sinking heart back on the USS Houston as the Exeter took the hit and began to slow, its movements labored and unsteady. Realizing the dire situation, he sprang into action.

"Make smoke, cover Exeter's withdrawal!" he commanded, his voice urgent and clear over the ship's intercom. "She's vulnerable. We need to give her cover! Now!"

The fleet responded immediately to Captain Rooks' command. The Houston and other ships began to emit thick clouds of smoke, creating a protective screen around the wounded Exeter. The sea around the Exeter transformed into a foggy veil, obscuring her from further enemy fire.

"Keep that smoke dense; we need to shield her from their sights!" yelled a Houston officer overseeing the operation.

Amid the chaos of damage control and firefighting efforts on the Exeter, the sight of smoke enveloping their ship buoyed the captain and his crew, providing a much-needed reprieve. "Steady on, lads! Houston's giving us a chance," he called out, rallying his crew.

The sight of the Exeter, wounded but defiant, surrounded by the protective embrace of the smoke screen, was a poignant moment in the battle. It was a testament to the solidarity and quick thinking of the Allied forces in the face of adversity.

As the smoke swirled around the Exeter, obscuring her from view, the crew of the Houston watched with bated breath, hoping their efforts would buy their ally enough time to withdraw to safety.

The Japanese, sensing an opportunity, intensified their attack. "Torpedoes in the water!" the lookout screamed. Captain Rooks expertly maneuvered the Houston, presenting as small a target as possible in the torpedo-infested waters.

In a tragic twist of fate, a torpedo struck the Netherlands East Indies destroyer Koertner, caught in the crossfire. A massive explosion sent a fountain of water sky-high, obscuring the ship from view. Only fragments of the Koertner remained when the water settled, with a few desperate survivors clinging to her overturned hull. "Godspeed," whispered Captain Rooks, knowing they could offer no aid without jeopardizing their own ship.

The Java Sea Battle raged on, a relentless dance of destruction and survival, with the fate of each ship hanging by a thread in the volatile waters of the Pacific.

As the sun descended towards the horizon, clouds of black smoke shrouded the sea around the USS Houston and her allied fleet, creating a smokescreen that obscured their vision and made spotting the enemy daunting.

Captain Rooks, peering through his binoculars, strained his eyes to discern the shapes of enemy ships in the murky haze.

"Captain, Japanese cruisers closing in on us," reported Commander Rice urgently from his station.

"Order our destroyers to launch a torpedo attack. We need to divert them, buy some time to regroup," Captain Rooks commanded, his voice steady despite the mounting tension.

The destroyers swiftly responded, darting forward to unleash their torpedoes. Although they reported no hits, the maneuver achieved the desired effect. "They're turning away!" exclaimed a sailor, relief evident in his tone.

With that, they broke off the engagement, ending the daylight battle without a decisive victory. Yet, the threat of the Japanese convoy loomed in the minds of the Allied commanders. "We'll try to catch them under cover of night," Captain Rooks mused, his gaze fixed on the darkening sea.

A somber assessment of their losses followed. "Koertner and H.M.S. Electra are gone," reported Commander Rice, his face etched with sorrow. "Exeter's had to pull back to Soerabaja, and the American destroyers are out of torpedoes and fuel."

The Houston, along with the Perth, De Ruyter, and Java, bore the scars of continuous gunfire. Of their destroyers, only H.M.S. Jupiter and H.M.S. Encounter remained. "We've fired 303 rounds per turret. Only fifty rounds per gun left," Captain Rooks announced, concern evident in his voice.

"The loss of turret three's hit us hard," added Commander Rice, "but we're still in the fight."

The Chief Engineer, emerging from below decks, added grimly, "My men are near breaking, Captain. Heat exhaustion's taken a toll in the fire rooms."

As the Houston and its crew navigated the treacherous waters of the Java Sea, the infamous voice of Tokyo Rose crackled over the radio, her words dripping with propaganda and mock sympathy. The crew, weary yet vigilant, gathered around the radio to listen with curiosity and defiance in their eyes.

"Hello again, boys of the Allied fleet," Tokyo Rose began, her tone falsely sweet. "I have some news that might interest you. The mighty 'Galloping Ghost of the Java Coast' has been sunk... again! It seems the Japanese Navy can't help but sink her repeatedly. How many lives does one ghost have, I wonder?"

In the mess hall of the Houston, the crew reacted to her words with a mixture of laughter and eye-rolling. One of the sailors, a young man with a mischievous grin, called out, "Hey, did anyone feel us sinking? I must have missed it while having my coffee!"

Another sailor chimed in, his voice laced with humor, "I think we're up to our ninth life now, aren't we? This ghost sure is resilient!"

The crew's laughter was a defiant response to Tokyo Rose's attempt to demoralize them. They were well aware of the psychological warfare at play and chose to meet it with humor and camaraderie.

Overhearing the banter, Captain Rooks couldn't help but crack a small smile. He admired the spirit of his men and their ability to find humor in the face of adversity. It was this unbreakable morale that kept them steadfast in their mission.

As night enveloped the sea, the USS Houston slipped away into the obscurity of the dark waters, creating distance from the lurking enemy. The ship's movement was stealthy, more a strategic repositioning than a capitulation. On the bridge, Captain Rooks, a man of steely resolve, convened his senior officers under the dim glow of the instruments. His eyes, reflecting a mix of determination and calculated risk, scanned the faces of his crew.

"We'll circle back around," he announced in a low, confident voice. "The darkness is our ally tonight. We'll use it to veil our approach and strike them when they least expect it."

Standing a step behind the Captain, Commander Rice furrowed his brow, concern etched on his face. "Sir, it's a risky move. They have superior firepower. If we're spotted, we'll be sitting ducks."

The Captain turned, locking eyes with Rice. His voice, though quiet, carried an unyielding edge. "Rice, I'm aware of the risks. But this is our only shot at turning the tables. They have outgunned and outmaneuvered us, but they won't anticipate this. It's our chance to hit them hard and fast."

Rice hesitated, the weight of the decision clear in his expression. "And if we fail, sir?"

Captain Rooks' gaze didn't waver. "Then we go down fighting on our terms. But I have faith in this crew and in our ship. We'll make it through."

The tension on the bridge was palpable as the officers exchanged glances, the gravity of the situation sinking in. Yet, there was a flicker of resolve in their eyes, a shared understanding of the stakes at hand.

The ship adjusted its course, its engines humming quietly as they slipped through the dark waters. The crew, aware of the plan, prepared for the impending engagement, their actions quiet but efficient.

A sense of anticipation hung in the air as the Houston turned back towards the enemy. The sailors, their laughter now replaced with focus, manned their stations. The ship, a silent predator in the night, readied itself to re-enter the fray.

The tension was intense, but underneath it lay a current of determination and a touch of the irrepressible humor that had carried them this far. "Let's show Tokyo Rose just how hard it is to keep a good ghost down," whispered one sailor to another, a grin spreading across his face.

In the darkness of the Java Sea, the USS Houston, the 'Galloping Ghost,' readied itself to defy the odds once more, its crew united in their resolve to fight on, buoyed by their unbreakable spirit and the bond that held them together.

The night brought new challenges. Suddenly, H.M.S. Jupiter, covering their port flank, exploded in a mystifying burst of flames, vanishing into the sea. "What in blazes happened?" Captain Rooks exclaimed, shock and confusion evident in his voice.

"We don't know, sir," replied Lieutenant Miller, his eyes wide with disbelief. "No enemy in sight, yet Jupiter's gone."

Undeterred but cautious, the fleet raced into the night, their minds filled with questions about Jupiter's fate and a relentless determination to locate the enemy transports. The night was fraught with uncertainty and danger, every shadow on the water a potential threat, every moment bringing them closer to an unseen enemy.

Chapter FOURTEEN

A Graveyard of Ships in the Java Sea

The USS Houston glided through the Pacific's inky depths, its presence marked only by a faint, rhythmic hum from the engines that resonated through the steel hull. This low thrum was a stark contrast to the tense silence that hung over the crew, each member acutely aware of the gravity of their nocturnal mission. An hour into their operation, the sea around them lay eerily still, its surface a glassy mirror reflecting the sparse, dim stars overhead.

Captain Rooks stood resolutely on the bridge, his posture rigid against the backdrop of the night. The cool sea breeze carried a faint saline tang, mingling with the subtle scent of machine oil that wafted from the ship's interior. His eyes, sharp and unblinking, scanned the horizon where the black sea merged with the starless sky.

To him, the ocean's calmness was deceptive, a serene façade hiding the perils that could lurk beneath its surface. The gentle lap of waves against the ship's hull was a soft, almost hypnotic sound, but to the Captain, it was a reminder of the lurking threats in the vast, dark waters.

Nearby, Commander Rice hunched over the radar, its green glow casting an eerie light on his focused expression. The faint, repetitive beeps of the radar punctuated the silence, each pulse a heartbeat in the quiet of the bridge. He scrutinized every blip and minor fluctuation on the screen, his senses heightened to detect any sign of danger. The radar's screen was a mosaic of greens and blacks, a digital representation of the ocean around them, where any unexpected spot of light could signify an enemy lying in wait.

The atmosphere on the bridge was thick with anticipation. The only sounds were the ship's structure's subtle creaks, the engines' distant hum, and the occasional murmur of hushed voices from the crew. They attuned every sense to the environment, with every sight and sound potentially signaling the dangers that the dark waters might conceal. Each absorbed in their vigil, Captain Rooks and Commander Rice stood as sentinels in the night, guardians of their vessel in the treacherous, unseen battlefield.

SUDDENLY, A FLARE BURSTING above them violently ruptured the tranquility, its brilliant light cascading down like a celestial waterfall. In an instant, an unnatural daylight bathed the Houston, throwing every line and contour of the ship into stark relief. The crew, momentarily blinded, squinted against the glaring light, their shadows long and distorted on the deck.

"We're sitting ducks," muttered Lieutenant Miller from his post, his voice barely above a whisper yet heavy with dread. His words echoed the unspoken fears of the anxious crew, each man acutely aware of their sudden exposure.

Captain Rooks clenched his jaw on the bridge, his eyes narrowing at the illuminated skies. "They're toying with us," he said, his voice laced with frustration. "Staying just out of range, like a predator circling its prey."

Commander Rice, standing beside him, nodded in grim agreement. "They're probing our defenses, Captain. Testing our reactions," he added, his hand moving unconsciously to adjust the dials on the radar console.

Each subsequent flare, following the first, ratcheted the tension higher. The crew waited, tense and silent, the only sounds being the steady rush of water against the hull and the distant roaring of the ship's blowers. The looming presence of death hung over them, a specter too ominous to acknowledge aloud.

When the fourth flare finally extinguished, snuffing out its ghostly luminescence, the crew breathed a sigh of relief. The return to darkness was a reprieve, albeit a brief and unsettling one. The shadowy night, once a cloak of concealment, now felt like a blanket of uncertainty.

Yet, the relief was ephemeral, quickly overshadowed by the realization that the enemy was out there, biding their time, playing a cat-and-mouse game with lethal stakes. Captain Rooks turned to Commander Rice, his voice low but resolute. "Prepare the crew, Commander. They'll strike when they think we've let our guard down."

Commander Rice nodded, his expression one of steely determination. "Aye, Captain. We'll be ready for them."

The moon's emergence brought some visibility, aiding their search for the enemy convoy. Ensign Stivers relieved Captain Rooks as the officer of the deck. Rooks sprawled on the forward anti-aircraft director platform, seeking a moment's rest. His respite was brief, interrupted by whistles and shouting. Rushing to the side, he saw groups of men in the water, yelling in an unfamiliar tongue.

"H.M.S. Encounter is staying behind for rescue," he announced, watching the figures in the water.

The USS Houston, flanked by her allies De Ruyter, Perth, and Java, pushed forward through the treacherous darkness of the night, navigating the unpredictable waters of the Java Sea.

Suddenly, an eerie phenomenon disrupted the thick, tense night — mysterious flares sparked to life in the water all around them.

Standing on the bridge, Captain Rooks squinted at the ghostly lights bobbing on the waves. "What are these?" he pondered aloud, his voice tinged with uncertainty. "Mines? Enemy markers?" The flickering lights cast an otherworldly glow, their intent and origin a puzzle wrapped in the shroud of night.

Peering through his binoculars, Commander Rice added, "They could be signaling our position, Captain. A trap, perhaps?" The notion hung in the air, heavy with implication.

The presence of the flares was unsettling, their purpose as yet unknown, adding another layer of complexity to the already fraught situation. The Allied fleet, unnerved but determined, maneuvered cautiously, steering clear of the mysterious lights. Yet, as they altered course, they encountered more flares, as if leading them into an unknown maze.

Suddenly, a sharp call from a lookout broke the tense silence. "Contact! Two large unidentified ships on the starboard side!" The voice crackled over the radio, urgent and alert.

Captain Rooks rushed to the side, his eyes searching the darkness. "Bring us about. Ready the guns," he commanded his voice a steady command in the chaos.

As the Houston and her companions turned to face the new threat, the silhouettes of the enemy ships loomed out of the darkness... out of nowhere! "Enemy vessels," Captain Rooks confirmed, a hint of resolve in his voice. "Engage at will!"

The Houston's guns roared to life, the sound thunderous in the quiet of the night. The flashes from the gun barrels momentarily illuminated the deck, casting stark shadows that danced with each volley. The smell of gunpowder filled the air, a sharp reminder of the battle at hand.

"Steady your aim, men!" shouted Lieutenant Miller from the gun deck, his voice rising over the cacophony of gunfire and crashing waves. "Make every shot count!"

The enemy, shadows against the night, returned fire, their presence betrayed by the muzzle flashes and the whistling of shells cutting through the air. The Houston shuddered as it braced against the assault, her crew undeterred, firing with disciplined precision.

But as swiftly as the engagement had begun, the enemy ships seemed to vanish into the night, their silhouettes melting away into the darkness, as elusive as phantoms. The firing ceased, leaving only the ringing echo of the guns in the ears of the crew.

Captain Rooks, peering into the darkness, his brow furrowed in thought, said to Commander Rice, "They're testing our strength and resolve. This won't be the last we see of them tonight."

Commander Rice nodded, his eyes still scanning the horizon. "We'll be ready, Captain. They'll find the Houston isn't easily outmaneuvered."

The fleet regrouped and continued its vigilant journey through the night.

The tension aboard the USS Houston was palpable, a tangible force that gripped every crew member as they peered into the oppressive darkness. The Allied fleet, with the Dutch cruiser De Ruyter at the helm, followed by the Houston, Java, and Perth, sailed in a new formation through the Java Sea, a strategic move aimed at countering the elusive enemy.

The radio crackled to life, a line of communication between the ships' captains. "De Ruyter to Houston, visibility is poor. Keep your eyes peeled," came the cautious voice of Captain Doorman of the De Ruyter.

"Roger, De Ruyter. Houston here. We're on high alert," replied Captain Rooks, his voice tense but calm.

Suddenly, the night's silence exploded into chaos with a massive blast. The Java took a direct hit, flames engulfing her in a monstrous fireball that turned the sea into a fiery canvas. She listed heavily, drifting out of formation like a burning ghost, her fate sealed within seconds.

"Java's hit!" shouted Lieutenant Morris, his voice cutting through the din. "She's going down fast!"

Captain Rooks, gripping the bridge's railing, peered into the inferno. "All hands, brace for impact! We might be next," he barked, his eyes fixed on the flaming wreck of the Java.

The ship's crew sprang into action, each man acutely aware of the imminent danger as the flames from the Java cast a haunting glow over their faces. The sound of the explosion still echoed in their ears, a grim reminder of the peril lurking in the darkness of the sea.

"Torpedo wakes spotted!" the radio crackled to life with a frantic shout. The voice, strained and urgent, pierced through the tense atmosphere of the bridge.

"Hard to starboard, now!" Captain Rooks commanded his voice a sharp contrast to the panic on the radio. His hands clenched the map table, eyes locked on the dark waters ahead.

"Java's been hit! She's going down!" another voice blared over the radio, the sounds of panic and chaos bleeding through the transmission.

Commander Rice, standing beside the Captain, grabbed the radio handset. "Report, Java! Status update!" he demanded, his tone a mix of authority and concern.

There was a brief, crackling silence before a reply came. "Java's aflame, losing power and...," the voice trailed off, overwhelmed by the sound of shouting and metal groaning under stress.

Captain Rooks turned to his crew, his expression grim yet resolute. "Prepare for evasive maneuvers! We need to avoid those torpedoes at all costs," he ordered, his voice cutting through the tension like a knife.

The crew members sprang into action, their movements swift and precise despite the fear that gripped them. The sound of the engines revved up, the ship heeling sharply as it changed course, trying desperately to outmaneuver the unseen enemy in the dark, treacherous waters. The air was thick with the tension of impending danger, every second stretching out as they awaited the fate that had just befallen the Java.

Then, in a cruel twist of fate, De Ruyter suffered a similar catastrophic hit. A violent explosion sent flames soaring above her bridge, engulfing the ship in an inferno. The once-proud cruiser began to succumb to the fire, a stark reminder of the enemy's lethal prowess.

Captain Rooks and his crew watched in horror on the Houston's bridge as their allies suffered decimation. "My God, they've hit De Ruyter," Captain Rooks uttered in disbelief. "All hands, prepare for evasive maneuvers!"

Commander Rice, standing beside him, echoed the urgency. "We must avoid their torpedoes at all costs!"

The night transformed into a nightmarish scene, the sea around them turning into a graveyard of ships. The shadows held unseen dangers, and every moment of silence was fraught with the anticipation of the next attack. The mission's end loomed ominously, the outcome hanging in the balance in the perilous waters of the Java Sea.

In a display of exceptional seamanship and quick thinking, Captain Rooks took command of the situation. "Hard to starboard!" he commanded, his voice cutting through the chaos. "Full speed ahead!"

The Houston's crew worked feverishly, their faces etched with determination and fear. The ship responded with agility, her engines roaring as she maneuvered through the deadly waters. Torpedoes, the harbingers of destruction, slipped by the Houston, missing her by mere feet on either side.

"Heads up, another torpedo on the port side!" yelled Lieutenant Miller, his eyes fixed on the dark water.

The crew held their breath, hearts pounding in their chests, as Captain Rooks guided the ship through the treacherous ballet of death. "Stay sharp, men! We're not out of this yet!" he barked, steering the Houston with a deft hand navigating through the minefield of torpedoes and debris.

As dawn approached, the Houston, battered but unbroken, continued to navigate the perilous waters, a testament to her crew's bravery and resilience and their captain's indomitable spirit.

As the USS Houston steered through the Java Sea's perilous waters, the onboard speakers' crackling momentarily diverted the crew's focus. Tokyo Rose's voice, infamous among the Allied forces, filled the air once more, her words laced with deceit and mockery.

"Good evening, boys of the Houston," Tokyo Rose began in her characteristically smooth, taunting tone. "I hope you're enjoying your little cruise in the Java Sea. Just so you know, we're keeping a very close eye on you."

A group of sailors gathered around the speakers rolled their eyes and exchanged knowing glances. They grew accustomed to her broadcasts, intended to demoralize but often achieving the opposite effect.

One sailor, a young man with a quick wit, retorted loudly enough for his mates to hear, "Oh, she's watching us, is she? Maybe she'll see how we danced around her torpedoes!"

Another chimed in, grinning despite the situation, "Yeah, tell her we're having a blast, would ya? Haven't had this much fun since basic training!"

The crew laughed humorously, a brief respite from the tension gripping them. Tokyo Rose continued, unaware of the mockery she was receiving at the hands of the Houston's sailors.

"And be careful out there, boys. It would be such a shame if something happened to your precious ship. Remember, the ocean is a big place, and accidents happen," she cooed, feigning concern.

This time, the ship's cook replied loud enough for those nearby to hear, "Accidents, huh? The only accident here is her thinking we'd fall for that baloney!"

Their laughter echoed through the ship, a sound of defiance in the face of Tokyo Rose's psychological warfare. Moments like these bolstered the crew's morale, a reminder that unity and humor could be just as powerful as any weapon in their arsenal.

Despite the levity, the men remained vigilant, their eyes scanning the horizon, their hands ready at their stations. Tokyo Rose's voice faded into the background as the Houston continued its perilous journey.

"Hard to port!" Rooks barked, his eyes fixed on the ominous wakes in the water. "Now, hard to starboard!"

The crew responded with precision, the Houston narrowly evading the lethal threats. They raced away from the carnage, leaving behind the stricken ships and the unseen enemy.

"It's horrible to leave them," muttered Commander Rice, his voice heavy with regret as they watched their allies succumb to the flames.

"We have no choice," Captain Rooks replied solemnly, his gaze lingering on the burning ships. "We must carry on."

With Admiral Karel Doorman lost with his flagship, command fell to Captain Rooks. The Houston set a new course for Batavia.

The night was an unending nightmare, filled with close calls and harrowing escapes.

"I never thought we'd see the sun again," Captain Rooks confessed, his voice reflecting the exhaustion and relief of his crew.

The Houston bore the scars of the battle. The concussions from the eight-inch guns had wreaked havoc within the ship. Captain

Rooks surveyed the damage, his heart sinking at the sight. Desks were upended, and their contents strewn across the deck. Lockers were open, their contents in disarray.

"Pictures, radios, books... everything's been tossed around like toys," said Commander Rice, picking his way through the debris. "She's a wreck, but she's still afloat."

The ship's interior was a testament to the ferocity of their battle. Yet, despite the chaos and destruction, the crew's spirit remained unbroken. They had survived the infernal night, which would stay in their memories forever.

As the Houston steamed towards Batavia, the crew set about restoring order amid the chaos, each one silently grateful for the dawn many feared they would never see. The journey ahead was uncertain, but the Houston and her crew were ready to face whatever challenges lay in wait.

The Admiral's cabin aboard the USS Houston, once a symbol of prestige and honor during President Roosevelt's stay, was now a scene of utter devastation. Clocks lay shattered on the deck, the once elegant furniture overturned, and mirrors cracked. Torn charts fluttered from the bulkheads, and chunks of soundproofing material scattered among the debris.

Captain Rooks surveyed the damage, his heart heavy. "This place is unrecognizable," he remarked solemnly to Lieutenant Miller, who stood beside him, equally dismayed.

"It's a mess, sir," Miller replied, picking up a broken clock. "Looks like a battlefield itself."

The ship had endured significant damage.

Prior bombings had damaged the plates, which were now alarmingly bent and leaking. The shattered glass of the bridge windows was a testament to the violence they had faced.

Punctured fire hoses, meant to be their lifeline in emergencies, added to the chaos with minor floods along the passageways. Yet, amid the destruction, Captain Rooks sensed an unyielding spirit. "She's wounded, nearly out of ammo, but the Houston's still got fight in her," he declared with a fierce determination.

The intercom on the USS Houston, still miraculously operational despite the relentless assault they had endured, crackled to life once again with the taunting voice of Tokyo Rose. Her words, dripping with sarcasm and feigned concern, echoed through Captain Rooks' quarters.

"My oh my, my navy boys," she cooed mockingly. "Not giving up the ship yet? Or, do you not hear me because you are at the bottom of the sea?" Her smirking laugh grated on the nerves, a calculated attempt to demoralize and provoke.

Captain Rooks and Commander Rice, who were in the quarters discussing their strategy, turned their heads toward the speaker. They exchanged a look, a mix of annoyance and amusement at the brazenness of the broadcast.

With a wry smile, Rooks responded to the unseen propagandist, "Well, Commander, it seems we're ghosts now, haunting the Java Sea. Tokyo Rose seems to think we're at the bottom of it."

Commander Rice, unable to resist joining in, added with a chuckle, "Seems like our ghost ship is still giving them a good chase. Maybe we should ask Tokyo Rose for our exact location since she seems to know more about our whereabouts than we do."

Their shared moment of levity in the face of Tokyo Rose's taunts was a small but significant act of defiance. It demonstrated the unbreakable spirit of the Houston's crew and their unwavering resolve to not let enemy propaganda shake their morale.

Turning away from the speaker, Rooks and Rice refocused on the more pressing matters.

These thoughts and countless others swirled in Captain Rooks' mind until he eventually succumbed to a fitful sleep, only for the "General Alarm" at 2400 hours to rudely awaken him. The clanging gong, a harbinger of danger, jolted him awake. Instinctively, he found himself in his shoes before he was fully conscious.

"Clang! Clang! Clang! Clang!" The sound reverberated through the ship. Captain Rooks hurried through the dimly lit wardroom, wondering what new peril they faced. "What are we up against now?" he muttered, feeling a sense of foreboding.

As he exited his room, a salvo from the main battery thundered overhead, throwing him against the bulkhead. "They're not firing for nothing," he thought, rushing through the passageways.

Passing a group of stretcher-bearers and corpsmen, he paused briefly. "Do you know what's happening?" he asked urgently. They shook their heads, just as in the dark as he was.

Ascending the ladder to the bridge, the firing intensified. The five-inch guns joined in, creating a deafening symphony of warfare. "This is going to be one Hell of a fight," Captain Rooks realized, his pace quickening.

On the Communication Deck, the gun crews worked swiftly and efficiently in the darkness, their one-point-ones joining the fray. Tracers streaked into the night, painting a deadly yet mesmerizing pattern against the dark sky.

Captain Rooks reached the bridge, his heart racing with adrenaline. The Houston was again embroiled in a fierce battle, her guns blazing in defiance. Every crew member, including the Marines, was a part of this desperate struggle for survival, their actions a dance of precision and urgency in the face of overwhelming odds. The night sky was alive with the sounds and lights of battle, a testament to the resilience and bravery of the USS Houston and her crew.

As Captain Rooks hurried towards the bridge of the USS Houston, the ship transformed, its very steel seeming to resonate with the tension of battle. Each corridor and deck echoed with the urgency of war, the air charged with anticipation and adrenaline.

The ship's guns were already thundering, their sounds melding into a formidable symphony of defiance. The main battery unleashed deep, blinding crashes that reverberated through the hull, each salvo a testament to the ship's power and resolve. The sharp, staccato cracks of the five-inch guns punctuated the air, a relentless rhythm in the chaotic ballet of battle.

Amid the cacophony, the rhythmic pom-pom-pom of the one-point-ones added a rapid, persistent beat. Their gunfire was a constant stream, tracing lines of deadly intent across the sea's surface.

Above it all, the continuous volleys from the fifty-caliber machine guns dominated the soundscape.

Initially intended for anti-aircraft defense, the crew now turned these formidable weapons against enemy surface targets, with their barrels glowing red-hot as they spat out a relentless stream of bullets.

On the bridge, the atmosphere was electric. Officers and crew members shouted orders and updates, their voices cutting through the din.

"Main battery, adjust fire two degrees starboard!" Captain Rooks commanded, his eyes fixed on the enemy through the haze of battle.

"Five-inch crews, focus on their lead ship! Let's break their formation!" barked Commander Rice, coordinating the gunnery teams with practiced precision.

The gun crews responded with disciplined efficiency, their actions honed by endless drills now put to the ultimate test. The Houston, shuddering under the recoil of her guns, felt alive with the spirit of battle.

Through the dense smoke and chaos of battle, the enemy ships relentlessly returned fire. Their shells tore through the air ferociously, leaving blazing fire and smoke trails in their wake. Explosions erupted around the USS Houston, violently rocking the vessel and sending towering plumes of water skyward, drenching the deck.

But the Houston remained steadfast. "Keep firing, men! We've got them on their heels!" Lieutenant Miller shouted from his station. His voice, loud and clear, served as a rallying cry amid the tumultuous storm of battle, infusing the crew with renewed determination.

Captain Rooks stepped onto the bridge, immediately engulfed in the blinding glare of enemy searchlights. Through the dazzling light, he could barely discern the menacing silhouettes of Japanese destroyers closing in, their bright beams strategically illuminating the Houston for their heavy units hidden in the dark abyss.

"The destroyers are lighting us up for their cruisers!" As he yelled, Lieutenant Miller strained to be heard over the thunderous din of war.

"Target those searchlights!" Captain Rooks commanded, his authoritative voice cutting through the chaos. The Houston's guns swung around, aiming at the glaring lights, obliterating them one by one as they appeared.

The bridge, typically a sanctuary of strategic command and calm decision-making, had transformed into a maelstrom of intense activity and barely contained chaos. Focused energy buzzed through the space as officers and crew members were deeply engrossed in their vital roles. The air was thick with tension, the sound of rapid-fire orders and urgent status reports melding with the distant, continuous thunder of gunfire and explosions.

"Status report!" Captain Rooks demanded, scanning the room.

"Port side guns still operational, sir! Starboard side taking heavy fire!" reported a crew member, his voice laced with urgency.

"Maneuver us out of their line of fire, and keep our guns hot!" the Captain retorted, his eyes scanning the hostile waters.

Lieutenant Miller, who was still standing nearby, replied, "Aye, Captain! Helm, hard to starboard! Prepare for evasive maneuvers!"

The ship's helmsman swiftly responded, "Hard to starboard, aye, sir!"

Captain Rooks then turned to Ensign Johnson, who was overseeing the gunnery crew, and barked, "Johnson, I want those turrets firing on anything that moves out there. Give 'em hell!"

Ensign Johnson nodded firmly. "You heard the Captain! Load and fire, boys! Let's show 'em what the Houston can do!"

The crew responded with a flurry of activity, each member acutely aware of the precariousness of their situation. The sound of shells whistling through the air, the crackle of radio communications, and the shouted commands created a symphony of warfare, a testament to the crew's unyielding spirit.

Captain Rooks stood at the center of this maelstrom, his eyes darting between the instruments, maps, and the sea visible through the smoke-stained windows. The weight of command rested heavily on his shoulders, the responsibility for his ship and crew a constant, unyielding pressure. Around him, the crew moved with frenzied efficiency, their faces set in grim determination.

Despite the urgency of the situation, Captain Rooks hesitated to interrupt the focused rhythm of his officers. Each man was a cog in the finely-tuned machine of naval warfare. Their actions synchronized to respond to the rapidly evolving situation.

The battle outside was a tempest of fire and steel. Reports from lookouts and radar operators painted a daunting picture — they had stumbled into a colossal enemy force. "Sir, intel suggests we're facing sixty transports, twenty destroyers, and at least six cruisers," reported Commander Rice, his voice steady but laced with the gravity of their situation.

Captain Rooks absorbed the information, a cold realization settling in. They were vastly outnumbered, a David against a Goliath force. "Keep our guns firing and stay nimble," he responded, his voice betraying none of his inner turmoil. "We'll need to outmaneuver them at every turn."

The bridge crew nodded, understanding the monumental task ahead. Each update from the radar room brought more urgency: "Enemy cruiser on the port side!" "Destroyer flanking to starboard!" The Houston's responses were immediate, her movements agile despite her size, her guns roaring in defiance.

In these chaotic moments, the bridge was a microcosm of the larger battle — a place of tense decisions, rapid responses, and the unspoken fear of what the next wave of reports might bring. Amid the pandemonium, Captain Rooks and his crew clung to their training and each other, united in their determination to navigate the perilous dance of naval warfare against overwhelming odds.

The night, once an ally to the USS Houston, had betrayed them, revealing a sea swarming with enemy vessels. The realization hit with the force of a physical blow. "We're in the thick of it!" Captain Rooks bellowed, his voice cutting through the chaos that erupted around him. The situation was dire, the air thick with the scent of gunpowder and the growing fear of encirclement.

Without hesitation, the mighty Houston continued to fight, their guns roaring to life with a fury that shook the air. The Houston veered sharply to starboard, their engines roaring in a desperate bid for escape. The deck vibrated under the crew's feet as the guns thundered, firing broadsides at the encroaching enemy ships.

"Another one of our ships has been hit!" The cry came from a crew member on the Houston, his voice laced with horror and disbelief. The eyes of the Houston's crew turned in unison to witness the unfolding tragedy.

The gallant vessel that had stood shoulder to shoulder with the Houston was reeling from the impact of multiple torpedo hits. Flames engulfed her decks, casting an eerie glow on the water. The sound of her steel hull groaning under the strain of the damage was almost drowned out by the continued gunfire.

Amid the inferno, the crew of the Perth fought with courage that bordered on the surreal. Their guns continued to blaze, a defiant answer to the relentless assault, even as the ship began to list dangerously.

Witnessing the horror, Captain Rooks shouted orders above the din of battle. "Keep firing! Cover that ship as best we can!" His voice was a mix of command and a barely concealed rage at the loss of their ally.

The crew of the Houston responded with a renewed fervor, their actions fueled by a mixture of fear, adrenaline, and grim determination. The ship shuddered with each discharge of her guns, the sound echoing across the chaotic seascape.

But the other ally, mortally wounded and fighting against the inevitable, was soon overwhelmed. Once proud and formidable, her silhouette began to sink beneath the waves, succumbing to the sea that had been her domain.

The crew of the Houston watched in stunned silence, the screams and shouts of battle replaced by heavy, collective grief. The loss of another brave ship was not just a tactical blow but a personal one, felt deeply by each man aboard the Houston.

As the vessel disappeared beneath the water, her guns fell silent, marking the end of her valiant struggle. The Houston, now alone amid a sea of enemies, prepared to continue the fight, her crew united in their resolve to honor the memory of their fallen comrades. The night was far from over, and the battle raged on.

Realizing the dire situation, Captain Rooks made a fateful decision. "Turn us back into the convoy," he ordered, his voice resolute. "If there's no escape, we'll make them pay dearly for the Houston!"

The ship pivoted, heading straight for the heart of the enemy fleet. Understanding their captain's intent, the crew braced for the ferocious battle ahead. Gunfire echoed around them, a relentless storm as the Houston cut through the night, a lone warrior set on a final, defiant stand. The air was thick with the smell of gunpowder, the sound of shells whistling past, and the tension of imminent danger, creating an atmosphere charged with both fear and determination.

The brave men of the Houston, in a desperate bid for survival, engaged the Japanese transports at close range. Captain Rooks, standing firm on the bridge, directed the onslaught. "Hit them with everything we've got!" he ordered his voice a beacon of resolve in all the chaos.

As the Houston unleashed her fury, she simultaneously fended off the attacking destroyers, their torpedoes, and shellfire, adding to the bedlam. Japanese cruisers, lurking in the background, pummeled the Houston with relentless salvos.

The bridge of the Houston was a scene of controlled chaos, illuminated by the flashing lights of instruments and the occasional flicker of gunfire from outside. Lieutenant Miller, stationed at his post, his face set in a grim expression, relayed the dire situation to Captain Rooks.

"We're taking heavy fire, Captain. They're hitting us hard!" he shouted above the din of battle. His voice was tense, the weight of each report heavy with the reality of their situation.

"Our starboard side is compromised!" he continued, his eyes scanning the reports coming in. "The aft gun turret has taken a direct hit. We've got casualties there!"

Gripping the edge of the navigation table, Captain Rooks responded with urgency. "Get the medics to the turret, now! And return fire with everything we've got."

Outside, a storm of enemy fire engulfed the Houston. The sound of shells continually striking the ship was a constant terror. Each hit a bone-jarring shock that reverberated through the steel hull. Explosions rocked the deck, sending shrapnel flying and causing devastating damage.

"Main deck's been breached!" came another frantic report from a crew member. "We've got fires near the ammunition storage!"

The smell of burning metal and the acrid stench of explosives filled the air, mingling with the sharp tang of fear and adrenaline. The crew worked desperately to douse the flames, their efforts a race against time to prevent a catastrophic explosion.

Amid the chaos, the loudness of battle almost drowned out the screams of injured men. Medics, their faces set in grim determination, rushed to tend to the wounded, dragging the injured to whatever cover they could find.

The Houston, battered and bruised, continued to fight back with a ferocity born of desperation. Her guns, though diminished, still roared in defiance, answering the enemy's barrage with one of their own.

Captain Rooks, his face a mask of resolve, continued to issue commands, his voice steady in the tumult. "Hold the line, men! We're not done yet!"

During the reports of damage and loss, Lieutenant Miller maintained his post, his voice unwavering as he continued to relay information.

The impact was like a hammer blow, reverberating through the decks and corridors, sending tremors of dread through the hearts of every man aboard.

In the engine room, the scene was one of instant, catastrophic destruction. The torpedo's impact tore through the thick steel hull, unleashing a Hellish inferno. Flames erupted, consuming everything in their path with merciless speed. The roar of the explosion mingled with the sounds of rending metal and shattering machinery, creating a symphony of destruction. The men stationed there stood no chance, their lives claimed in an instant by the merciless blast.

On the bridge, they felt the impact both physically and emotionally. "Engine room's been hit!" shouted a crewman, his voice laden with panic and disbelief. The words hung heavy in the air, a grim testament to the brutal reality of their situation.

Captain Rooks, his face set in a grimace of pain and anger, grasped the situation immediately. "Godspeed to their souls," he murmured, a brief invocation for the fallen. Then, louder, "Damage report, now! We need to assess our capabilities."

The ship, now severely crippled, groaned under the strain of the damage. The once powerful engines, the heart of the Houston, fell silent, drastically reducing the ship's speed and maneuverability. The eerie creaking of stressed metal and the distant crackle of fires battled throughout the vessel and replaced the hum of the engines.

"Captain, we've lost significant propulsion capabilities," reported Lieutenant Miller, his voice steady despite the chaos around him. "We're sitting ducks if we don't get some power back."

Around them, the crew moved frantically, trying to contain the damage, put out fires, and tend to the wounded. The smell of smoke, fuel, and seared metal filled the air, a potent reminder of their danger.

Taking a moment to steady himself amid the turmoil, Captain Rooks issued his commands. "All hands, stay sharp. We're not out of this fight yet. Let's show them what the Houston is made of!"

The resulting thick smoke and scorching steam momentarily forced men away from their guns, but their resolve remained unshaken. "Back to your stations!" Captain Rooks commanded, his tone unwavering despite the dire circumstances. The crew, driven by duty and courage, returned to their posts, facing the inferno.

The damage was severe. The loss of power to the shell hoists halted the flow of ammunition.

Men tried to bring shells up by hand, but debris and fires impeded them. "Keep firing with whatever we have!" Captain Rooks ordered, determination etched on his face.

The USS Houston, already reeling from the devastating torpedo strike, was rocked yet again by a new calamity. A shell, fired with lethal precision by the enemy, found its mark on Turret Two. The impact was catastrophic, a direct hit that set off a massive explosion. The force of the blast sent a shockwave through the ship, rattling every rivet and bulkhead.

In an instant, a monstrous inferno engulfed Turret Two. Flames erupted skyward, a fiery pillar visible for miles, casting an ominous glow over the chaotic battle scene. The intense heat radiated outwards, warping metal and shattering glass.

On the bridge, the situation turned from dire to catastrophic. The explosion sent a wave of heat and flames billowing into the conning tower, the heart of the ship's command. Windows shattered, showering the interior with glass, while instruments and controls sparked and fizzed, their functionality compromised by the blaze.

The crew on the bridge, engulfed by smoke and searing heat, scrambled to escape the inferno. Coughing and shielding their faces from the heat, they stumbled out of the conning tower, desperate for air.

"Get those flames out!" Captain Rooks bellowed above the roar of the fire. His voice was a commanding force, rallying his crew amid the chaos. He grabbed a fire extinguisher, joining the efforts to battle the blaze.

The crew, despite the overwhelming heat and smoke, responded with urgency. They fought the fire with extinguishers and water, a desperate struggle against the unrelenting flames. The sound of hissing steam and the crackling of fire mixed with the shouts and coughs of the men.

The fire disrupted communications and severed vital lines of command and coordination. The ship, now partially blind and deaf, was more vulnerable than ever. In the middle of the chaos, they made makeshift efforts to re-establish contact with the rest of the ship and coordinate their response.

Captain Rooks, still standing firm in the smoke and flames, continued to issue orders, his voice a beacon of hope in the desperate situation. "We need to maintain control. Keep fighting!"

The situation aboard the USS Houston had deteriorated rapidly, pushing the ship and her crew to the brink. In a devastating blow, the sprinkler system, activated in response to the raging fires, had inadvertently flooded the magazine.

The last supply of eight-inch ammunition, crucial for their main battery, had become utterly ruined, drenched, and useless. Stripped of her main artillery, the Houston was left severely crippled, like a lion without its claws amid a merciless hunt.

As if sensing her vulnerability, another torpedo, a lethal messenger of the enemy's intent, struck the Houston with unerring accuracy. The explosion was a monstrous force, an eruption that sent violent shivers through the entire ship structure. Standing resolute on the bridge, Captain Rooks felt the ship tremble under his feet, a quiver that spoke of a mortal wound.

At that moment, he knew that the fate of the Houston had been sealed. The ship, his proud command, began to list dangerously to starboard. Yet, in these final moments, the Houston's remaining guns continued to fire, a last, defiant roar against the encroaching shadows of defeat.

"Abandon ship! Abandon ship!" Captain Rooks ordered, his voice echoing through the ship, each word resounding with the gravity of their dire situation. The order, though necessary, tore through him with a heart-wrenching finality.

Lieutenant Miller, stationed on the bridge, made a swift and decisive move. He leaped over the railing with the bridge taking fire, landing with a heavy thud on the deck below. He narrowly avoided a shell that exploded where he had stood just moments before, a stroke of luck amid the relentless onslaught.

Rushing to the port catapult tower, Lieutenant Miller's eyes landed on the last airplane, a forlorn sight against the backdrop of destruction. It stood there, a useless relic, its wings shrouded in the darkness of the night, a silent witness to the ship's final moments.

Below deck, the scene was one of grim orderliness. Despite the continuous shelling, the imminent sinking of the ship, and the knowledge of what lay ahead, there was no panic among the men. They abandoned ship with a methodical calmness, their faces stoic, etched with the resignation of those who have accepted their fate.

The crew, each man carrying the weight of the night's horrors, descended into lifeboats and rafts, the sea's cold embrace awaiting them. They left the Houston, a ship that had been their home, their protector, now a sinking testament to their bravery and sacrifice.

In the waning moments of the USS Houston's final battle, Captain Rooks stood resolutely on the bridge, his eyes surveying the chaos around him. He was issuing last orders, his voice steady but laden with the unspoken knowledge that these would be his final commands. The crew, battered and exhausted, responded to his every word, their actions driven by adrenaline and deep respect for their captain.

Rooks moved among his crew with a calm, steady presence, offering words of encouragement as the USS Houston weathered the storm of battle. "Hold the line, boys! We're not done yet!" he called out, his voice a beacon of strength in the tumultuous chaos.

As he laid a reassuring hand on a young gunner's shoulder, a sudden, deafening explosion erupted from a nearby gun mount. The blast tore through the brief calm, a violent reminder of the battle's fury.

"Captain, get down!" shouted Lieutenant Miller, his warning cry slicing through the air just moments too late.

A lethal shard of shrapnel, propelled with violent force by the explosion, struck Captain Rooks. The impact was swift and devastating. Crew members rushed to his side, their faces etched with shock and fear.

"Captain!" cried a young sailor, kneeling beside him, his hands trembling as he tried to stem the blood flow.

His strength fading rapidly, Captain Rooks managed a faint, reassuring smile. "Keep... fighting," he whispered, his voice barely audible over the din of battle. "For... the ship..."

Once filled with the fire of leadership and determination, his eyes slowly closed, and his head fell to one side, a final, peaceful gesture amid the raging chaos around him.

The crew stood in stunned silence for a heartbeat, the reality of their loss sinking in. Then, as if ignited by their Captain's final words, they returned to their stations with a renewed sense of purpose, fighting not just for survival but to honor the memory of a leader who had given everything for his ship and crew.

The air was thick with grief and determination, the sounds of battle now underscored by a deep, collective resolve. Captain Rooks's sacrifice would not be in vain; his spirit would live on in the hearts and actions of his brave crew.

Below deck, Buda, the Captain's Chinese cook, learned of the heartbreaking news. His face, ordinarily warm and full of life, crumpled in anguish. Refusing to leave his post, he seated himself outside the Captain's cabin, his body rocking gently back and forth in a rhythm of mourning. "Captain dead, Houston dead, Buda die too," he repeated, his voice a whisper of despair. His loyalty to Captain Rooks and the ship was unwavering, and his decision to go down with the Houston was a testament to the profound bond he shared with the ship and her captain.

Commander Rice's recount of the harrowing experience began with the urgent order to abandon the ship. Chaos ensued as his second-in-command, designated to take over in emergencies, jumped overboard without hesitation, disappearing into the depths thirty feet below. Despite the urgency, Rice noted his lack of a lifejacket, recalling that sailors at his gun station occupied his usual one. Aware of surplus lifejackets stored in the hangers, he made his way there amidst the mayhem.

As Rice navigated from the port to the starboard side, he passed the warm, yeasty aroma of the bake shop and the rich, oily scents of the ship's galley. Suddenly, the ear-splitting roar of shells shattering the air struck the boat. The impact was catastrophic, ripping through the metal and wood with ferocious explosive force, sending a cacophony of screams and tearing metal echoing through the air. The blast knocked Rice to the deck, the taste of gunpowder and saltwater filling his mouth.

Shaken, he scrambled to his feet, the realization dawning on him that a lifejacket might be a futile gesture for a man facing such imminent death. The ship, now groaning and creaking as it heavily listed to starboard, forced him to stagger back towards the port side. Amidst the chaos, he locked eyes with another sailor, Johnson.

"We're going down, aren't we, Commander?" Johnson shouted over the din, his face a mask of fear and determination.

Rice nodded grimly. "Looks like it, but let's not wait for the ship to decide our fate!"

The smell of smoke and burning fuel was overwhelming now, the sounds of men shouting orders and cries of fear melding into a terrifying symphony. With a determined breath, Rice leaped into the churning, oil-slicked water, foregoing the lifejacket. His Navy training kicked in, his strokes strong and purposeful, as he swam away from the doomed vessel, the sounds of the sinking ship hauntingly echoing in his ears.

In the water, Rice's situation worsened. As he resurfaced for air, another person jumped in, causing him to ingest fuel oil and saltwater. This led to severe sickness, vomiting, and impaired vision under the moonlit sky. Rice's survival instinct strengthened despite the discomfort, and he called for assistance.

Two men responded, including Marvin Bain from Arkansas. Equipped with a lifejacket, Bain supported the ailing Rice, helping him stay afloat in the buoyant saltwater.

Together, Rice and the other sailor navigated towards a life raft that the crew had jettisoned earlier. Rice regretted discarding his shoes, realizing too late their potential usefulness. Reaching the life raft, they found it occupied by several wounded, including Tsao, who refused to leave the raft. Traditionally, one should swim alongside a raft rather than ride on it, but the situation dictated otherwise. The group, including Rice and Bain, clung to the raft's tow lines, attempting to maneuver it through the strong currents.

The currents in the straits between Java and Sumatra were notably powerful, sweeping them far from land and pushing them closer to the shore. Throughout this ordeal, the USS Houston had not yet sunk, and the survivors were at the mercy of the sea's unpredictable movements, highlighting the perilous nature of their situation.

The sea around them churned violently, still heaving under the relentless bombardment. The Japanese shells, arcing through the night sky, exploded upon impact with the water, sending shockwaves that reverberated through Rice and his men's bodies with each detonation. The survivors, clinging to their makeshift raft, felt each concussion as a physical blow, similar to a kick in the stomach.

"Boy, we've had it!" Rice thought grimly as the current dragged them inexorably towards the maelstrom of shellfire. The merciless barrage continued, the Japanese seemingly firing indiscriminately, unaware or uncaring of the survivors in the water.

Amid the chaos, a Japanese submarine sliced through the water, its diesel engines emitting fumes that nearly suffocated all of us searching for breath. Its wake tossed the raft, jostling them violently. Soon after, a Japanese transport appeared, its soldiers crowding the rails. Under the clear night sky, illuminated by a bright moon, the soldiers spotted the survivors, shouting "Hey Joe!" taunts as they passed.

On the raft, Rice conferred with Lieutenant Barrett, a surviving sailor on the ship. "Lieutenant, we're in the middle of a landing force here," Rice informed him, the realization dawning on them that they were amid a convoy, the very target of their prior engagements. The proximity to the shore became alarmingly evident as they spotted sandy beaches and a mountainous promontory.

"Lieutenant, let's aim for those mountains," Rice suggested, wary of landing amid the enemy. They attempted to steer the raft, but the strong currents thwarted their efforts. By daybreak, the scope of the Japanese operation was clear – a vast convoy as far as the eyes could see surrounding them, beginning its assault on the beaches.

Their situation seemed increasingly dire. The long hours in the water, battling oil and saltwater sickness, had taken their toll. By midday, when the Japanese finally approached to pick them up, Rice and his men were beyond exhaustion, having spent nearly eleven hours fighting for survival in the treacherous waters.

As the Houston sank into the depths of the Java Sea, Commander Rice and the remaining members of his crew, adrift and exhausted, witnessed the solemn demise of their once-mighty vessel.

The cacophony of battle, distant booms of artillery, and sharp cries of men locked in an unforgiving struggle for survival pierced the morning air. Waves slapped rhythmically against the sinking hull, a haunting requiem for the ship that had been their sanctuary and protector.

Silhouetted against the early morning war-ravaged sky, the survivors floated amid the wreckage. Their faces, slick with oil and sea spray, reflected a mix of despair, exhaustion, and a deep-seated resolve. They watched, some in stoic silence, others with quiet sobs, as the Houston slowly succumbed to the sea, her outline growing fainter with each passing moment.

In this eerie stillness, broken only by the sea's relentless murmurs and distant warfare, there was a shared, unspoken reverence among the crew. This was more than the loss of a ship; it was the end of an era, the loss of comrades, and a stark reminder of the brutal reality of war.

Commander Rice, his uniform drenched and clinging to his weary frame felt an overwhelming sense of loss. Yet, even in this moment of despair, his leadership remained steadfast. Though heavy with fatigue, his eyes scanned the horizon, ever watchful, ever protective of his men.

The Houston, their home and fortress on the sea, slipped beneath the waves in a final, dignified act of surrender to the ocean. And with her, Captain Rooks, a leader who had embodied honor and bravery, and Buda, whose loyalty transcended the boundaries of duty.

The sea, an unforgiving witness to their sacrifice, closed over the Houston, enveloping her in its depths.

The memories of the ship and her captain, defined by courage, resilience, and an unbreakable spirit, would endure in the crew's hearts. This legacy, as lasting as the waves carrying the few survivors, overshadowed the grim reality that the Japanese might use them as target practice. As they trod water, awaiting possible strikes from enemy machine guns, the legacy of their bravery stood undiminished.

Chapter FIFTEEN

Lieutenant Johnathan Miller Abandons Ship

Let's back up a moment and follow our Lieutenant Miller out the other side of the Houston as she began to sink quickly. As the vessel reeled under the relentless assault of enemy fire, her final moments unfolding with brutal swiftness, Lieutenant Miller navigated his way toward the quarterdeck. The journey was a gauntlet of chaos and destruction. Once a proud and formidable vessel, the ship was now a scene of catastrophic ruin.

The quarterdeck was a grim tableau of the war's unforgiving nature. The fallen sailors, who had fought valiantly to the end, covered the deck. Their bodies sprawled in a haphazard array, offering a stark and haunting reminder of the human cost of battle. Some draped lifelessly over their stations, while others lay crumpled on the deck where shrapnel or the concussive force of explosions had struck them down.

Each position told a silent story of bravery and sacrifice in the face of overwhelming odds. The air was thick with the acrid stench of smoke and burning metal, mingling with the sharp tang of gunpowder. The sound of the ship's structure groaning under the strain of damage and the distant, muffled explosions created a dissonant symphony that underscored the chaos.

His heart heavy with grief and adrenaline, Lieutenant Miller pushed through the devastation. His mind was a whirlwind of thoughts - memories of fallen comrades, the weight of loss, the instinctive urge for survival. There was no time for mourning or reflection in this maelstrom. The pressing need to survive, to keep moving, overrode all else.

His footsteps echoed hollowly on the metal deck, each step a grim reminder of the situation's gravity. Once a place of command and control, the quarterdeck was now a bastion of desperation. The ship's demise was imminent, its once mighty form succumbing to the relentless onslaught.

The screams and orders of his fellow sailors were a distant noise as if muffled by the surreal nature of the moment. Lieutenant Miller's focus narrowed to the immediate task at hand - reaching the lifeboats, a slim chance at survival in the vast, merciless ocean.

As he moved, the stark reality of the situation enveloped him. The Houston, a ship that had been a home and protector, was now a dying giant, her final moments a testament to the bravery of those who served aboard her.

Miller saw his division's men working feverishly in the starboard hangar. They were struggling to bring out a seaplane pontoon and two wing-tip floats, hastily filled with food and water in anticipation of such a dire situation. "Get those floats out!" he shouted, urging them on. "We can use them as a raft!"

He rushed to the base of the catapult tower, working rapidly to release the lifelines. "We need to get these overboard, now!" he called out, uncoupling one line and starting on the next.

Suddenly, a torpedo struck directly below, its impact sending shockwaves through the deck.

Miller lost his balance, suddenly finding himself drenched in a deluge of fuel oil and saltwater. Panic set in as he fully grasped the reality of their perilous situation.

"Fire! We've got to move!" Miller yelled, his voice laced with fear as he imagined the flames engulfing him. Driven by a desperate need to survive, he sprang into action. The rest of the crew, echoing his fear, scrambled frantically away from the inferno on the starboard side towards the safer port hangar. Shouts and cries filled the air as they navigated through the chaos.

"Everything's burning! Move!" one of the soldiers screamed as they cleared the quarterdeck. At that moment, a salvo of shells tore through it, the explosions resonating deep below, shaking the very core of the ship. The deck vibrated violently under their feet, a foreboding sign of the ship's rapid descent into the depths.

"We need to get off this ship now!" Miller shouted back at the other sailors urgently, his voice cutting through the noise. The sounds of metal groaning, men shouting, and shells exploding created a cacophony of despair and urgency around him.

Emerging from the depths, Miller found himself amid a sea of men, all struggling for survival. Frantic screams and shouts filled the night, turning the water into a chaotic battlefield. The lieutenant swam with all his might, desperate to escape the pull of the sinking ship.

"I can't go down with her," he thought, his strokes fueled by adrenaline and a fierce will to live.

Around him, men fought against the overwhelming odds, their cries a haunting chorus in the dark sea. Miller and the other survivors swam, determined to survive, as the Houston, the ship he had called home, descended into its watery grave, taking with it a piece of each man who had served upon her. The night was a maelstrom of desperation and bravery, a testament to the human spirit's relentless fight against the inexorable grasp of death. The early morning dawn was an eye-opener when Miller saw the number of ships still surrounding them from the Japanese.

Having swum a few hundred yards from the USS Houston, Commander Rice turned back, gasping for breath, to witness the final moments of his ship. The Houston was listing heavily to starboard, caught in the merciless glare of Japanese destroyers' searchlights. As the enemy raked her decks with machine-gun fire, men in the water struggled for survival while others clung to overloaded life rafts.

"Look at them!" Rice cried out, disbelief and horror in his voice as he saw the Japanese destroyers deliberately firing at the men in the water. "They're shooting our crew!"

The concussions from the exploding shells sent shockwaves through the water, pummeling Rice's body with brutal force.

He winced in pain, aware that the concussions from the blasts were killing those closer to them.

Rice, adrift in the tumultuous waters of the Java Sea, was a solitary figure in a vast, chaotic expanse. His mind struggled to process the nightmarish reality unfolding around him. The end of the USS Houston, a ship he had served with pride and dedication, was a sight that seemed almost too surreal to believe.

The sea around him was an uproar of activity, illuminated eerily by the harsh, unyielding beams of Japanese searchlights, although the morning glow had grown to where Rice could see just how outnumbered they were. These beams cut through the early morning haze, spotlighting the final moments of the once-proud Houston. The ship wounded grievously, listed further to starboard, her silhouette a dark, haunting shape against the backdrop of the searchlights.

The sounds of battle continued unabated, a cacophony of machine gun fire coming from every direction, the rapid staccato bursts creating a terrifying symphony that underscored the chaos. The gunfire seemed to come from all sides, an inescapable barrage that filled the air with the sound of lethal intent.

Above the din of gunfire and the roar of the sea, Rice could see the Stars and Stripes still proudly flying on the mainmast of the Houston. The flag fluttered defiantly, a poignant symbol of resilience and courage against the backdrop of the morning sky. For a brief, heart-wrenching moment, it stood as a testament to the bravery of the ship and her crew, a final act of defiance in the face of overwhelming odds.

Then, with a tired, almost resigned shudder, the Houston began her final descent. The ship, battered and broken by the relentless assault, slowly slipped beneath the waves of the Java Sea. As she sank, the sounds of battle faded into a muffled echo, the chaos giving way to a somber, grave silence.

Floating amid the wreckage and turmoil, Rice watched in stunned silence as the Houston disappeared, swallowed by the sea. The reality of the moment was overwhelming - the loss of his ship, the uncertain fate of his crew, and the end of a chapter written in bravery and sacrifice.

Miller looked around at the oily water, now a graveyard for the Houston and many of his shipmates. But, in the middle of the chaos, he saw hundreds of Japanese soldiers and sailors struggling in the debris from their own sunken ships.

As he watched them, a grim sense of satisfaction overcame him. Despite the overwhelming odds, the Houston fought valiantly to the end.

"Well done, Houston!" he repeated to himself, a small smile on his face of tragedy. The memory of the ship and her courageous crew would live on. Their final stand was a testament to their bravery and sacrifice.

Around him, the sea was a chaotic assortment of friends and foes battling against the merciless ocean. The sounds of battle and the cries of men pierced the early morning sky, hauntingly reminding everyone of the horrors of war. Rice, Miller, and the other survivors, surrounded by the aftermath of the Houston's last battle, swam on, determined to survive and carry the memory of their fallen ship and shipmates.

Chapter SIXTEEN

Prisoners of War

The USS Houston, a fallen giant of the American Navy, lay deep beneath the Java Sea, leaving her crew to battle the merciless ocean. Seaman John Thompson struggled for survival amid the churning waves while Sergeant William 'Bill' Davis, his voice barely audible over the sea's roar, shouted encouragement, "Keep your head up, John! Don't let the sea take you!"

The survivors scattered, each clinging to debris, their faces painted with fear and desperation. Commander Rice, now the highest-ranking officer after the valiant Captain Rooks went down with the ship, floated among his men, his expression solemn in the face of their desperate plight.

"*The Houston's gone,*" Rice said quietly to himself, feeling the weight of command now resting on his shoulders.

As dawn broke further, adding more light to the day, the distant hum of engines signaled the approach of new danger. "Japanese boats!" someone cried out in alarm, turning the survivors' hope of rescue into dread.

Japanese forces moved swiftly, hauling the exhausted men out of the water. Confusion and fear dominated as they rounded up the crew.

"Stay together as best as you can!" Davis yelled, trying to maintain some order within all the chaos.

Aboard one of the Japanese vessels, Thompson and other crew members stumbled into a cramped space below deck. A Japanese officer barked orders, his voice harsh and unforgiving, echoing off the metal walls. The American sailors shoved and jostled found themselves treated with cold indifference. The air was tense, the confined space amplifying every sound and movement.

Commander Rice, aboard another vessel, scanned the faces of his crew, some injured, all wearing the unmistakable look of defeat. "Stay strong," he urged them, his voice resonating with authority and empathy.

The reality of their loss hit them hard. "What now, Commander?" a young sailor asked Rice, his voice shaking with uncertainty.

"We stay united, and we endure," Rice responded, his heart heavy with losing their ship and captain.

Commander Rice, now the senior officer among the survivors, tried to maintain a semblance of order among his men. He stood on the deck of the Japanese vessel, watching as his crew, beaten and bedraggled, were herded like cattle. "Stick together," he urged them, though he knew the chances of staying united were slim.

Seaman John Thompson, shivering from both cold and fear, clung to the words of Sergeant William 'Bill' Davis. "We'll get through this, right, Sarge?" John asked, his eyes searching for some reassurance.

Now tinged with uncertainty, Davis's usual stoic demeanor replied, "One day at a time, kid. One day at a time."

Their arrival at the POW camp was a journey filled with dread and despair. The men crammed themselves into the holds of ships, received minimal food and water, and wondered about their fate. The once solid and determined crew of the Houston now faced the harsh reality of captivity, where hope was a scarce commodity.

THEIR JOURNEY TO THE POW camp was a harrowing experience, marked by deprivation and uncertainty. The camp itself, surrounded by barbed wire, was a stark reminder of their grim new reality.

On their first night, the men lay awake, haunted by the memories of the sinking and their harrowing ordeal in the water. As days turned into weeks, the harshness of life in the camp began to take its toll.

Despite their dire circumstances, the men found a glimmer of solace in shared memories of the Houston. Thompson initiated a conversation to lift their spirits in the dimly lit and cramped space.

"Remember the times in the mess hall?" Thompson would begin, his voice tinged with nostalgia. "The laughter, the clatter of trays, and the smell of coffee in the air?"

"Yeah," another sailor, Johnson, chimed in, a faint smile crossing his worn face. "And those endless debates over which coast had the best beaches, East or West?"

"Don't forget the cook's special on Sundays," added Martinez from a corner, his eyes briefly lighting up. "How he somehow made even powdered eggs taste good."

Their subdued but genuine laughter filled the space, temporarily transporting each man back to better days aboard their ship. For a moment, the harsh reality of their current situation faded into the background, replaced by the warmth of camaraderie and the comfort of shared experiences.

Rice, alongside other senior crew members, worked tirelessly to keep morale up. "We're in this together," he would remind them during their brief, clandestine gatherings.

The mental torment of their situation, exacerbated by the lack of information about the war and their families, was almost unbearable. Yet, the spirit of camaraderie among the Houston crew remained steadfast.

The men spoke often of the Houston, honoring her memory and the sacrifice of those who went down with her, including Captain Rooks. They vowed to survive and return home, keeping the spirit of the Houston alive.

Their physical health waned as time passed, but their resolve never faltered. They faced each day with determination, drawing strength from one another, and the memories of their ship united in the hope of returning home one day.

In the evenings, the men gathered in their barracks, sharing stories of the Houston and their lives before the war. These moments of camaraderie were their only respite from the grim reality of their existence.

"I remember the first time I saw the Houston," Thompson reminisced one evening. "She was the most beautiful thing I'd ever seen."

Fitting on his thin mattress, Davis added, "She was more than a ship. She was home."

Amid the hardship, there were minor acts of defiance. Men would subtly sabotage their work or steal extra food when the opportunity presented itself. They celebrated these small victories quietly, reminding themselves that their spirits were not yet broken.

Yet, as the days turned into weeks, the harsh conditions began to take their toll. Food was scarce and often inedible, and clean water was a luxury. Men fell ill, and the infirmary, a small, overcrowded shack, offered little in the way of actual medical care.

Commander Rice, witnessing the suffering of his men, felt a deep sense of responsibility. "We have to keep each other alive," he told them. "Look out for your buddy. Share what you have."

The guards, ever watchful and cruel, would often beat prisoners for minor infractions. The sound of their boots and the crack of their rifles were a constant reminder of the prisoners' powerlessness.

One day, news arrived that sent shockwaves through the camp. The war was not going well for the Allies. The men gathered, listening in heavy silence, their faces etched with worry and exhaustion.

"We can't lose hope," Commander Rice said quietly, his voice steady despite the weight of the news. "The tide of war can change."

"But sir, the situation seems so bleak," a young sailor named Jenkins spoke up, his voice trembling slightly.

Rice looked at him, his eyes reflecting a mix of resolve and understanding. "I know, Jenkins. It's hard to see any light in this darkness. But history has its turns, and we must believe in our cause."

Another sailor, Peterson, added with a hint of defiance, "We've faced tough odds before. We're still here, aren't we?"

"That's the spirit," Rice affirmed, nodding at Peterson. "We've weathered storms, and we can weather this. Our resolve must be stronger than our circumstances."

The group nodded, drawing a small measure of strength from Rice's words. Amid the despair, his leadership was a beacon, however faint, guiding them through the uncertainty.

But as weeks turned into months, hope became more challenging. Letters from home were nonexistent, and the outside world seemed a distant, unreachable place.

In the middle of this despair, there were moments of humanity. A guard, showing a rare act of kindness, shared extra food with a sick prisoner. These small gestures were like rays of light in the overwhelming darkness.

The men of the Houston, bound by their shared ordeal, became a family. They cared for the sick, shared their meager rations, and held each other up when the weight of captivity became too much to bear.

As the first year of captivity drew to a close, the men settled into a grim routine. They woke each day to face the same hard labor, scant food, oppressive fences, and guards. Yet, they met each day together, their bond forged in the fires of adversity, their spirits still unbroken.

Looking at his men's faces, Commander Rice knew the road ahead was long and uncertain. But he also knew that as long as they stayed together, they had a chance. The Houston might be gone, but her crew remained united and resilient, a testament to the enduring spirit of those who serve.

The POW camp, a grim expanse of wooden barracks and barbed wire, became the new reality for the crew of the USS Houston. The days were long and arduous, marked by grueling labor, scarce food, and the ever-present threat of abuse from the guards.

Rice tried to keep morale high despite the dire conditions. As the sun rose over the bleak landscape every morning, he would pass among the men, offering words of encouragement. "Stay strong," he would say. "We're still a crew and must look out for each other."

Now gaunt and weary, John Thompson found solace in Rice's words. He, Sergeant William 'Bill' Davis, and other former Houston crew members stuck together. The camaraderie they had developed on the ship was their lifeline in the camp.

Each day, the men went out to labor under the unforgiving sun. Their tasks varied, but all were grueling and designed to test the limits of their endurance.

In the fields, a group of sailors bent over rows of crops. "Keep it up. We're almost done with this row," encouraged Thompson, wiping the sweat from his brow as he pulled another weed from the dry soil.

"Yeah, just to start on the next one," muttered Davis, his hands raw and blistered.

Meanwhile, at a construction site, another group toiled under the watchful eyes of their captors. "Hand me that hammer, will you?" Johnson asked as he struggled to fit a wooden beam into place. The structure they were building was unclear, but the physical toll it took was evident.

"Got it," replied Martinez, passing the tool. "Who knew we'd become carpenters in the Navy," he added with a wry smile, trying to lighten the mood.

Elsewhere, a team received the assignment to haul heavy rocks and debris. "One step at a time, boys," Rice said as he lifted a huge stone. His leadership was a constant source of motivation, even in the most back-breaking tasks.

The relentless and exhausting work was meant to break their spirits as much as their bodies. Yet, amid this hardship, the men found small ways to support each other, their camaraderie an unspoken pact of resilience against their daunting circumstances.

"Keep at it, lads," Davis would grunt as he swung his pickaxe. "Can't let these bastards see us break."

Food was a constant concern. The rations were meager – a small rice ball, sometimes accompanied by a watery soup with a few floating vegetables. "Gourmet meal, right here," John would joke weakly, trying to lift the spirits of his friends.

Illness was rampant. Malaria, dysentery, and other diseases swept through the camp, preying on the weakened prisoners. The camp's infirmary was little more than a shack, lacking supplies and proper medical staff. "I'll be fine," John insisted once when he fell ill, though his pallor and shaking hands said otherwise. Davis, acting as a makeshift nurse, tended to him with a grim determination.

Abuse from the guards was frequent and brutal. Beatings for minor infractions were common, and the prisoners learned to brace themselves for the worst.

"Stand tall; don't give them the satisfaction," Rice would advise, his voice firm yet carrying an undertone of empathy. Despite his scars from similar encounters, he remained a pillar of strength.

"You're right, sir," Jenkins replied, trying to muster a brave front. His hands trembled slightly, a natural response to fear, but his resolve was evident in his eyes.

The air was heavy with the stench of sweat and fear. The sounds of distant shouts and the occasional harsh command from the guards created a constant, unsettling background noise.

"We've got to stick together," murmured Thompson, glancing around at his fellow prisoners. Like the others, his face appeared drawn and weary, yet his spirit remained unbroken.

Rice nodded, his gaze sweeping over the men. "Remember who we are and what we stand for. Our bodies may be trapped, but our spirits remain free."

The men drew a deep breath, the smell of damp earth and their unwashed bodies filling their nostrils. At that moment, amid their despair and harsh reality, Rice's words offered hope, a reminder of their inner strength and unity.

Despite the hardships, the men tried to keep each other's spirits up. They would gather in the evenings, sharing stories of their time on the Houston. "Remember back before the war when Captain Rooks hit the Admiral in the head in softball. Remember how quiet it got?" one sailor would say, prompting laughter from the others.

They spoke of their plans for after the war, of the things they would do and the places they would see. "First thing I'm doing is getting a big, juicy T-bone steak," John would declare, his eyes distant with longing.

Rice, seeing the importance of these gatherings, encouraged them. "We need to remember who we are where we come from. It's what will get us through this."

As one month after another dragged on, the men's physical condition deteriorated, but their resolve did not. They supported each other, sharing their meager rations with those who were too sick to work and offering a shoulder to lean on when the memories of their situation became too much.

In the face of their suffering, the former crew of the Houston became a symbol of resilience. Their solidarity, born of shared hardship and a common past, was a beacon of hope in the desolation of the POW camp.

The days turned into weeks, and the weeks into months, each one marked by the relentless cycle of hard labor, scarce food, and the struggle to maintain their dignity in the face of relentless dehumanization.

But through it all, the men held onto each other, their memories of the Houston, and their plans for the future. These were the things that kept them going and the flame of hope alive in their hearts. They were more than prisoners; they were survivors, bound by an unbreakable bond, determined to return home and tell the story of the Houston and her brave crew.

Chapter SEVENTEEN

A Struggle to Survive

In the oppressive shadows of a cramped, makeshift shelter within the POW camp, where the air was thick with the stifling heat of a tropical night, Commander Rice convened a covert meeting.

A single, flickering candle cast elongated shadows on the walls of the shelter, which consisted of little more than scrap wood and tattered canvas. The candle's flame danced in the still, heavy air, filled with the mingled scents of damp earth and the sweat of weary men.

Rice, a figure of quiet authority even in captivity, hunched over a frayed and creased map on an improvised table made from an old crate. Beside him were his most trusted crew members, Sergeant William 'Bill' Davis, a man weathered by years of service and hardened by the trials of war, and Seaman John Thompson, the youngest among them, whose once youthful face now bore the etchings of premature maturity.

"We may be prisoners, but we're not beaten," Rice spoke in a hushed, urgent tone, his eyes intensely focused on the map. His words echoed softly in the confined space, a declaration of defiance.

Davis, his arms crossed, leaned against the rickety wall, the muscles in his jaw clenching in agreement. "We've weathered worse on the Houston, sir," he replied in a deep, gravelly voice, his demeanor unyielding despite their dire circumstances.

Thompson perched uneasily in dark, musty barracks on an ancient stool that groaned under his weight. In his hands, he fidgeted with a small, jagged piece of metal he'd found, a rare find in the camp. His eyes, clouded with uncertainty, lifted to meet Rice's steady gaze. "Sir, what are we going to do?" he murmured, his voice barely more than a breath.

Commander Rice leaned over a worn-out map, his finger tracing a path to the makeshift kitchen. "John, your role there is critical. Keep sneaking out food. It's not just sustenance; it's a lifeline of hope for everyone here."

Thompson's face softened into a sly grin. "A bit extra for strength, then," he said, a glimmer of defiance lighting up his eyes.

Rice then turned to Davis, who stood with his arms crossed, his face set in a mask of determination. "Davis, keep up the 'work' in construction. Each nail you misplace, every beam you skew, it's a silent rebellion."

Davis clenched his fists, his voice a low growl of resistance. "We'll keep up the charade of being broken. But inside, we're as sturdy as the Houston ever was. They can't break our spirits."

Distant shouting abruptly disrupted the strategy session in the barracks, starkly reminding them of their captors' omnipresent threat. Commander Rice acted quickly, extinguishing the candle and casting the room into impenetrable darkness. In this sudden void, his voice cut through the fear, a pillar of strength and resilience. "Remember, men, we're all under the same stars, under God's watchful gaze. Hold onto your faith. It'll guide us back home," he whispered with a powerful undercurrent of conviction in his words. The men, huddled in the blackness, felt a surge of hope, their resolve fortified by Rice's unwavering belief in their eventual return to freedom.

After their secret meeting, the soldiers moved quietly, returning to his bunk in the sparsely lit barracks. A profound sense of unity and determination enveloped them, an unspoken bond forged through shared hardship. The air was heavy with a blend of resolute determination and deep camaraderie, enveloping each weary soul in an intangible cloak of solidarity. Their quiet steps and the soft rustle of the movement were the only sounds punctuating the solemn atmosphere of their temporary sanctuary.

In the hushed atmosphere of the barracks, the soldiers took to heart Commander Rice's words. One of them, his low and intense voice, reinforced the message to his comrade, "You heard the Commander, boys. We've got to keep believing." Another soldier's voice, a soft echo in the darkness, responded with a simple truth, "Yeah, faith's all we've got in this darkness." Their words, spoken in whispers, reflected the deep resolve and shared belief that sustained them in these darkest hours.

As the soldiers lay in their bunks, a sea of personal reflections enveloped each of them. One soldier imagined the warm embrace of family, the laughter of his children echoing in his mind. Another envisioned the comforting sight of his hometown, its streets, and familiar faces bringing a sense of peace. A third soldier clung to memories of his beloved, her smile lighting up the dark recesses of his thoughts. Amid these vivid images, they found a shared comfort.

Within the daunting, barbed-wire boundaries of the POW camp, a sense of resistance kindled among the captured crew of the USS Houston. In this grim world, John had found his quiet way to rebel. Assigned to the dilapidated kitchen, he adopted the role of a covert guardian. With every opportunity, he'd stealthily pocket extra food scraps, the fabric of his worn uniform bulging slightly with the stolen bounty.

Under the veil of night, he became a furtive distributor of hope. "Here, take this," he murmured softly, passing a morsel to a frail comrade, his voice tinged with empathy. His eyes, alight with a subtle defiance, communicated more than words could. "We all need to keep our strength up," he added, his smile a small, rebellious act.

The recipients of his generosity nodded in gratitude, their faces etched with the hardships of captivity yet illuminated by the flicker of solidarity. "Thanks, John. You're a lifesaver," one sailor whispered, his voice laced with weariness and gratitude.

Though minor in the grand scheme, this clandestine operation was a powerful act of defiance against the captors.

In the oppressive environment of the POW camp, Davis, a man of robust build and unyielding spirit, channeled his defiance into the construction tasks assigned by their captors. He had the task of building essential structures like barracks and storage facilities. With each nail he hammered, he would deliberately place it slightly off-center, and every wooden beam he set, he ensured it was subtly misaligned, creating a hidden fragility in the structures.

In the dim evening light, huddled with his fellow crew members, Davis's voice was a low rumble of defiance. "We'll play along with their games," he'd say, a sly grin crossing his face, "Let them believe we're just doing as told."

Another prisoner, catching on to Davis's sabotage, whispered, "Won't they notice something's off?"

Davis shook his head, his eyes gleaming with mischief. "Not if we're careful. Every weak beam, every loose nail, it's our silent rebellion. Remember, we're the crew of the Houston, not just their prisoners."

His words spread a quiet fire of resistance among the men, their chests swelling with a renewed sense of purpose.

The grim reality of their situation deepened when the vigilant guards uncovered the acts of sabotage within the camp. The men knew the risks, but the discovery led to harsh and ruthless punishments. When the officers demanded accountability, Davis bravely stepped forward, accepting the fate that awaited him. The tension among the remaining crew was palpable as they watched their comrade led away.

Later, only a few of those taken for punishment returned, their faces marked by the ordeal. The absence of the others was a silent, somber reminder of the cost of their defiance.

Their fellow prisoners greeted those who returned with reverence and sorrow. In hushed tones, one whispered to another, "They may break our bodies, but not our spirit." Their quiet acts of rebellion continued each a tribute to their lost comrades' bravery and sacrifice.

In the faint-lit barracks, humor was a cherished respite for the sailors. As they huddled together, their laughter was a brief escape from the grimness surrounding them. "Hey, do you remember when Captain Rooks walked in on Thompson trying to take an extra piece of cake?" one sailor began, his eyes twinkling with mischief. Laughter erupted as they recalled Thompson's startled expression and the captain's reaction. Another chimed in with a story about a seagull landing on the sergeant's head during a drill, adding more lightness to their somber surroundings. These shared moments of humor, weaving tales from their past, brought a sense of normalcy and camaraderie, momentarily lifting the weight of the crew's situation.

In the somber barracks, illuminated by the moonlight seeping through small windows, the air was heavy with the fatigue and resilience of the men. Amid the worn cots and personal items carrying memories of home, they gathered, seeking solace in shared faith. Though not deeply religious, Commander Rice continued to be a beacon of hope in these gatherings.

"We're more than just soldiers; we're children under God's watch," Rice began, his voice a calm anchor in the sea of uncertainty. "In these trying times, remember, we are never truly alone. Our faith, our belief in something greater, binds us, gives us strength."

One of the men added, "Faith is what keeps the flame of hope alive in this darkness."

Rice nodded, then offered a simple prayer, "Lord, watch over us, your humble servants. Grant us strength to endure, hope to sustain, and the courage to face each day. May we find solace in Your presence and hold onto the promise of returning home. In Jesus Christ's name, we pray. Amen."

The men echoed a soft "Amen," each finding a measure of peace in the prayer, a spiritual anchor amid the storm of their captivity. The night seemed less oppressive, their bonds a little stronger, united by their faith and the hope of seeing home again.

In the shadowed barracks, a young sailor, more a boy than a man, embodied their collective courage. He stood defiantly against a guard to shield a fellow prisoner, an act that earned him a brutal beating. Despite his youth, his spirit was unyielding.

"I couldn't just stand there," he whispered painfully to his bunkmate when he returned, his body a canvas of bruises and resolve. "We have to look out for each other, right?"

His bunkmate, eyes wet with unshed tears, clasped his hand. "You did more than that. You showed us what bravery looks like. And... you returned to tell about it!"

The story of the young sailor's courage spread like wildfire through the camp. Each retelling added a layer of admiration and a renewed sense of purpose. Though it came at a tremendous personal cost, his defiance ignited a flame of resilience in their hearts.

"We need to remember what he did for one of us," another sailor said in a hushed, reverent tone. "It's about more than just surviving. It's about standing up for each other."

Even in the darkest times, the young sailor's bravery was a beacon of hope, reminding them that they couldn't break their spirits, even in captivity.

The camp's medic, a usually reserved man, emerged as an unsung hero. His role transcended his duties; he became a guardian angel to many. Risking severe punishment, he cleverly smuggled medicine and supplies from the infirmary, providing essential care to those in dire need.

At night, he'd tiptoe from bunk to bunk, administering aid. "Hang in there, buddy," he would say softly, offering a reassuring pat on the shoulder along with the much-needed medicine.

One night, weak from illness, a fellow prisoner murmured, "You're risking everything for us..."

The medic replied quietly, preparing a dose, "We're all in this Hell hole together. If I can ease some pain, then it's worth it. We're all we've got, and we've got to look after each other."

His actions, often carried out under the cover of darkness, became a silent testament to the unspoken bond of solidarity among the prisoners. Each pill, each bandage he provided, was not just medical aid; it was a symbol of hope,

In moments of reflection, the prisoners found comfort in their shared memories of the Houston. They recounted tales of battles fought, storms weathered, and ports visited, keeping the spirit of their beloved ship alive within them. These stories reminded them of their identity as proud sailors of the US Navy, a bond unbroken by captivity.

As the harsh months stretched into years, the indomitable spirit of the Houston crew shone as a beacon of hope. Their acts of resistance, unbreakable spirit, and unwavering faith and humor became the threads that held them together against all odds.

Working on the Bridge over the River Kwai as prisoners of war (POWs) was an experience marked by hardship, resilience, and a constant struggle for survival. The tropical heat was oppressive, the humidity suffocating, and the conditions under which the men worked were brutal.

Early in the morning, as the sun began to rise, casting long shadows over the dense jungle, the sound of a guard's whistle pierced the air. "Up! Up! Work awaits!" barked Sergeant Ito, a Japanese guard known for his ruthless efficiency.

The men, weary and malnourished, slowly rose from their makeshift shelters. "Another day, another test of will," muttered Thompson, rubbing his sore muscles.

"We'll get through this, just like we always do," replied Jenkins, offering a weak but determined smile.

As they made their way to the worksite, the sounds of the jungle were all around them - the distant calls of exotic birds and the rustling of leaves in the gentle morning breeze.

But the cacophony of construction soon drowned out these natural sounds—the clanging of metal, the shouts of overseers, and the grunts of exertion from the men filled the air.

"Keep it moving, keep it moving!" yelled an overseer as the POWs worked tirelessly, hauling heavy logs, laying tracks, and assembling the massive structure piece by piece. The smell of sweat and earth mingled in the air, a constant reminder of their toil.

"I can't feel my hands anymore," said Martinez as he struggled to lift a heavy beam.

"Just hold on a bit longer. We'll get a break soon," encouraged Rice, always trying to keep morale up despite the dire circumstances.

The sun climbed higher in the sky, its rays merciless. The heat was relentless, and the men's shirts clung to their backs, soaked with sweat.

"Water... I need water," gasped a young sailor, his face pale and his lips cracked.

"Here, take mine," offered Miller, passing his meager water ration. "We have to look out for each other."

As the day wore on, the progress on the bridge was evident, but so was the toll it took on the men.

Their captors pushed them to their limits, both physically and mentally. Yet, amid this grueling labor, small acts of defiance and camaraderie kept their spirits alive.

"We're building their bridge, but they can't break our spirit," said Rice, his voice a steady force of hope.

"That's right, sir. They can take our freedom, but they can't take who we are," echoed Jenkins, his voice strong despite his exhaustion.

As the sun began to set, casting the bridge in a golden light, their captors allowed the POWs to return to camp. Exhausted, they walked back, their bodies aching but their resolve unbroken. The Bridge over the River Kwai was a testament to their unwillingness to give in, symbolizing their endurance against all odds.

Seeing his men's strength and courage, Rice knew their story was one of extraordinary resilience. "We are more than survivors," he would often reflect. "We are the unbroken spirit of the Houston, and we will endure."

The camaraderie within the group went beyond mere survival; it was a lifeline in the storm. They shared everything they had, from the last bite of their meager rations to the thin, threadbare blankets that offered little reprieve from the cold.

"One day, we'll look back on this as just a bad memory," Rice said one evening as he watched his men divide their rations, ensuring those who were weakest got a larger share. His heart swelled with pride at their selflessness in such dire times.

Their sense of brotherhood was palpable. They celebrated birthdays with makeshift cakes made from scraps and shared stories of their lives before the war, holding onto the dreams and hopes for the future.

"I always wanted to travel," John Miller shared one night, trying to sound upbeat despite the gloom. "See the world, not like this, but... you know, the real world."

Davis, from his bunk, joined in. "When we get out of here, I'm first taking a long, hot bath. Then, I'm eating a meal that doesn't look like slop... maybe a T-bone, a lobster tail, and a giant baked potato!"

The infrequent arrival of letters from home was like a ray of sunlight piercing their dark world. The men would gather around, eagerly listening as they read each letter aloud, cherishing this precious connection to their loved ones.

"I got a letter from my sister," one sailor said softly, his voice laced with homesickness. "She's keeping the farm running. Says she can't wait to see me."

Rice's letter from home was a bittersweet reminder of what was at stake. Holding the letter close, he shared its contents with a small group of men. "My wife says she's proud of us. Proud of what we're standing for here," he said, his voice betraying a rare vulnerability.

In their darkest hours, the crew found solace in their shared humanity. They talked about their fears, shared the little they had, and found reasons to laugh despite the hopelessness of their situation.

"We're in this together," Rice often reminded them as they sat in the faint twilight. "As a family. As brothers. That's our strength. That's how we'll survive this."

Their story, shaped by the trials of war and the harsh reality of captivity, became a testament to the unyielding human spirit. In the face of overwhelming adversity, they discovered an unbreakable bond of brotherhood that sustained them, a bond that the camp's brutality could never diminish.

As the days turned into weeks, weeks into months, and months into the end of their third year of captivity, the grind of captivity continued its relentless assault.

Sweat and grime streaked Davis's face as he wiped his brow with a ragged cloth, his hands trembling slightly from exhaustion. He turned to John, his voice tinged with fatigue. "Just focus on the next one, John. That's all we can do. One day at a time... one year at a time."

The camp's infirmary was a tragic sight, a ramshackle hut filled with the moans of the sick and wounded. It was woefully under-equipped, its shelves sparsely stocked with the most basic medical supplies. The air inside was heavy with the scent of antiseptic and despair.

The death of a young sailor, once a beacon of life and optimism, cast a deep, somber shadow over the crew. His battle with dysentery, a common yet deadly ailment in the camp, ended tragically, leaving a void where once there was youthful exuberance.

"Remember how he'd always have a joke ready, no matter how tough the day was?" one sailor said, his voice breaking with emotion.

"Yeah," another replied, wiping away tears. "He kept us smiling when there was little to smile about. Can't believe he's gone."

The reality of their loss was a harsh reminder of their own vulnerability and the cruel circumstances they were enduring.

John's voice was barely a whisper as he broke the news to Davis. "We lost Jimmy," he said, his words barely audible. "He didn't make it."

Davis lay on his bunk, his gaze fixed on the ceiling, lost in a sea of thoughts. He exhaled a deep, weary sigh that seemed to carry the world's weight. "It's getting tougher, John," he whispered, his voice barely audible in the stillness of the barracks. "Every day, we're losing too many good men."

Sitting on the edge of his own bunk, John turned to Davis. The same heavy sorrow filled his eyes as well. "I know, Davis," he replied quietly. "It feels like we're losing a part of ourselves with each one gone."

Davis nodded slowly, his eyes never leaving the ceiling. "Remember Thompson? Always the first to volunteer for anything. And now..."

Grief tinged John's voice as he added, "Yeah, he always had a smile, even in this Hell. "It's just... it's hard to make sense of it all."

A heavy silence enveloped the room, with the only sound being the distant, muffled footsteps of the guards outside. The sorrow was palpable at that moment, a shared burden beyond words.

In the forlorn barracks, the air was thick with grief, each loss of a comrade intensifying the already heavy atmosphere. The sounds of solemn whispers filled the space as Commander Rice stood before his men for a memorial. His voice, firm yet laden with sorrow, echoed through the barracks. "We remember them," he declared, his words a tribute to the fallen. "We honor them by carrying on. We must keep their memory alive."

The men, their faces etched with despair, gathered closely, sharing a moment of collective mourning. The flickering candlelight cast long shadows, mirroring the sadness within them.

In a quiet corner, John's voice trembled with emotion, "The not knowing... it's eating me up inside. Are we forgotten out here? Does the world even know we're still alive? Are we all just destined to die in this stink hole?"

Sensing John's deepening despair, Davis reached out, placing a comforting hand on his shoulder. "Listen, kid," he said with a steadfast resolve, "we're not forgotten. We can't lose hope. Someone out there is looking for us. We just have to hold on."

Their conversation was a small but potent act of defiance against the uncertainty and fear that haunted them.

The arrival of Red Cross packages was a rare but cherished event. When a package arrived, the men would gather around, their faces lighting up with anticipation. "Chocolate!" John exclaimed jubilantly one day, holding up a small bar.

For a brief moment, sounds of joy filled the barracks, offering a rare respite from their daily struggles.

But these moments of joy were fleeting. The relentless cycle of hard labor, hunger, sickness, and the looming threat of violence from their captors continued unabated.

Through it all, Rice remained a beacon of hope. "We've come this far together, gentlemen," he'd say during their darkest moments. "We can't lose hope now. We owe it to ourselves and to the brothers we've lost."

In the evenings, the men would gather, sharing stories of the Houston, their families, and dreams for the future. These conversations were a lifeline, a reminder of the world beyond the barbed wire.

Yet, as the war dragged on with no end in sight, hope became an increasingly scarce commodity. The daily toll of captivity was relentless, each man grappling with his own inner demons.

In their hearts, however, a flicker of hope persisted.

AFTER THE ALLIES BOMBED the Bridge they had worked on for two long years, the Japanese put the POWs to work, moving the mountains of material that were coming ashore during the general off-loading phase of the landing operation on the west coast of Java. One night, very late in the night...probably near the hour of midnight...they permitted the men to lay down and sleep. They got very little sleep... it was so cold. They'd been in the water all day, and, of course, they were terribly chilled at nighttime.

Commander Rice reminiscences with some of his crew one night. "The one thing I will never forget is if you are ever aboard a ship that sinks, well, believe me... keep your shoes. Leaving them was terrible, but I kicked them off in the water. I had reason and ample cause to regret that many times afterward.

Then, the following day, the remaining crew of the Houston resumed the business of unloading all the supplies coming in during the last phase of the landing operation. About the middle of the morning, the Japanese had the men load many of these supplies on carts of one sort or another. Most of them were wooden two-wheeled carts.

It was the intent that they were to load all this material of various sorts...rice and other sorts of preserved rations, not C-rations as we know combat rations to be, but great tubs of plums and pickled seaweed and such items as that. The men loaded these carts, and then they... those captured at that particular place... were to be the motive power for all these carts and move away from the beach area.

The combat forces treated the POWs well on the first day they worked on the beach. Of course, many of the troops who came in followed the infantry. Usually, the infantry would first land, and then you land your supporting troops... your artillery, engineers, and mechanized forces.

We had preceded the landing of these units, and we saw them land the artillery... most of it was horse-drawn artillery that day... and some light, mechanized forces, and other motor-transport equipment.

As these combat troops formed up on the beach and then made preparations to move on to the combat zone... if there was a combat zone... they would break out their packaged rations, the combat rations. Mostly, it would be tin cans of prepared meat like meatballs and some sort of fruit and then little bitty, tiny, hardtack, cracker-like things with hard-sugared candy.

Members of the Houston relied on the food that combat troops shared with them for the day. These individuals, responsible for getting equipment ashore and ensuring it reached its intended destination, earned the titles of rear echelon, communication zone personnel, or combat support units, and we referred to them as beach master parties.

They were part of the Navy and part of Marine Corps personnel. The only abuse the men had at all was from these people. Sometimes, people referred to individuals of that sort as rear area commandos because they rarely engaged in combat. This was the thing that we were to note pretty much throughout our time as prisoners-of-war... anytime we were around front-line combat troops, we usually received good treatment from them.

The crew's challenges often stemmed from administrative and auxiliary personnel far from the front lines. As they loaded a heavily burdened cart, Miller oversaw a water buffalo-powered cart. The Japanese had seized this buffalo, much to the dismay of the local owner.

"Seems we got lucky with this one, eh Miller?" one of his crew members remarked, hoisting a sack onto the cart.

Miller grunted in response, "Lucky if you call hauling loads with a buffalo lucky. But hey, beats carrying it ourselves."

They strategically loaded the cart, heavier at the front, allowing the buffalo to bear some weight. Despite the grim situation, Miller and his crew found a slight reprieve in this small advantage, sharing a moment of camaraderie amidst their arduous task.

As the POWs prepared to move from the beach zone, the water buffalo, burdened with the heavy cart, had plans. Suddenly, it veered off course, heading determinedly towards the jungle. The men tried to control it, but the buffalo was resolute.

"Hey, where's he going?" one POW exclaimed as they watched the animal disappear into the dense foliage.

"Looks like he's had enough of this," another said wryly.

The buffalo reached the jungle, but the cart remained stranded, unable to cross the four-foot ditch in its path. The POWs, realizing their predicament, shared resigned looks. "Well, guess it's on us now," one of them muttered, bracing for the arduous task ahead.

As the POWs faced the daunting task of pulling the cart themselves, a Japanese guard barked orders in broken English. "Push cart now! Move!" he commanded, gesturing impatiently towards the road.

The crew members grumbled among themselves, feeling the scorching heat of the concrete under their bare feet. "Feels like we're walking on hot coals," one remarked, wincing with every step.

Another added, "This road's like a frying pan. Can't imagine it getting any hotter."

The air was heavy with the scent of the sea mingled with their sweat. The sound of their labored breathing and the relentless scorch of the sun beating down created an oppressive atmosphere. They trudged along, the heat from the road almost tangible, burning their tender feet, a relentless reminder of their harsh reality.

Chapter EIGHTEEN

Whispers of the War's End

The sun beat down mercilessly on the POW camp, a stark, barbed-wire enclosed compound that had been home to the crew of the USS Houston for almost four long years. A substantial change was brewing amid the oppressive heat and dusty air. Rumors, those fickle harbingers of hope and despair, whispered of the war's end. They meandered through the cramped barracks and overworked mess halls, igniting a cautious optimism in the hearts of the weary prisoners.

Commander Rice, a pillar of strength throughout the ordeal, felt the shift in the air. He moved among his men, calming in the rising tide of excitement. "Keep level heads," he advised his voice a blend of hope and caution. "Rumors are just that until we hear it from the commandant himself."

In their barracks, John Thompson and Sergeant William 'Bill' Davis sat side by side on their cots, the weight of years of captivity etched on their faces. John turned to Davis, his eyes reflecting hope and disbelief. "Could it be true, Sarge? Are we finally going home?" he asked, his voice barely above a whisper.

Davis, a man of few words but deep thoughts, put a reassuring hand on John's shoulder. "Let's hope, John. Let's hope. But let's not count our chickens before they hatch," he said, trying to temper the young man's expectations.

The following day, as the sun reached its zenith, the camp commandant, a stoic figure who had been the face of their captivity, called for assembly. The men lined up, their bodies worn but their spirits kindling with anticipation. The commandant, his face impassive, delivered the news: the war was over. The Axis had surrendered.

A stunned silence fell over the camp, the gravity of the words sinking in. Then, as if on cue, a cheer erupted, raw and cathartic, a sound that encapsulated years of suffering, longing, and suppressed hope. Rice, standing tall amid his men, felt a surge of emotion. "We've made it, gentlemen. We're going home," he announced, his voice steady but his eyes glistening with unshed tears.

Days later, the arrival of the USS Enterprise, part of Operation Magic Carpet, marked the beginning of freedom for the prisoners. As the storied vessel approached, the camp gates swung open, signaling liberation, not further captivity. Davis, stepping out into the open, took a deep breath of freedom's air. Overwhelmed by emotion, he said, "Never thought I'd see this day," tears of relief and joy streaming down his sun-beaten face as the silhouette of the USS Enterprise stood proudly in the distance, a symbol of their long-awaited return home.

The journey back home also included a ride for many on the battleship, the USS Iowa, repurposed for the mission of Operation Magic Carpet. The men boarded the vessel bound for the United States, their hearts heavy with memories but lightened by the prospect of return.

ON THE DECK OF THE Enterprise, John stood by the railing, watching the endless expanse of the ocean. "I can't wait to see my family, to have a proper meal, to sleep in my own bed," he shared with Rice, who stood beside him, gazing into the horizon.

"It was an honor to serve with each of you," Rice said, his voice laden with emotion. "What we endured, what we survived... it speaks to the strength of each man here."

The ship's arrival at the port in San Francisco was a moment that seemed to suspend reality. As the vessel approached, the iconic Golden Gate Bridge loomed in the distance, symbolizing hope and homecoming. The docks were alive with activity, a vibrant tapestry of color and movement.

Crowds lined the docks as far as the eye could see, waving flags and banners that fluttered in the gentle sea breeze. Their cheers and applause rose in a crescendo, a welcome symphony to the returning heroes. The air filled with the smell of the ocean, mingled with the faint aroma of street food from nearby vendors, enhancing the festive atmosphere.

"Look at all those people!" exclaimed Jenkins, his eyes wide with disbelief as he leaned on the railing, gazing at the crowd.

"They're here for us, can you believe it?" Thompson added, his voice choked with emotion.

The weary yet elated sailors lined the deck, waving back at the crowd. Many had dreamed of this moment, but the reality was more overwhelming than they had imagined.

"Never thought I'd see this again," murmured Martinez, a tear trailing down his cheek.

Parents hoisted children onto their shoulders for a better view, and their excited chatter contributed to the joyous noise. Veterans from previous conflicts stood proudly, their medals glinting in the sunlight, a silent nod of respect and camaraderie to the men aboard the ship.

"We made it, boys, we made it back home," said Rice, his voice steady but filled with a profound relief.

As the ship docked, the band on the shore struck up a patriotic tune, its lively notes dancing in the air.

The scent of fresh flowers brought by those waiting to greet their loved ones mingled with the smell of the sea.

"It's good to be home," said Jenkins, a sentiment echoed in the hearts of all the men aboard. They had returned to a nation grateful for their service, a community ready to welcome them back into its embrace. The ship's arrival at the port marked not just the end of a journey but the beginning of a new chapter for all the brave men returning home after a long time away.

As John stepped off the ship, his heart pounding with a mix of anxiety and excitement, he eagerly scanned the crowd. His eyes darted from face to face until they finally locked onto those of his family. Overwhelmed with a surge of joy, he broke into a run, closing the distance rapidly. "Mom! Dad!" he shouted, his voice breaking with a torrent of pent-up emotions.

With tears streaming down her face like rivers of relief, his mother reached out with open arms. "John, my boy!" she cried out, her voice a mix of laughter and sobs. She embraced him tightly, holding him like she'd never let go. Her familiar perfume, a faint floral fragrance, filled his senses, grounding him in the moment's reality.

His father, a man of few words but deep emotions, stood with tears glistening in his eyes. He stepped forward and clapped John firmly on the back. "Welcome home, son," he said, his voice thick and husky with emotion, betraying the stoic facade he often wore.

John's younger sister jumped up and down beside them, barely containing her bubbling excitement. "I missed you so much, John!" she exclaimed, her voice a high-pitched bell of joy. She held his hand tightly as if anchoring him to the spot.

Around them, the sounds of the dock - the cries of seagulls, the distant horn of another ship, the murmur of other reunions - seemed to fade into the background. The smell of the salty sea air mixed with the familiar scents of home, creating a tapestry of memories.

The reunion was a whirlwind of emotions - joy, relief, love - each feeling intensifying the next. They clung to each other, their tears a testament to the long and arduous journey that had finally brought them back together mercifully.

At that moment, nothing else mattered except the fact that they had reunited, becoming a whole family once more.

Davis stood for a moment, absorbing the poignant scene around him. The sounds of joyful reunions filled the air, with the salty tang of the sea mingling with the earthy scent of the dock. Then, he saw them - his family.

His wife, tears cascading down her cheeks, raced toward him, their children in tow. "Billy Lloyd!" she cried, voice quivering with emotion.

As they embraced, their tears mixed, each drop a symbol of the pain of separation and the joy of reunion. "I missed you so much," his wife whispered.

"Daddy, you're home!" his children exclaimed, clinging to him.

Davis, overwhelmed, could only hold them tighter, murmuring, "I'm here now, I'm here." The war had left its scars, but at that moment, only love and relief mattered, enveloping them in a cocoon of happiness.

IN THE FOLLOWING DAYS, Paul Rice, John Thompson, and Bill Davis found themselves grappling with their experiences. Sitting together in Rice's backyard, a world away from the POW camp, they shared a bottle of Jack Daniel's Single Barrel and their thoughts.

"How do we move on from this?" John asked, his voice reflecting the turmoil within.

Paul Rice sipped his whiskey, his gaze distant but resolute. "We remember, Bill. We honor those we lost and live the best life possible.

We tell our stories, not just for us but for them. That's how we move forward."

Davis nodded and added, "We survived Hell together. That counts for something. It has to."

Their conversation meandered into the night, a cathartic release of years of pent-up emotions. They spoke of the friends they had lost, the hardships they had endured, and the future that lay ahead. The war might have ended, but its impact forever lingered in their minds and hearts.

Their journey from the depths of captivity to the freedom they now enjoyed was a testament to their resilience, their unbreakable spirit, and the bonds of brotherhood that had sustained them. They were more than survivors; they were the legacy of the USS Houston, a legacy that would endure through their stories, their memories, and the lessons they carried forward into a world forever changed by war.

John Thompson faced a struggle upon returning to civilian life, a battle that many veterans encounter, which is less visible but no less challenging than what he had experienced during the war.

The small garage he opened became his sanctuary, where he could immerse himself in the simplicity of engines and gears, away from the complexities of a world that had moved on without him. At night, however, the nightmares would come, vivid and terrifying, pulling him back to the POW camp. It was in the loving embrace of his family, in the laughter of his children, that John found his solace, his anchor in the tumultuous sea of post-war life.

Sergeant William 'Bill' Davis returned to his hometown a hero, greeted with parades and accolades, a stark contrast to the quiet internal turmoil he faced. Speaking about his experiences proved difficult; the words seemed too frail to bear the weight of what he had endured. Instead, Davis found his purpose in helping fellow veterans, channeling his efforts into veterans' affairs where he could offer support and understanding, a silent acknowledgment of their shared burden.

Compelled by a need to ensure that the story of the USS Houston and her valiant crew would never be forgotten, Commander Rice authored a book in which he poured his memories and insights. It was a tribute, a memorial in words, to his shipmates' bravery, sacrifice, and enduring spirit.

THE ANNUAL REUNIONS of the Houston crew became a sacred tradition. Every year, the surviving members would gather, their numbers dwindling with time, to reminisce, laugh, cry, and remember those who were no longer with them. These reunions were not just gatherings but rituals of remembrance, a testament to the bonds forged in the crucible of war.

The unveiling of the memorial dedicated to the USS Houston and her crew was poignant. Paul, John, and Bill stood side by side as they had in the camp, united in their respect and loss. As they each laid a wreath, the silence that fell over the crowd was a powerful tribute, speaking volumes where words fell short.

In their later years, the men of the Houston found themselves stepping into the role of educators, imparting the lessons of their experiences to younger generations. John would often speak to his children, his words tinged with the wisdom of someone who had faced the darkest depths of human experience. "What we went through, it taught me about the strength we all have inside," he would say, hoping to instill in them the values of resilience and hope.

At veterans' meetings, Davis became a voice for the importance of camaraderie and mutual support. "We got through it because we had each other," he would remind his fellow veterans, emphasizing the strength found in unity.

Rice often spoke of the broader implications of their ordeal through his book and in interviews. "Our story is a testament to survival, hope, and the unbreakable human spirit," he would say. "These themes are timeless, as relevant today as they were during the war. They remind us of what we can endure and what we can overcome."

The legacy of the USS Houston lived on not just in monuments and books but in the lives of its crew, in the lessons they imparted, and in the enduring spirit of brotherhood that continued to unite them. Their story, a narrative of unimaginable hardship and remarkable resilience, remained a powerful testament to the strength of the human spirit, echoing through time and continuing to inspire future generations.

Chapter NINETEEN

The Journey of the USS Houston Ends

As the author wrote the final chapters of this remarkable saga, the epic journey of the USS Houston's crew now reaches its poignant conclusion.

From the terrifying moment the depths of the Java Sea claimed their ship and to their long-awaited return to American soil, their experiences became an indelible part of American naval history.

Their tale began with the thunderous roar of cannons and the chaos of battle on tumultuous seas, a stark reminder of the perils they faced in service to their country. The sinking of the Houston was not just the loss of a ship but the fracturing of a family bound by steel and saltwater. Survivors, clinging to life in the unforgiving sea, held onto each other and the memories of those they had lost.

As prisoners of war, they endured tests of endurance in ways unimaginable. The squalid conditions, the unending toil, the gnawing hunger, and the ever-present shadow of despair could not break their spirit. Each day was a battle for survival and preserving their dignity and the memories of the USS Houston.

Their eventual liberation and return home were moments of bittersweet triumph. As they stepped onto their homeland, each footfall was a testament to their resilience. They received greetings as soldiers returning from war and as embodiments of courage and perseverance.

They have woven the tales of their individual and collective heroism, the friendships forged in the crucible of conflict, and the sacrifices made, both great and small, into the very fabric of American naval history. Their journey, marked by extraordinary moments of brotherhood and sacrifice, stands as a profound testament to the unyielding human spirit.

The sinking of the Houston was not just the loss of a ship; it marked the beginning of an odyssey for her crew. Cast into the merciless waters and then corralled into the brutal confines of POW camps, these men endured what few could imagine. Their survival was not solely a battle against the physical deprivations of war but a relentless fight to maintain their humanity in the face of despair.

John Thompson, the young sailor whose dreams were once as vast as the ocean he sailed, returned home a changed man. A depth of understanding born from suffering and endurance replaced the wide-eyed innocence with which he had viewed the world. Yet, in captivity, the forge tempered his spirit of resilience. He found solace not in forgetting his past but in embracing it, using his experiences to shape a life of purpose and meaning.

Sergeant William 'Bill' Davis, the embodiment of stoic strength, became a beacon for other veterans grappling with the shadows of war. His journey was not just one of physical survival but of emotional reconciliation. In helping others, he found his path to healing, understanding that the bonds of brotherhood forged in the crucible of war were the threads that could guide him through the labyrinth of post-war life.

Commander Dave Rice's resolve to document their story was more than a quest for historical preservation; it was a tribute to the indomitable spirit of his crew. His book became a vessel carrying the legacy of the Houston and her crew into the future, ensuring that their sacrifices and heroism would not fade into the annals of history but continue to inspire.

The legacy of the USS Houston and her crew resonates far beyond the book chapters or the confines of history. It is a narrative that echoes the enduring themes of human struggle and triumph. The resilience they displayed, the unbreakable bonds of brotherhood they formed, and their sacrifices speak to the human experience's core.

Their story, set against the backdrop of one of the most tumultuous periods in world history, is not just a record of events; it is a journey of the human spirit. From the depths of despair in POW camps to the joyous reunions with families, their experiences encompass the spectrum of human emotion.

As we reflect on the journey of the Houston crew, we need to remind ourselves of the extraordinary capabilities of ordinary people. Faced with unimaginable challenges, they showed that resilience is not the absence of fear or despair but the decision to keep moving forward despite them. They taught us that brotherhood was not just a bond formed in easy camaraderie but one that was forged and solidified in adversity. Their sacrifices remind us of the price of freedom and the value of fighting for what we hold dear.

The story of the USS Houston and her crew of the Galloping Ghost of the Java Coast remains a poignant chapter in American naval history and a timeless narrative of courage, hope, and the unyielding strength of the human spirit. In their story, we find reflections of our struggles and aspirations, making their journey not just a tale of the past but a mirror to our own lives.

EPILOGUE

The Dance of the Devil

As the sun set on February 28, 1942, the USS Houston, alongside the Australian light cruiser HMAS Perth, faced an overwhelming enemy force in the Sunda Strait. That night marked a tragic yet valorous chapter in U.S. Naval history that would resonate for decades.

The USS Houston, known as "The Galloping Ghost of the Java Coast," was a Northampton-class cruiser with a distinguished service record. Under the command of Captain Albert H. Rooks, the ship became a symbol of American naval prowess in the Pacific. However, during the ill-fated Battle of Sunda Strait, the Houston, heavily outnumbered and outgunned, fought fiercely against a formidable Japanese fleet. The battle, a desperate effort to stem the tide of Japanese advances in the region, saw the Houston and Perth fighting valiantly against insurmountable odds.

On February 28, the USS Houston and HMAS Perth faced a formidable Japanese fleet in the early hours, resulting in a valiant but overwhelming battle. The Houston sustained severe damage from torpedoes and gunfire, leading to its tragic sinking, with over 600 Sailors and Marines perishing. This night's horror extended to the survivors, who endured brutal captivity marked by torture, neglect, and harsh conditions. Yet, the extraordinary resilience and fortitude these men displayed throughout their imprisonment are a testament to their unwavering courage and dedication.

The true fate of the USS Houston and HMAS Perth remained a mystery until the conclusion of World War II. The full extent of the tragedy that befell the USS Houston and the harrowing experiences of the survivors only became apparent after the war, thanks to the detailed accounts provided by the liberated POWs. Their testimonies shed light on the events and the incredible endurance they displayed during their captivity.

Recognizing their extraordinary bravery, the USS Houston received the Presidential Unit Citation. Captain Rooks, who valiantly led his crew in the Battles of the Flores Sea and Java Sea, received the Medal of Honor posthumously. He was in Missing-in-Action status at the time of the award, a somber reminder of his ultimate sacrifice for his country.

The legacy of Captain Rooks and his crew was further honored with the commissioning of a Fletcher-class destroyer, the USS Rooks (DD-804), named in his memory. This ship served as a lasting tribute to the heroism and sacrifice of the Houston's crew.

The Navy decommissioned the USS Rooks (DD-804) on July 26, 1962, and transferred it to Chile. The ship had a distinguished history, participating in various deployments from its commissioning in September 1944 until its decommissioning. For more detailed information about the USS Rooks and its history, you can visit HullNumber.com.

Today, the story of the USS Houston and her valiant crew remains a powerful part of U.S. naval heritage. Their incredible tale of bravery, resilience, and sacrifice in the face of overwhelming odds is an enduring inspiration to the Navy and its Sailors.

The legacy of the Houston and her crew—a legacy of honor, courage, and unwavering commitment—continues to echo on and on through the annals of naval history, reminding us of the price of freedom and the valor of those who defend it.

The End

Biography of Captain John H. Rooks

ALBERT HAROLD ROOKS, a true hero, was born on December 29, 1891, in Colville, Washington. His remarkable journey in the United States Navy began when he entered the Naval Academy as a midshipman on July 13, 1910.

On June 6, 1914, he graduated from the Naval Academy and received his commission as an ensign, marking the commencement of a remarkable and illustrious career.

In the following seven years, which included the tumultuous years of World War I in 1917-18, Rooks served on various ships, including the USS West Virginia (ACR-5) and the USS St. Louis (C-20). Notably, he also took command of submarines, including the USS Pike (SS-6), USS B-2 (SS-11), USS F-2 (SS-21), and USS H-4 (SS-147).

In 1921, Lieutenant Rooks joined the staff of the Twelfth Naval District in San Francisco, California, where he served until 1925. While serving during this time, he earned a well-deserved promotion to lieutenant commander. His naval journey continued with duty on the USS New Mexico (BB-40) battleship for three years, followed by service at the U.S. Naval Academy. In 1930, he played a pivotal role in commissioning the new cruiser USS Northampton (CA-26) and served on her until 1933, when he returned to the Naval Academy for a second tour.

Commander Rooks achieved another milestone in February 1936 when he commissioned the new destroyer USS Phelps (DD-360) and remained her commanding officer until 1938. Continuing his dedication to professional development, he attended the Naval War College and later served on the college's staff. Captain Rooks received a promotion to the rank of captain on July 1, 1940, while still at the War College.

In 1941, Captain Rooks took command of the heavy cruiser USS Houston (CA-30), becoming the flagship of the Asiatic Fleet. He led his ship through the challenging initial three months of the Pacific War, where the Asiatic Fleet and its British and Dutch counterparts fiercely battled against overwhelming Japanese forces in Southeast Asia, the Philippines, and the East Indies.

Unfortunately, the USS Houston and her valiant commanding officer met a tragic end in the Battle of Sunda Strait on March 1, 1942.

Captain Rooks posthumously received the Medal of Honor for his "extraordinary heroism, outstanding courage, gallantry in action, and distinguished service" as the USS Houston's Commanding Officer during intense combat with superior Japanese enemy forces. This included surviving multiple air attacks and a major naval engagement, inflicting significant damage on the enemy despite enduring heavy damage to his ship. Captain Rooks remained on the bridge until the end, going down with the USS Houston.

Albert Rooks' path to greatness commenced when he received his appointment to the Naval Academy, leading him to leave high school to prepare for entry into this prestigious institution.

His father's role as a steward at the state penitentiary in Walla Walla characterized his family history. His sister, Edna Bernadine, married professional baseball player Wallace "Wally" James Hood, Jr., in October 1922.

Throughout his naval career, Edith, his wife, supported him. A marker in Washington commemorates his memory. Captain Albert Harold Rooks is a true American hero, and his posthumous Medal of Honor is a testament to his extraordinary bravery and unwavering commitment to duty. His legacy symbolizes courage and sacrifice, forever etched into the annals of American naval history.

| Page

Don't miss out!

Visit the website below and you can sign up to receive emails whenever Sidney St. James publishes a new book. There's no charge and no obligation.

https://books2read.com/r/B-A-HKSI-XKUTC

BOOKS 2 READ

Connecting independent readers to independent writers.

Did you love *USS Houston - Galloping Ghost of the Java Coast*? Then you should read *I Am Woman - Hear Me Roar*[1] by Sidney St. James!

[2]

Our story has its quiet beginning at a convention in Seneca Falls, New York, in 1848. Susan B. Anthony attended, and it was here her legacy began. This convention launched the suffrage movement. This novel is based on actual events in history, although it is written as creative fiction. There are two parts to this Victorian Romance, Women's Rights, and State's Rights.

It gets underway after the convention in the summer of 1860 with four young women, known throughout the reading as the four musketeers, who are all single and graduate from the Hampton Women's College in Virginia. It follows their courtship with handsome men from all walks of life, Colonel Richard 'Dick'

---

1. https://books2read.com/u/bpDdal

2. https://books2read.com/u/bpDdal

Jackson, Reverend Russell James Keiner, Brett Meyer, and an Italian opera star, Carlos Orsi. The lead character in the novel is Dianne Jenkins, who is portrayed as man-hater... but is she really!

The rights usually enjoyed by women were often taken away when she married. As a matter of fact, a woman gave up so many civil and property rights upon walking across that threshold that she was said to be entering a state of "civil death." One such woman who would not stand for this inequality was Dianne Jenkins. She loves Reverend Russell Keiner with all her heart but hates him with all her mind. Her moving speech as Magna Cum Laude at Hampton's College describes her feeling toward inequality while not pulling any punches.

Married women were not allowed to make contracts, devise their last will and testament, or take part in other legal transactions. Women, once married, were not in control of the wages they earned.

In our story, Dianne Jenkins is an outspoken woman. She disliked the fact that women were expected once they married to do the maintenance of the family from sewing a pair of socks to doing the laundry to cooking the meals and, of course, bearing as many children as she could until it killed her. Because the laws were written by men, a married woman was supposed to remain home and take care of the cooking, cleaning, and getting pregnant every time she hung her husband's pants on the clothes' line.

As the first of this two-volume novel unfolds, we find our four women standing beside their fathers while our country splits, and they fight for the glory of the 'Star-Spangled Banner' in State's Rights. Or, do they take up arms with the Confederacy? At the same time, one of our women fights not to be controlled by a man she so dearly loves. The problem is that she loves him and desires him with her heart, but something from her past keeps her mind from letting him into her heart!

Some quotes from women during this story:

"The best protection any woman can have is courage." – Elizabeth Cady Stanton

"I distrust those people who know so well what God wants them to do because I notice it always coincides with their own desires." – Susan B. Anthony

"There shall never be another season of silence until women have the same rights men have on this green earth." – Susan B. Anthony

"I never doubted that equal rights were the right direction. Most reforms, most problems are complicated. But to me, there's nothing complicated about ordinary equality." – Alice Paul

Read more at https://www.facebook.com/sidneystjamesshow.

Also by Sidney St. James

Beneath the Waves Series
Throwback - Terror Beneath the Waves

Bridget Flynn Detective Series
Bridget Flynn - A Female Detective
Bridget Flynn - A Female Detective
A Prince of Their Own

Demon Gorge Trilogy
Room of Death - Here Today and Gone Tomorrow
Fate - Eventually Everything Connects
Standing in the Shadow of Death - The Sword of Damascus
Demon Gorge Trilogy Box Set

Gideon Detective Series
Rosenthall - Bete Malefique des Bois
Gideon Returns - A Damsel in Distress
The Dusty Adler Murder Mystery

Phantom of Black Rock Cove
The Transformist
El Transformista
Ace of Spades
Gideon - The Final Chapter (Volume 2)
The Final Curtain Call - The Illusion of Innocence
Lady in Red
Ace of Spades (Vol. 1) & Gideon - The Final Chapter (Vol. 2)
Gideon Detective Murder Mysteries Box Set: Books 7-9

James' Recipe Series
Wild Game Recipes - Squirrels, Bullfrogs, Alligators, Rabbits,
Armadillos and More
Recipes that Won Chili Cookoffs in Texas
Duck and Goose Recipes from the Wilds of Eagle Lake, Texas and
the Rock Island Prairies
Grandma's Homestyle Cooking Recipes

Lincoln Assassination Series
The Lost Cause - Lincoln Assassination
Lincoln Assassination Series Box Set: Books 1 - 5
Lincoln - Pursuit and Capture of John Wilkes Booth
Lewis Thornton Powell - The Conspiracy to Kill Abraham Lincoln
The Knights of the Golden Circle
Mary Elizabeth Surratt - "Please Don't Let Me Fall!"

Love Lost Series
It Takes Two to Tango (Volume 1)

It Takes Two to Tango (Volume 2)
Tears Are Words from the Heart
Let Me Drive
Belem Towers - Only Two Will Ever Know
The Curse of Knight's Island
Norderney Island
The Winds of Destiny

Omega Chronicles
Omega - The Lost City of Altinova
Nevaeh - The Lost City of Nemea
Bonaventure - Three Years on the Island
Crux Ansata - The Lost City of Ankara
Nevaeh & Crux Ansata Part I & 2 Anthology in the Omega
Chronicles
Omega Chronicles Books 1 - 3 - An Anthology

Planetary Romance Trilogy
The Secrets of the Mist
Secrets of the Golden Cliffs
Wrath of Nevaeh

Self-Guided Creative Writing Series
Taglines Unveiled - Crafting Memorable Dialogue Hooks

Texas Outlaw Series

Sam Bass - A Dead Man's Hand, Aces and Eights

The Faith Chronicles
The Rose of Brays Bayou - The Runaway Scrape
Adversity - Keeping the Faith
Faith - Seventy Times Seven
Genesis - Stepping Onto the Shore and Finding It is Heaven
Hallelujah - He is not Here; He Has Risen (Luke 24: 6)
Seeing the Power of God
Living in God's Word
The Faith Chronicles: Books 1 - 3: An Anthology
The Faith Chronicles Box Set: Books 4-6

The Storm Lord Trilogy Series
The Flaming Blue Sword
Nine Months Will Tell
The Three Keys to Armageddon
The Storm Lord Trilogy Box Set: Books 1 - 3 An Anthology

The Whodunnit Series
Murder in Horseshoe Bay - Death Comes Quietly
Jaded Lover - Things Are Getting Heavy
Under Cover Queen - Sequel to Jaded Lover
The Amaryllis Murder Mystery
Murder at Morgan Park
Checker Cab Murder Mystery
Destiny Waits - Murder at the Lakeside Museum
Lollapalooza - The Case of the Woman in Black

Time Travel Series
Quantum Echoes - RX-7: An AI Detective

Victorian Mystery Series
This Old House - A Lily Blooms in the Jaws of Hell
I Am Woman - I Am Invincible

Victorian Romance Series
I Am Woman - Hear Me Roar

World War 2 Series
USS Houston - Galloping Ghost of the Java Coast

Standalone
True Love Ways
I Go to Pieces - Part 2: Sequel to True Love Ways
Guitar - Truth is Strange - Stranger Than Fiction
Refuge of Death - A Kiss for a Kiss
The Runaway Scrape
Das Ausser Kontrolle Geratene Kratzen
La Raspado Fuera de Control

Watch for more at https://www.facebook.com/sidneystjamesshow.

About the Author

Step into the world of Sidney St. James, a master of the written word whose enthralling tales blend imagination and history into an extraordinary tapestry of creative nonfiction. St. James weaves captivating narratives that transport readers to distant eras, revealing untold stories and breathing life into forgotten characters with a pen that dances across the pages.

Growing up surrounded by books and immersed in the tales of the past, he developed a keen eye for historical details and an uncanny ability to breathe life into bygone eras.

Drawing inspiration from the annals of time, St. James embarked on a literary journey that would captivate the hearts and minds of readers worldwide. With meticulous research and vivid imagination, he skillfully resurrects forgotten events, peeling back the layers of time to expose the untold truths that lay dormant in history's shadows.

Each stroke of his pen creates a portal, transporting readers to ancient civilizations, turbulent revolutions, and untamed frontiers. Through his meticulously crafted prose, the past springs to life as battles thunder, intrigues unfold, and heroes and heroines emerge from the forgotten corners of time.

His works have transcended mere entertainment, leaving an indelible mark on the literary world. He has garnered critical acclaim, topping bestseller lists and captivating readers across continents. St. James invites us to traverse the corridors of time with each new release, immersing ourselves in familiar and foreign worlds where history blends seamlessly with imagination.

Beyond his literary achievements, St. James is known for his unwavering commitment to historical accuracy. His exhaustive research and attention to detail lend authenticity to his narratives, allowing readers to embark on an immersive and genuine journey. Through his creative nonfiction, he breathes fresh life into the past, igniting a love for history within his readers and reminding us that our collective past is a treasure trove waiting to be explored.

As Sidney St. James' pen becomes a time machine, transporting us to distant and familiar realms, bridging the gap between the past and present. With each turn of the page, St. James invites us to unlock the secrets of history, awed and inspired by the extraordinary lives that came before us.

Read more at https://www.facebook.com/sidneystjamesshow.

About the Publisher

Welcome to BeeBop Publishing Group, a vanguard in the realm of independent publishing. As a pioneering and forward-thinking publishing house, we are committed to the cultivation and advancement of indie authors and emerging writers. Our core mission is to establish a vibrant platform that enables creative minds to flourish and disseminate their narratives globally.

At BeeBop Publishing, we are acutely aware of the hurdles and impediments that burgeoning authors frequently encounter in the traditional publishing landscape. In response, our foundation is built upon the principle of empowering authors, providing them with the necessary tools and opportunities to actualize their literary aspirations.

Comprising a cadre of industry veterans with a fervent zeal for literature, BeeBop Publishing offers an all-encompassing suite of services to assist authors at each juncture of their publishing odyssey. Our array of services encompasses meticulous manuscript editing, scrupulous proofreading, innovative cover design, and professional formatting. Our adept team is dedicated to ensuring that your publication epitomizes excellence in quality and professionalism.

Beyond the realm of publishing, our commitment to our authors extends into cultivating a collaborative and nurturing environment. We advocate for a milieu where writers can engage with peers, exchange insights, and gain knowledge from shared experiences. Our dynamic online community, alongside author-centric events and workshops, is designed to forge a network of impassioned writers who mutually inspire and elevate each other.

A distinctive feature of partnering with BeeBop Publishing Group is our bespoke approach to the publishing process. Recognizing the uniqueness of each author, we invest time in comprehending your specific vision and objectives. Irrespective of your genre – be it a suspense-filled thriller, an enchanting romance, or a boundary-pushing science fiction tale – our services are customized to align with your distinct needs, ensuring your publication is a true reflection of your creative vision.

For indie authors and debut writers, the prospect of marketing and distribution can often appear daunting. BeeBop Publishing assuages these concerns with a proficient marketing team adept at devising comprehensive promotional strategies to elevate your book's visibility. Utilizing a blend of modern social media tactics, online marketing, book events, and traditional marketing avenues, we aim to target and captivate your intended audience, creating a buzz around your literary work.

Additionally, we offer extensive distribution channels, making your book accessible in both print and digital formats through major online retailers, bookstores, and libraries. We are advocates for the belief that exceptional stories should be universally accessible, endeavoring to bridge your book with avid readers across the globe, eager for new and captivating narratives.

Embark on your publishing journey with BeeBop Publishing Group. Whether your manuscript is in its final stages or you're crafting your initial draft, our team is poised to guide and support you at every phase. Allow us to be your steadfast ally in transforming your writing ambitions into a tangible reality.

Together, we will amplify your voice, uncover your story, and actualize your dreams. Unleash your creativity and carve out your unique success story with BeeBop Publishing Company – where your literary vision becomes our shared mission.